Thalgor's Witch

THALGOR'S WITCH

NANCY HOLLAND

Best Wishes,
Nancy Holland

TULE
PUBLISHING

CHAPTER ONE

E RWYN BLESSED THE hated dark. Not the familiar black of night, but the cold time of year when the sun retreated from the land and filled the days with gloom.

The shadows allowed her to all but disappear when she pulled the cloak around herself and the child by her side. Huddled behind a dense evergreen thicket at the edge of the leafless forest, they were near enough to the road not to lose their way once it was safe to move on, but well hidden from the warriors who tramped past them back to their camp.

The victors, almost a hundred of them, sauntered along the road talking among themselves about the battle they had won, the women they had taken.

The child beside her, barely five years old, whimpered with fear. Erwyn slipped one hand over the girl's mouth. Luckily, the men on the road talked and laughed too loudly to hear. Felyn clung closer.

Soon only stragglers still ambled down the road. Erwyn and the child would soon be free to escape to the Sea Mountains.

The slightest stir of the air warned her of the sword that

brushed her back.

Fear turned her blood to ice. Even her magic froze.

"Is this how your men scout a forest, Gurdek?" asked the man who held the sword.

"It is the cold time," came the reply. "And they are weary from battle, Thalgor."

"I wonder if I should kill this lurker or you."

The words held more amusement than menace, but Felyn cried out in terror. She threw off the cloak and fled into the underbrush.

Exposed, Erwyn stood. Her knees wobbled, but she held her head high and blinked in the pale-yellow glow of the shuttered lantern carried by the smaller of the two men.

Before she made out more than their shapes—one very tall, the other short and broad—the child cried out again.

Erwyn moved toward the sound, but the sword the larger man held now at her belly stopped her.

Something flailed about in the bushes. A third man appeared, the child thrown over one shoulder. This man was filthy, his clothes in tatters, his hair matted to his head. Erwyn's stomach clenched with disgust as much as fear.

"Small, but female," the man declared with an ugly laugh.

Erwyn made another involuntary move against the sword. It gave way slightly rather than wound her.

"Drop her," the man who held it, Thalgor, told the newcomer.

The third man complied, but grumbled darkly.

The child froze in the light then ran to Erwyn, who again felt the unwelcome need to comfort her.

"A full-size female," the third man said, his toothless leer close enough for Erwyn to smell the rot of his breath.

When he reached a hand toward her breast, she murmured a few words to turn his own evil against him. He crumpled to the ground and began to vomit black bile.

Gurdek watched the man fall, a look of horror on his face.

"A witch." He let the lantern sink.

"Perhaps." The tall man, Thalgor, moved his sword from Erwyn's belly to her throat. Her heart beat wildly and rose to meet it there. "But witches can heal as well as harm."

The man writhing on the forest floor cried, "Yes. Make it stop!"

Thalgor pushed him aside with his foot. "Not heal you. You deserved the curse. But…"

Above the stench of vomit, the sickly sweet smell of the tall man's deadly wound flowed over Erwyn.

Her duty as a witch claimed her. She tossed her cloak over the child and opened the leather bag she wore on a strap across her chest.

"Down," she commanded, freed of the fear that had held her.

To the obvious amazement of the others, the tall man fell to his knees at her feet, his sharply angled face raised to her.

The reason became clear when she pulled back his cloak to expose the gaping wound cut under his heart, clear through the leather breastplate.

As she fled the battle she had seen the headless body of the leader who had destroyed her own camp and enslaved her. None but this great man could have struck such a blow.

"So, the enemy wounded to kill even as he died."

Thalgor struggled to his feet again, sword still in hand.

"As will I, should you attempt any treachery."

The blood-splattered weapon glinted in the lantern light as he raised it over his head.

Unafraid in the face of his weakness, she put her hand on the skin exposed by the severed breastplate. His flesh burned and shifted under her touch.

"It is not your time yet."

He lowered the sword, but held it ready.

"Bring the lantern," she commanded.

Gurdek sidled closer. He nervously eyed the vial of glowing blue liquid and the stone bowl she pulled from her bag.

"I need light and heat." She took the lantern and set it on the ground. "Remove his breastplate."

She unshuttered the lantern, poured the ocean-scented liquid into the bowl, and set it near the flicker of the yellow flame.

"Why would you heal an enemy too weak to harm you or your child?" Thalgor asked through teeth gritted against Gurdek's jostling.

She is not my child, Erwyn began to say, but thought better of it. Would these strangers value an untouched woman or a mother more?

"Magic has laws of its own," she said instead. "My gift does not belong to me. I must heal wherever I can." She'd learned the ancient formula from her mother long ago. "Besides, your friend here seems fit enough to harm us both."

Freed from the blood-soaked breastplate, Thalgor looked the shorter man up and down.

"Fit, perhaps, but too afraid of witches to do more than throw the lantern at you." He smiled, then drew a sharp breath as she painted the heated oil on his wound.

Charmed in spite of herself by the smile and the way his long brown hair framed his face, she offered a smaller bag. "I have herbs to bring sleep while I work."

"No. I am the leader of my band. Pain and death are nothing to me."

Which sounded like another ancient formula.

She felt the weakness of his body under her hands, could touch his pain with her mind, and knew it was far from nothing. Without her magic, he would be dead by dawn. Even now his body swayed and sweated with the stress of not crying out whenever she touched the wound.

She chanted the magic words in the silent clearing. The man she'd made sick lay frozen on the ground, no doubt afraid any movement would make the pain in his belly worse. Gurdek held the light close to where she worked, his eyes still wide with terror. The child under the cloak no longer wept. Probably she'd fallen asleep.

Suddenly Thalgor's powerful body slumped to the ground.

Erwyn dodged his fall, but it startled Gurdek so much he dropped the lantern with a cry of panic and fled down the road.

Now she was free to carry out her promise to her dying mother and take Felyn to the Wise Witches. Only they might be able to free the child of her curse. And, perhaps, provide them both with the home they had lost when their camp was destroyed in the last dark time.

She turned to wake the child, then looked back at the unconscious man at her feet.

She could not yet be certain he would live. The laws that ruled her magic required her to save him if she could. Her vow to her mother, what she herself might want or fear as a woman—neither mattered in the face of her duty as a witch. Escape would have to wait.

"I hope your other lieutenants have more fortitude in the face of a simple witch," she muttered as she righted the lantern and shifted Thalgor's body so she could reach his wound. "You should have taken the herbs, great man."

"I have no need of them." Eyes dark and hard as stone fluttered open. "Gurdek was cursed once by a witch, so he is more afraid than most."

"Cursed how?"

As she began to bind the wound with cobwebs from her bag, long habit made her try to distract him from the pain. Too late she realized if he fainted again, once she had safely bound his wound, she could escape without violating the laws of her magic.

"Cursed in a way only a man can be. For a whole year."

He began to laugh, but the movement tore at his wound. His face whitened and fresh beads of sweat dotted his brow.

She could not make herself hurt him more, but she didn't try to distract him again.

She helped him sit before she tore his tunic into strips to wrap the wound. When she pulled hard to knot it, he gave a thunderous moan and fell back to the ground.

Her heart pounded as she gathered her things, roused the sleeping child, and wrapped the cloak around them both. She took a moment to release the man she had cursed from his pain. He fell at once into a deep sleep. Duty done, she turned to flee.

An icy hand, relentless as the leather hobbles that had kept her a slave, wrapped itself around her ankle. The chill that ran through her was fear and more than fear.

"No, witch." Thalgor's voice was thick with pain. "I am not done with you yet."

"GURDEK!" THALGOR KNEW his lieutenant would have circled around and returned by now.

He appeared at once, sword drawn.

"Tie her."

Gurdek eyed the witch, as tall as he, if half as wide, then he looked back at Thalgor, who kept his eyes fixed on the rope at his lieutenant's waist. With a barely perceptible sigh, Gurdek took the rope and started to cut it in two pieces.

"No. Only tie the witch. The child will stay with her mother." Thalgor shot a sharp glance at their prisoner. "And the witch will allow it as long as we have her child."

He wondered if the child's father lay dead among the dozens of men he had killed this day. The witch did not act like a woman who had just lost her man. But he knew little of what went on between men and women, beyond the most basic.

And she is not a woman, he reminded himself when his blood began to heat at the thought of that most basic.

Perhaps witches did not mourn. Or perhaps this one did not. She surely showed no sign of love toward her child. Not as his mother had on that far ago night when she and his childhood self had hidden from a warrior who found them after all.

The child was the image of her mother—the same oval face with dainty features, the same dark hair pulled back in a long braid, the same large eyes under a strong brow. But the child had darker skin and cat-green eyes with slitted centers.

The witch's eyes were a pale blue that should have been weak and watery, but instead shone like the sky on a summer morning. Shone with anger as she submitted to the rope.

If not for the child, he was certain, she would fight both him and Gurdek to the death, with her magic or without it. She might even take one of them with her.

Both her courage and her submission made his blood churn in a way that distressed him.

Thalgor lifted himself to his knees, then his feet. He felt the wound heal, but pain still burned a black edge to his vision. Once on his feet, he took an unsteady step forward. He had lost a lot of blood and the witch's magic had not restored it, but his legs held him. He walked on, as if he never doubted he could, and gestured for Gurdek to follow.

"What do you want with a witch?" Gurdek grumbled with the familiarity of an old comrade as they followed the road toward their camp.

Preoccupied with walking normally despite the pain, Thalgor leered at him in response.

Gurdek knew him too well to settle for such an answer. "You do not allow the men to rape, and even if you wished to take a witch to your bed, you know magic protects witches from men. I doubt this one will give herself to you freely."

Thalgor's body heated again with an unwanted vision of the witch struggling beneath him as he buried himself in the soft wetness of her body. But the flash of lust dissolved into memories of all the nights he had lain awake and listened to his mother scream and beg. Revulsion twisted inside him.

He knew now he should never have allowed the vile man they had left behind into the band when he came to them as a starving renegade. What he would do about the depraved pleasure his own imagination had given him Thalgor did not know. He could almost be grateful for his pain, as if it were a magic charm against the danger he might become as cruel as his mother's tormentor.

"Witches heal," he replied. "And they have second sight. To know how many warriors an enemy has, and where, could make us invincible."

"Her second sight did not save the band we defeated today."

"Perhaps their leader did not listen to her." He gestured with his sword to the bit of leather still wrapped around the witch's ankle. "He kept her a slave. Who listens to a slave?"

"But why should she share her gift with us?"

Thalgor looked back at the woman, who walked straight and proud despite the ropes and the child who clung to her cloak. "Perhaps she can be convinced to throw her lot in with ours. It might prove interesting to try."

A seduction either way, he thought with a shiver of desire.

ERWYN STRUGGLED AGAINST the indignity of the ropes with

small movements she hoped the men could not see in the deepening purple of evening, but she could not free herself. Even if she could, as the panic of the battle faded she realized her plan to flee to the Sea Mountains was worse than hopeless.

She had no food and the barren dark-time countryside offered little. Felyn could only walk so far in a day, and she was too heavy for Erwyn to carry. Despite her magic, they would starve long before they reached the Sea Mountains.

Best to let these men feed them well now and escape with stolen food, and perhaps an ox. If they hobbled her with rope, she could free herself when the time came. Until then, her magic would protect her, and she could protect the child.

Still, the rope chafed her pride as well as her wrists. From her hiding place in the evergreens, she had watched the victorious warriors herd the other captured women with the old men and the children toward the victor's camp, all walking freely. Despite his words, perhaps this big man doubted his strength and his companion's willingness to take on a witch unaided.

Or perhaps he likes the sight of a woman bound, a voice inside her warned.

The child who clung to her cloak stumbled, but Erwyn could not steady her with her hands tied. She watched as Gurdek righted the girl, and sensed a kind heart under the full beard and warlike bluster. His leader, though, was all ice and stone.

Anger shaped another plan in her mind, one more liable to succeed, if also more liable to prove fatal to her in the end.

When they reached the camp, she could hand Felyn over to the other captured women. None of them could raise her as a witch, if she was one, but freed of the child, Erwyn could take her revenge on their captors and make her escape.

The laws laid down at the end of the war between witches and men would keep her from using magic to kill, but her power offered other forms of vengeance. The big, handsome warrior with the ropes and the sly smile would suffer first and most.

But, she remembered with regret, the promise to her mother made revenge impossible.

Soon they emerged from the dark silence of the forest to the noise and firelight of Thalgor's camp. A camp so like the home she had lost that her eyes stung with tears.

Oxen lowed as boys took the goods and food captured in the battle from the baskets the animals carried. Smaller boys herded the cattle already freed of their burdens deeper into the meadow with the sheep. Somewhere a pipe played a dancing tune. Women cooked around campfires. A whole ox roasted on the largest fire.

Erwyn stomach reminded her a dismal meal at dawn was the last she had eaten.

Everyone around her talked and laughed and sang.

All but the captives from the defeated band at one side of the camp. The captured women knelt to shelter their children, wept on each other's shoulders, or clung to the few old men. They and the older boys stood at the edge, as if they could protect the others from the ring of well-armed warriors that encircled them.

She did not look for her aunt among the others from the camp where they'd both been enslaved. She had seen a misdirected arrow pierce the old woman's body through as she tried to flee the battle. A shattering wave of grief washed over Erwyn at the memory.

She remembered, too, the look of horror on the face of the archer who had shot the arrow, a tall, slender young man with immense brown eyes in a too thin face.

Thalgor walked into the camp without any sign of his injury, although she still felt the aching weakness inside him. His people fell silent as they saw him, until the entire camp was quiet except for the weeping captives at its edge. Even the cattle seemed awed to silence by their triumphant leader.

"My people," Thalgor said in a voice gone from mocking to majestic. "We have done well. Our warriors are great, and brave, and strong. We have taken food, livestock, and goods from many tents. We have taken women who in time will belong to our men who have none, children who will become as our own, old men to help with the work of the camp. Remember what they have lost this day."

His people murmured and nodded as if this were a speech they heard after every victory. But how could that be? Let the old men live? Take the children as their own? The women were not simply to be used and sold as slaves? Yet

Gurdek had said their men were not allowed to rape, and Erwyn felt the truth in Thalgor's words.

The other captives fell silent, no doubt as surprised as she was by his strange speech.

With a gesture to Gurdek to keep Erwyn and the child where they were, Thalgor walked to the circle where the remnants of the defeated band huddled together. Only the small children still wept.

"When we leave this meadow, you may come with us and have our protection." He spoke in the same majestic voice, softer now because his listeners were fewer. "Or you may venture out on your own. You will not be harmed if you stay with us. In any way," he emphasized as he looked at the women. "But you must work to keep yourselves. Your children will learn our ways. Those women who choose may become the women of our warriors who have none. We do not take slaves."

The captives stared at him in disbelief, then fell to talking among themselves. The conversations gradually took on clear patterns. Mothers argued with sons old enough to wish to join what warriors might be left from their band to become marauders and seek revenge. Old men argued with women reluctant to leave their men behind if any hope remained that they still lived. All of them hungry, cold, and frightened. All aware the choice Thalgor offered was for most of them a choice between life and death.

Slowly, in ones and twos and family groups, they stepped outside the circle of warriors.

"We are now of you." The voice of the old man who led them was rough with grief.

Thalgor nodded and gestured for food to be brought to the larger group who had joined his camp, and to the few who remained inside the circle–boys old enough to brave a life on their own, childless women who would leave in the morning to search for their men. A fire was lit for them as well.

Felyn began to cry.

"Let me take her to the other women," Erwyn urged Gurdek. "She is hungry."

"You will both eat." Thalgor had reappeared at her side. "In my tent."

She looked up into eyes that seemed carved from agate.

"I thought you took no slaves." She schooled the fear, and that other emotion she had no name for, from her voice.

"We take no human slaves."

Her blood ran cold, then hot.

"Make sure the men know she is a witch," he told Gurdek as he took the rope from him.

Then he turned back to Erwyn. "As for the child, without her within my reach, I would not dare keep you in my camp, much less in my tent."

Erwyn shivered with a fear her magic could not lessen. A dread darker, deeper than of death.

Thalgor saw her fear. He smiled.

CHAPTER TWO

THEY MADE SLOW progress through the camp because the people crowded around Thalgor as they always did, eager to speak to him or even touch the cloak he kept wrapped closely around him to hide his wound. He spoke to those he knew by name, now and then stroked a child's head as he talked with its parents.

Dara waited for him outside her mother's tent as she had after every battle since the last cold time. Until recently he had been glad for the distraction from battle and death she provided.

Her cloak hung open to expose the gown pulled tight across her ample breasts. Her lips would taste of the berry juice that stained them red.

"Thalgor." She smiled at him with hungry eyes.

He could not simply ignore her.

"Dara."

He gestured for Gurdek to take the witch and her child on to his tent, but the witch refused to follow, and Gurdek was clearly afraid to force her to move. With a shrug, Thalgor turned back to the woman who had until recently been his lover.

"Who's that?" Dara pointed at the prisoner.

"A witch. I think she might be useful in battle."

Dara raised one eyebrow, then turned to him with a dismissive shrug. She stroked a hand down his sword arm.

Once her touch would have made him smile in anticipation. Now it irritated, but he didn't push her hand away.

"I watched the battle from a tree on the hillside." She paused to lick her lips. "You killed so many men." She stroked his sword arm again. A familiar flush tinged her face. "And I saw you cut their leader's head off."

Her eyes glowed with a desire that always made him uneasy. Now, drenched in his own blood and that of the men he had killed, her passion for battle repelled him more than ever before. He gently pushed her hand away from his weary arm.

"He wounded me in the process. Badly."

"I don't see any wound." Her wide, red mouth formed a pout.

"The witch healed it."

"Oh. The witch." Dara turned to where his prisoner watched them and gave her a malevolent smile. "She has a child, and you can't force a witch. What use is she to you?" Dara rubbed her breasts against his arm.

Her touch chilled him. He took half a step back.

Between that chill and the wound, he feared he would be sick if he didn't soon make his escape.

"I told you. I think she might be useful in battle."

"But not in your bed?"

Dara licked her lips, which made her look like nothing so much as a viper. His stomach clenched tighter.

"My wound makes my bed beside the point." He eased another half step back. "For anyone."

Dara stroked his sword arm again. His belly churned.

"Perhaps tomorrow? Right after a battle is always best, but I could come to tend your wound…"

"You never tend anything of mine. You refuse to carry my water or cook my food. You only want to be my woman in bed."

Once that had pleased him well enough. All his lovers knew he only wanted a night's pleasure now and then. When they wanted more, they chose men who would give them the love he could not. Shame and rage had turned his heart to stone long ago. Dara was the first woman he had tired of before she was ready to move on.

"Isn't in bed enough?" She stepped closer again. A cold sweat beaded on his brow. "If I stay in my mother's tent she does the work and I can devote myself to pleasing you."

"And yourself."

"Of course."

She gave her hips a little shake so they made contact with the part of him that interested her most.

He refused to step away again, but pushed her gently back.

"Stay in your mother's tent, then. All the time."

She looked up at him in disbelief. Her eyes clouded. Not with hurt, to his relief, but with anger.

"Because of the witch?"

She stood feet apart, hands fisted on her hips. A man who challenged him so would already be dead. The people around them, who had politely pretended not to listen, suddenly turned to stare.

He took a deep breath against the anger. *Consider yourself lucky to be rid of her before you got her with child.*

"Because I have become tired of you."

"Tired of me!"

Repulsed by you, he wanted to say, but mindful of the people around them he replied, "Yes."

"No one gets tired of *me*. I…"

Dara clearly had more to say. Her lips moved, but no sound came out of her mouth. Her eyes opened wide in surprise, then fear as she turned toward the witch.

The witch smiled.

"Witches can make dangerous enemies," Thalgor commented when he was certain he could speak without laughing.

Others around them were less restrained. No one guffawed outright, but giggles and snorts moved through the small crowd.

Dara looked around at them, face scarlet with rage, but still couldn't utter a sound. She made a half move toward the witch, then spun around and disappeared into her mother's tent.

As she went he saw the witch give a small nod he knew released Dara from the spell.

The witch still smiled. Not an evil smile, but a contented one. The smile told him that fed and happy she might be beautiful.

But what had happened to Dara had made him even more aware of how dangerous it could be to trifle with a witch.

The heat that circled his body and settled low in his belly told him he wanted to do much more than trifle with this one.

FAIR WARNING GIVEN, Erwyn turned to follow her captors as they strode on toward Thalgor's tent, but Felyn refused to take another step. She plopped to the ground and sat like a stone. Tears flowed down her cheeks.

Thalgor and Gurdek both turned to see why their prisoner didn't respond to the tug of the rope.

"She is too heavy for me to carry," Erwyn pointed out.

"Tell her to get up and walk." Thalgor's tone still echoed with anger from the scene with the woman who clearly was, or recently had been, his lover.

Erwyn's nose twitched with the urge to turn that anger

against him and curse him in some painful and permanent way. She chose instead to bide her time and conserve her powers.

"She's tired and hungry. Were you never a child? I wouldn't walk any more, either, if I were she."

The two men looked at each other. Gurdek opened his mouth as if to say something, but seemed to reconsider Thalgor's mood and snapped his mouth shut. He handed the rope to the larger man with obvious reluctance and knelt beside the child to lift her to his shoulders with surprising gentleness.

Surprisingly, too, the child allowed him to do it without protest. In hopes of food, Erwyn concluded from a look at the mask-like little face so similar to her own.

Thalgor let Gurdek carry the child past him, then absently tugged on the rope for Erwyn to follow. That was too much. She stood her ground and jerked the rope back, heedless of the pain in her bound wrists.

Thalgor turned to look at her and her heart stalled. He came to within half a step of her, so he towered over her like a fox over a cornered rabbit. She refused to be afraid. She braced her feet apart, as that woman had, and glared at him.

"Don't challenge me," he growled. "I owed Dara a certain amount of forgiveness. I owe you nothing."

He spat the last word out with such vehemence that a few of the people nearby moved gingerly away.

"You owe me nothing," Erwyn agreed. "Except your life.

So much for your gratitude." She held up her bound hands.

"I let you live."

"And I let you live."

As they faced each other Erwyn felt the minds around them wonder. She knew the danger if they wondered too much about their leader's ability to control a witch. Torn between pride and that danger, she held Thalgor's gaze until the silent wondering around them grew too loud, then strode past him, head high, to follow Gurdek and the child.

Her surrender took Thalgor so much by surprise the rope almost pulled out of his hands when she reached its length. He recovered quickly and marched along behind her like a herdsman with his beast. He would pay for that, too.

Thalgor's tent was closest to the huge fire where the ox was roasting. Warriors stood around in small groups, eating battle gruel while they waited for the meat to cook.

Erwyn's eyes stung from the smoke while her mouth watered at the savory smell of the meat. *Food, food, food,* her whole body seemed to chant.

Thalgor pulled her to a stop to talk with his men. She allowed it only because she knew any wondering about his ability to control her could be especially dangerous here. Warriors were by nature suspicious of strangers, especially witches.

Gurdek disappeared into Thalgor's tent with his burden. As soon as the flap closed a wail went up from behind the wall of tight-woven wool. A loud thump, then a string of curses. A small body rocketed from the tent and flew to Erwyn's side.

Gurdek lumbered after the child, limping slightly.

Erwyn yanked the rope free of hands Thalgor had let relax and turned to face Gurdek, shielding the child with her body. "What did you do to her?"

Thalgor came to her side, but she couldn't tell if he did it to intimidate her or his comrade.

"I-I...? Nothing," Gurdek protested.

"She screamed. And she trembles."

"I did nothing." He appealed past her to Thalgor, who made an impatient noise low in his throat.

"As soon as we were in the tent," Gurdek explained, "she started to wail and pounded on my head. When I tried to put her down, she kicked me in the chest so hard I fell over."

"I see," Thalgor murmured with barely concealed amusement as he took the rope and tugged more gently for Erwyn to follow. The child came, too, clutching her cloak.

"So, the daughter is as fierce as the mother. Is she a witch as well?" Thalgor asked Erwyn.

Danger lurked behind any possible answer to that question. Before she could decide which danger was least, she saw a tall, thin young man come around the corner of Thalgor's tent.

The archer who had killed her aunt.

He must have recognized her, too, because he gasped, and his face went white with horror, as it had when her aunt fell.

She stopped in front of him. The young man's hand went to the knife on his belt.

"A knife isn't much use against a witch, Rygar," Thalgor said casually. "But I will not let her harm you."

You can't stop me, she wanted to say, but his warriors still listened.

And while she glared, she did not intend to harm the young man. He had not meant to kill an old woman who only fled the battle. Still, Erwyn did not want him to think she would ever forget, or ever forgive him.

"Will you eat with me, Rygar?" Thalgor asked the archer.

"Does the witch eat with you?"

"Tonight, yes."

"Then I will not. Thank you."

As Rygar left, Erwyn felt the guilt gnaw inside him. Perhaps Thalgor sensed it, too, because he gave her a questioning look.

What linked the two men? Rygar was too old to be Thalgor's son. A man-lover? No. Not alike enough for brothers. She shrugged the question off and followed Thalgor into his tent.

A single torch dimly lit the dark space inside. Gurdek, who had come in after them, took it to light the others around the room, then lit the braziers by each of the four doorways. Shadows danced on the pale brown ox hide roof.

The growing light revealed a large room dominated by a

massive table at its center. Benches surrounded it on three sides, with a large chair on the fourth. More benches lined the walls. Three sets of curtains marked three rooms similar to the anteroom where they had entered, one on each side. The tent was similar enough to her uncle's she could guess the two side rooms would be sleeping chambers, the one across the room a scullery and larder that led to a small cooking fire outside.

The glow of the torches glinted off the gold inlay on the carved chair opposite them and a small pile of gold and a rainbow of jewels on the table. Taken from the defeated band, but displayed far more carelessly than they had been in her former captor's tent, or her uncle's before that.

Thalgor let the inner curtain fall behind them. The double walls kept out the cold and deadened the sounds outside. The sudden warmth and quiet, the flicker of light made it seem as if they had stepped into another world, both eerie and familiar.

No wonder the child had screamed and run away. She still clung, trembling, to one of Erwyn's tied hands. Erwyn turned her hand in the ropes to cup the child's face in an awkward, almost involuntary effort to comfort her.

"You never told me if she is also a witch." Thalgor sat on the bench in front of them and drew his knife from its sheath.

Frightened into honesty, Erwyn replied, "I don't know."

He stopped. The edge of the knife glimmered in mid-air.

"I don't think so," she added under the prod of his stare.

"How could you not know if your man was of witch blood?" He pulled her hand from the child's grasp and cut the ropes in a single stroke that froze Erwyn's heart with fear.

She rubbed her sore wrists and waited for her heart to start to beat normally again.

"Or don't you know who her father was?"

She chose the risk of defiance over the pain of confession and remained silent.

Gurdek disappeared through the curtain in the back of the tent and returned with a bowl of gruel. An old woman carried in two more bowls behind him.

Despite the age lined on her face and the silver braid over her shoulder, the woman walked straight, with more pride than Erwyn would have expected from a servant.

"Rygar?" the old woman asked in lieu of a greeting.

"No, Gee," Thalgor answered. "Your pet fears my witch."

The woman set the bowls on the table. She looked Erwyn up and down, then her warm brown eyes came to rest on the child.

Despite her age, she crouched down and held out a hand. "Come here, girl."

Much to Erwyn's surprise, the child went to Gee, who sat her on one of the benches by the table and pushed a bowl of gruel toward her. With a cry of delight, the girl began to eat while the old woman beamed happily down at her.

Gurdek claimed another of the benches, and ate, too.

"Which of us do you mean to starve?" Thalgor pointed lazily at the single remaining bowl. "Me or the witch?"

The old woman frowned at him and went out again. She came back with another bowl of gruel and a piece of honeycomb on a plate, which she put on the table near the child.

Thalgor gave a huff of laughter as he took off his cloak. Gee took one look at the blood-soaked bandage, went into one of the side chambers and brought him back a clean tunic. He pulled it on before he sat at the table and began to eat.

Erwyn took the last bowl from the table and sat on one of the benches by the wall, well away from Thalgor and the child.

Suddenly the noise that seeped through the walls from around the campfire outside grew louder.

"Meat." Gee grinned and hurried out.

The sounds of the happy camp outside flooded briefly in. When the tent flap fell, it plunged the room back into quiet. Erwyn felt very much alone with the child and the two men. More alone when the child emptied her bowl, quickly chewed up the honeycomb, and fell asleep curled up on the hard wooden bench.

Gurdek wolfed his food down with an occasional wary glance at Erwyn. Thalgor simply ate as if no one else were there.

Erwyn sniffed the savory mixture of crushed grain, herbs,

and vegetable broth. She had to curb the urge to bolt it down as the child had.

She scraped the last of the thin gruel from the bowl as Gee returned with a platter of meat and set it on the table by Thalgor. Gurdek pulled out his knife, cut a huge piece of roasted flesh, then began to devour it. The old woman sat beside him and held out a plate where he put a smaller slice of meat.

Erwyn was shocked by their brazenness. In the camp of her captors, everyone ate by rank. The same had been true in her own camp. Her uncle had eaten, and her aunt, then his lieutenants, the warriors, the old men and the older boys, finally the other women and children. Often there was only gruel for them. In very bad years, some of the women and children had died from hunger, even when her father led the band. Some might go hungry in Thalgor's camp, but perhaps the children would not starve.

Thalgor drew his knife and cut a large piece of meat. He surprised her even more when he walked over to drop it in her now empty bowl. He looked down at her expectantly.

"Thank you." The words nearly choked her.

He barked a laugh, then cut a piece for himself.

The roasted meat melted in her mouth, and filled her belly with warm comfort. She wanted to gobble it up, too, but ate slowly to savor every bite.

When Gurdek finished, he muttered something about the need to post guards and left. Gee gathered up the dishes and went into the scullery. Erwyn was left alone with Thalgor and the child. She stood with a sigh and went to wake her charge.

But nothing she did could rouse the girl. Erwyn sat on the bench next to her and buried her hands in her hair in frustration.

"Let her sleep there," Thalgor suggested quietly.

"She'll wake up in the night and set up a wail when she realizes she's in a strange place."

"Are you sure you can't carry her to bed?"

She stared at him and probed his mind to see why he sounded angry. A wall protected his thoughts from her.

Witch blood! This man carried witch blood so powerful it was almost a presence in the room.

An icy chill ran through her. The same witch blood that protected his thoughts from her could open her mind to him, unless she remained constantly on her guard against him.

Almost as if she felt the impact of Erwyn's dismay, the child stirred, whimpered and sat up, blinking slightly.

"Come," Erwyn said coolly. "Which way?"

Thalgor gave her a black look and started to say something, but instead he gestured to the side of the tent opposite where Gee had fetched his clean tunic.

Erwyn led the child through the drape that separated the sleeping chamber from the main room. A single torch lit the comfortable space. She put the child on the bed along one wall. The girl fell asleep at once, Erwyn's hand held tight in hers.

Erwyn waited a while before she pulled her hand free gently so as not to wake the child. When she looked up, Thalgor stood in the doorway, a leather strap in his hand.

Her heart began to race, not with fear but with a mixture of dread and excitement she'd never felt before. She took a step backward and almost toppled over the sleeping child.

He stopped her fall and pulled her closer to him.

Close enough in the half-light that she saw his face had tightened, not with desire, but with anger. Her heart skidded to a halt after all, paused, then resumed its frantic rhythm.

"You are an unnatural mother." He stepped away from her. "Is that true of all witches?"

Pain shot through her at the sudden reminder of her mother's love, but she gave no sign.

"Witches are unnatural," she replied.

He cursed under his breath, then gestured for her to sit on the bed on the wall opposite the child. Unsure of his intent, but confident in her power to protect herself with magic if necessary, she complied.

To her surprise, he fell to one knee in front of her and lifted her foot. The same foot he had branded with his icy touch in the forest now burned beneath his fingers. He freed it of her sandal, pulled a rope from his belt and tied one end of it around her ankle.

"They say our ancestors lived in stone houses." He

stooped to tie the other end of the rope to a post by the doorway. "But we live in tents, and tents are easily escaped from. You know now I would not harm your child, if only because the old woman would not let me, so I must find another way to keep you here. Your hands," he commanded as he stood.

The strap dangled from his hand. Her heart beat wildly.

"You mean me to think you cannot untie a rope?" he asked.

Still she sat silent, hands clasped in her lap.

"I will not have to bind you if you sleep in my chamber."

"Sleep?"

"Among other things."

His arrogant smile would probably have had any other woman in his bed in a heartbeat.

Not Erwyn. Arrogant men–the father who had not believed, the uncle who had not listened–had already cost her both mother and home.

With cold dignity, she lifted her hands to him.

After he bound her wrists with the leather, more loosely than Gurdek had with the rope, he left her alone with the child.

He must have known, as her previous captor had quickly learned, that her magic could not burn leather as it could rope. She would have to undo the knots.

When she finally succeeded, Thalgor's people still laughed and sang by the fire outside. Drums beat a dance rhythm. Happy chatter and the sound of pipes crept in through the tent wall.

Her hands freed, she could make herself invisible to take some food and escape, but she would have to leave the child behind. She knew now no harm would come to the girl, but she had made a vow to her dying mother.

With a sigh, she lay back on the bed to wait until the camp was quiet, so she would be able to take the girl with her.

The day had begun before dawn and every moment of it had been hard. Long before the camp fell silent, she slept.

She dreamed her mother floated toward her across the sea. When the vision threw back its hood, she saw, not her mother's face, but that of a young man about the age of Rygar with Thalgor's body—even taller and more muscular than the archer's—and Thalgor's face, but dark hair and eyes as blue as her own.

"Who are you?" she asked, as the vision stepped from sea foam to sand.

"I am the Witch King." His voice was both tender and sad.

She shook her head. "You are a man."

"I am the Witch King."

"What do you want of me?"

"You must stay in this camp."

Her heart began to pound. "You know I cannot."

"You must. For my sake."

Confusion swirled around her like the fog that rose from the stormy sea behind the vision.

"I cannot. I must take the child to the Wise Witches."

"Stay for the sake of the child."

"No. She has already cost me too much."

"And what have you cost her?" A single tear traced a path down his cheek.

"Who are you?" she asked again.

"Stay for your own sake."

"I can't," she sobbed.

Then he disappeared. His absence felt like a death.

She awoke just before dawn, her face wet with tears. Thalgor stood beside her. He silently retied the leather strap around her wrists and left her to sleep again.

THALGOR SAT AT the table, discussing their next move with Rygar, Gurdek, and the rest of his council when the witch emerged from her chamber. Dark circles beneath those clear blue eyes showed the hours she'd spent in the effort to free herself. Silently she raised her hands.

Gee played a stone game with the child nearby. At his nod the old woman went and untied his prisoner's wrists. Once freed, the witch undid the rope from her ankle and threw the free end into the chamber behind her.

When Gee went into the scullery to get her breakfast, the

witch did not take the old woman's place beside the child as he expected, but stood where she was and rubbed her wrists.

The memory of how he had frightened her with his knife the night before shamed him. The ropes had been necessary, but not the terror in her eyes. This woman–this witch–pulled something evil out of his soul. He would have liked to think she put it there, but he knew better.

The child whimpered.

"Go to her," he ordered the witch, angry on the child's behalf more than his own.

The witch stayed where she was. "You have already said I am an unnatural mother."

"My grandmothers were both witches. From what I remember they were as loving as any grandmothers."

"I am not her grandmother."

His men snorted with surprised laughter. Even Thalgor had to admire his prisoner's spirit, and her wisdom in knowing she need not pretend she was under his control with these men, whose loyalty to him was unshakable.

"Does your child have a name?"

Why was the witch so driven to protect the girl, despite the cold way she treated her? And why did she pause before she answered such a simple question?

"Felyn," she finally said.

"Can she talk?"

The witch stepped between him and the child as if to fend off a physical attack.

"Of course she can talk."

"I haven't heard her speak. And those slitted eyes...I thought she might be a half-wit."

"She speaks—and hears—perfectly well." His prisoner tipped her head toward the child.

Thalgor felt an unwelcome shudder of recognition. He, too, had refused to speak after he and his mother were captured. Until he had been made to.

"Has her mother a name?" he asked to erase the memory.

The witch paused again before she answered, long enough for his witch blood to warn him she might not be the child's mother after all.

"I am Erwyn."

Gee came in then from the scullery with a bowl of their morning gruel, rich with sheep's milk and dried berries.

"Ah, here is your food. Eat it and be silent. We are in council and women do not speak in council."

The witch began to protest, but when Gee handed her the bowl, she took it and sat on the bench by the door, well away from where the old woman played with the child.

He turned his attention back to his lieutenants.

"You were saying we should move south," he prompted Gurdek. "Why?"

"We will find more forage for our livestock there. And my men fight better when it is not so dark and cold."

"So we should move south because your men fear the dark?" Batte challenged, only half in jest. He was not much older than Thalgor, a blond, wiry man, his handsome face marked by a jagged scar that ran from one side of his nose almost to his shoulder, a reminder of a long-ago battle they had nearly lost.

"Better than to move north," Gurdek half-joked in return, "where there are so many mountains and caves for raiding parties to hide simply because your men don't like to sweat."

"Why not stay where we are?" asked Rygar, always the peacemaker. "It will take time to assimilate all we took in the last battle–people, animals, and goods–into our camp. Let us rest here a while."

"Too exposed," Thalgor said. "And the grass grows thin. We must move our herds farther away each day to graze."

"East, toward the forest," Gurdek's second suggested. "Our women and children can hide there if we are attacked."

"If we aren't attacked from the shelter of the forest itself." Batte's second was prone to contradiction like his leader. "I say west, toward the moor. No one goes there."

"For good reason." Thalgor studied the map while the others continued to debate. Finally he made a decision. "South."

The others nodded, Batte more slowly than the rest.

"We move in two days."

"No!"

The witch stood behind Rygar, staring over his shoulder at the map.

CHAPTER THREE

"NO?" THALGOR ASKED the witch, more puzzled than angry.

"There is danger to the south. You must move north."

"North? Toward the Sea Mountains?"

She nodded.

"So you can more easily escape to the citadel of the Wise Witches?" He drew a circle with his finger around the mountains on the map. "Do you think I am a fool?"

"You are a fool if you ignore my warning and move south."

He took a deep breath to ease the anger that burned inside him. Had he not told her women did not speak at his council? Yet she openly called him a fool.

Unable to see her thoughts, he found trust hard. And the cold way she treated her child rankled. As did the curl of unwelcome lust low in his belly.

"A warning based on what? We send scouts in all directions each day. They have found no large forces anywhere. It makes the most sense to move south where there is more feed for our animals."

The witch closed her eyes to look into the future–or to make him think she did.

"Two small raiding parties can be as dangerous as one large one." The blue eyes opened and met his fearlessly. "Not enough men to capture your camp, but enough to weaken you badly for the next raiding party or band of marauders that comes along."

"Lies," Gurdek spat.

"Do not listen to the witch," Batte, for once, agreed.

"Did you not take me captive because of my power to see as well as my power to heal?"

"I do not know yet if you see, or see truly. But I do know two things. We are strong enough to resist any raiding party. Or any two. And you have good reason to trick me into going north."

"I could escape more easily in the chaos of battle."

"Or be killed, or captured by someone who would be much less kind to you than I."

"You mean to die in either case."

Her quiet defiance sent a strange thrill through him, but the distrust of witches was stronger.

"Why would you help us? We killed your men, captured your people."

"They were not my people, any more than yours are." A look of remembered loss softened the witch's face.

He wondered for a moment if she was even old enough to be the child's mother. Perhaps a very young witch could be taken by force after all. That might explain her coldness toward the child, and her uncertainty whether the girl was a witch.

Yet he remembered all too well how his mother had loved the child she bore to the brute who had captured them.

The possibility that Erwyn might also have been raped cut open old scars carved deep into his heart, reminding him of the cost of love. He pushed the unwanted memories away.

"Still, why should I trust that you wish to help us?"

The witch's face went cold again. "I only tell what I see."

"Why allow the witch to speak at all?" Batte grumbled, turning his back to them both.

She pulled herself up taller. "I tell you, you must move north. Tomorrow."

"And I tell you, you must be silent and let us decide based on what is, not what might be."

"What will be."

"Silence!"

He stood and leaned over the map toward her. The move brought him close enough that he smelled the sweet woman's scent of her body. His eyes fell against his will to the mound of her breasts as they rose and fell under her gown with each angry breath. Blood rushed through his ears, then flooded lower to harden his body with a burning want he could not wish away.

"Fool!" she spat at him.

"Get out!" He threw his arms wide toward her.

She picked up her cloak, wrapped it around her, and strode out of the tent. The child ran after her, and Gee followed them.

"A witch is nothing but trouble," Gurdek commented quietly.

The others nodded in another rare moment of harmony.

ERWYN STOOD OUTSIDE the tent and took deep breaths to calm herself. She took strength from the icy breeze in her hair, the dim sunlight on her face. The child came to play nearby and hummed tunelessly to herself. Gee watched them from a stool by the door and chatted with the other women who passed by.

At noon Gee went to feed the men who still met inside and Erwyn took her place on the stool. She must have dozed because suddenly Thalgor stood over her. His shadow chilled her.

"Do witches do no work?"

"I have worked today. I saw. That is more than heavy work. I saw, and you did not listen to my warning. My uncle did not listen either. He insisted his scouts knew more about what the enemy might do than I did. You might learn from his mistake. His arrogance cost me my home."

Her uncle's camp had not truly been her home since her mother's death, but this man would care little about that.

"Did the leader of the band we defeated not listen either, or did you tell him convincing lies, as you tell me?"

"He feared me. Another lesson you might consider. He feared me, and he did not ask."

"Nor did I."

She stared off into the bustling camp. "Do you know what it is to be a slave?"

"Yes."

The word carried so much pain she almost asked him the story behind it, but she knew he would not tell her.

"If I had spoken to him as I did to you today, he would have killed me by the second word."

Dark memories still shadowed his face. "Were you so sure I would not?"

"All praise you for not taking slaves. I merely hoped you would not treat even a witch in such a way."

"I would not kill you, no, but..." He let the words hang between them for a long moment, then said sharply, "Get up."

"If you were truly evil," she told him as she slowly stood, "I could turn that evil against you to make you so sick you'd wish for death. But you are merely bad tempered, so you are safe for now. A shame."

She pictured his wound in her mind and tightened it. His hand went to his chest to rub away the ache.

"Ingratitude is close to true evil," she added.

When she eased the tightness again, Thalgor looked puzzled for a moment, then dropped his hand.

"After you eat, follow the old woman and help her get water," he ordered in a softer tone. "Do not try to stray. You won't get far, and tomorrow I will have to hobble you with leather."

Erwyn shuddered inside at the reminder of her recent enslavement. "The child?"

"Will stay with me." He looked at Felyn and nodded.

To Erwyn's surprise, the child gravely nodded back.

"We ate together this morning while you still slept, and I taught her a game."

"Then you knew she is no half-wit."

"Still, she did not speak." His face hardened, as if he remembered something he would rather forget. "Water."

She nodded and went through the empty tent to where Gee waited in the scullery with her midday meal.

By evening Erwyn knew that, whatever other purpose Thalgor might have for her, he also meant for her to take over the more physical daily chores from the old woman.

Erwyn didn't mind the work. She had worked much harder as a slave and always worked in her own camp, even when her father led them. Besides, work made it easier to forget the Witch King and his strange message, which haunted her all day.

"Who helped you before?" she asked Gee as they carried the day's last jars of water from the river in the frigid gray of evening. Not far away, an early owl hooted.

"Sometimes I managed alone, sometimes Rygar helped me."

Erwyn wondered what connected Gee to the archer. But such speculation flew out of her mind when the old woman went on.

"Now and then Thalgor."

That the fierce leader of this large camp would ever carry water was unthinkable.

"They're both good boys."

"Hardly boys," Erwyn protested.

"Thalgor was barely sixteen when he became our leader. Rygar was just a child."

Could the image of the Witch King that haunted her be Thalgor at that age? No. The Witch King was darker, and for all his witch blood, Thalgor was no witch, nor was any man.

They dined well that night on roast sheep. Gurdek ate with his men. Rygar joined them instead, but sat as far as he could from Erwyn.

Over the meal she tried again to convince Thalgor to travel north, but he refused to listen, as her uncle had.

"I have no desire to be captured by an even worse man than you," she told him when he finally roared at her to be silent.

"Perhaps he will have enough evil for you to turn against him and torment him. You would enjoy that."

Erwyn threw her bowl on the table and stomped out

again. With as much dignity as she could muster, she strode past the startled guard but knew better than to go farther than the edge of the light cast by the torch next to the tent door.

She stood between light and dark for a long time. Her mind filled with the call of night birds, the banter of the guards, and the familiar sounds of the camp as it settled for the night.

How could she get Thalgor to believe her?

When she felt calm enough, she closed her eyes to see the danger that waited to the south. Perhaps she could at least find a way to help the band survive the double onslaught she foresaw.

Help the band survive! Her eyes flew open.

As she had told Thalgor, a battle would give her a chance to escape. She and Felyn, with food and an ox, would be well on their way to the Sea Mountains before he could even think to come after her.

Why did it please her to be so certain Thalgor would come after her?

She took a deep breath of the cold night air and pushed the question from her mind, then went back into the tent.

"Go to the child." Thalgor turned away from the stone game he played with Rygar. "Gee can't settle her for the night."

Erwyn went into the sleeping chamber where the old woman held the sobbing child.

"She feared you were gone entirely."

Erwyn sat and allowed Felyn to crawl into her lap. The girl quieted at once.

When the old woman left them, Erwyn put the child to bed and stayed beside her until she slept.

When she finally stood, Thalgor waited in the doorway.

"You are clever as well as a witch." He swung the strap he held in his hand. "Too clever, perhaps."

He fastened the rope still tied to the tent post securely around her ankle, then he wove the leather strap around her wrists before he knotted it tightly.

"Last night I did not want to pain you so much you could not sleep. A mistake I will not make again." He reached out one hand and ran it slowly along her cheek. "Be careful, witch."

She made her face so hot he jerked his hand away with a small cry.

"Be careful yourself, warrior."

He gave a rueful smile and left her to wonder if the whimper she barely suppressed when he touched her was fear or something else entirely.

The heat faded from her face more slowly than it should have. The unfamiliar heat in her body ebbed more slowly still.

She spent the night trying to undo the leather woven around her wrists. Eventually exhaustion won out and she slept.

She dreamed she stood in the citadel of the Wise Witch-es. She searched for them so she could learn the truth about Felyn, but dark passage led only to dark passage. Just as she decided to turn back, afraid she might become lost in the maze forever, she entered a sea-scented chamber where the solid stone walls glowed blue.

In the middle of the sacred light waited not the oldest and wisest of all witches, as she expected, but the young man from her dream the night before.

"Who are you?" she asked him again.

"I am the Witch King."

"What do you want of me?"

"You must stay in this camp."

"No." Panic swelled inside her. "No!"

With an effort of will she cried "No" a third time and forced herself awake. Already the light of full day filtered through the walls of the tent.

She emerged from the sleeping chamber to find only Gee and the child in the large room. She held up her hands for the old woman to untie. Gee shook her head as she did so.

Erwyn spent the day helping the old woman load an ox cart with the contents of Thalgor's tent. Guards lifted the heaviest things—four to load the table, two to load the chair Thalgor never used—but much else had to be packed in the wooden cart.

Erwyn found it unsettling to pack for the trip south she knew could only bring more bloodshed. Stranger still to load jewels, gold, and weapons that had belonged to her captors, and to her uncle and her father before that, into a cart for Thalgor to carry away so another warrior could kill him and take them in turn.

She tried to imagine how Thalgor's warriors might resist the attacks she foresaw, but the hard work and many interruptions made deep thought hard.

Thalgor and his council met most of the day in the tent. Boys carried messages back and forth. Warriors came for their orders. The old men who would lead the march in case of an attack came to study the map.

Felyn, disturbed by the activity and noise, clung to Erwyn most of the day. Gee tempted the child away briefly for a game after lunch, but otherwise every time Erwyn turned around she found the child under foot, her cursed eyes dark with fear.

"She is still afraid you will leave her," Gee commented when Erwyn finally did stumble over the child. "Why don't you tell her you won't?"

Erwyn picked herself up and righted the basket of cooking pots she'd been carrying. Luckily, none had broken. She repacked the basket's fragile contents carefully, as if too absorbed in the task to respond to Gee's question. After a minute the old woman shrugged and went on with her work, but Erwyn knew the girl had heard the words she did not say.

In mid-afternoon, the woman named Dara stopped outside the tent. She stood a while and watched Erwyn, then sidled closer.

"Have you no witchcraft to keep Thalgor from making you work?" She glanced around to make sure no one heard. "I did that without any magic. You must be more witch than woman if he is so ungrateful for what you did for him last night."

"I would not let him touch me," Erwyn hissed back, then realized too late she had been tricked into telling Dara what she wanted to know.

"Ah! That's your mistake and my gain."

The other woman gave her an unpleasant grin, licked her lips, and went into the tent. She quickly came out again, her face twisted in anger.

Which made Erwyn smile, although she didn't know why.

By evening she was more exhausted than the day before, too weary even to grumble when she had to sit on the ground because only one bench remained in the tent.

Rygar ate with them. He must have seen her exhaustion because after his meal he left and returned with a jug of water.

"Women's work, Rygar." Thalgor's teasing smile took the sting from his words.

"I remember when we all worked."

Rygar went through to the scullery with the water, then came back and sat again on the other end of the bench.

"You do not think being leader is work?" Thalgor asked him.

"I've been at your side long enough to know it is. But I wonder when you became a man who worked captives like slaves and made them sit on the ground."

Thalgor shifted uneasily. "The men carried out one bench too many. I didn't think it worth the time to have them bring it back. The witch did not object to sitting on the ground."

"And you like to have the witch at your feet." Batte had come in and leaned against a tent pole. "Not that I blame you."

Erwyn shot the newcomer a look so venomous he blanched.

Thalgor and Rygar looked at Batte, then at each other as if deciding how to respond. They both chose silence with the same small shrug.

Erwyn almost saw the Witch King sitting between them. Was her dream nothing more than the mix of these two men, so alike in some ways, so different in others?

She shook her head and pulled herself to her feet to rouse Felyn, who dozed beside her.

Thalgor followed them into the sleeping chamber. Once she'd settled the child, he tied Erwyn's wrists, but not as tightly as he had the night before.

After he left, she began to undo the knots, finishing near sunrise. She untied the rope around her ankle, threw her cloak across her shoulders and went to wake the child.

Felyn refused to stir. Erwyn shook her and whispered her name fiercely, but still the child slept.

An owl called. Dawn drew closer. Too late for the darkness to cover their escape, and she could make only herself invisible.

If she waited until tomorrow, they would be that much farther south, another day added to the already perilously long journey to the Sea Mountains.

If she went to the Wise Witches alone, perhaps they could remove Felyn's curse without the child being there, or give Erwyn the power to remove it when she came back to this camp. If the curse could not be removed, Erwyn might find a home in the citadel of the Wise Witches, and Felyn a home here with Gee. In either case, the Wise Witches would be able to give Erwyn the truth she craved about the child's father.

"Forgive me, Mother, Aunt," she whispered. "Gee will keep her safe for you."

She slipped into the scullery, filled a basket with bread, cheese, and dried fruit, and slung it on her back. No need for an ox without the child. She stirred the air to make herself invisible and fled the sleeping camp.

She went north, toward what little would remain of her captors' camp.

At sunrise she stopped close to where Thalgor had discovered them. A panther screamed not far away. She stirred the air backward to end the spell, then sat to rest.

She might have slept, despite the cold and damp. One moment, she sat alone in the blue-gray of the slow cold time dawn. The next moment, three cloaked figures stood before her.

The one on her left lifted her hood.

"Mother!" Erwyn gasped and rose to her knees.

The one on her right lifted her hood to reveal a face pale and indistinct, as if hidden behind a veil or lost on a foggy night. A face much like her own, but strangely incomplete.

Erwyn felt no fear, only familiar warmth toward the fragile wraith.

"Sister," she wanted to say, but the word came out "Child."

The middle figure lifted his hood. The Witch King.

Panic overwhelmed her. She stumbled to her feet and ran as if all the evil in the world howled at her heels. Ran hard and fast, with no thought of where she went.

"Stay!" She heard her mother's voice behind her.

"Stay." A ghostly voice, hollow as a broken promise.

"Stay." The Witch King's voice.

She stopped and turned to confront the three specters, but they had vanished. She looked about for them wildly, then took her bearings in the early morning mist.

The guards of Thalgor's camp stood only a few feet away, swords drawn. Too late to make herself invisible. She held her head high and walked past them into the camp as if on her way back from a morning stroll. The guards stared at her dumbfounded, as did the women by their fires and the boys who herded livestock as she walked through the camp to Thalgor's tent.

He obviously knew she had escaped because she found him pacing the empty center room and cursing her under his breath so as not to wake Rygar, who slept in a makeshift bed on the ground.

When Thalgor saw her, he ran to her and grabbed her by the shoulders. He shook her once, then dropped his hands and turned away, cursing again under his breath, but now he cursed himself. Finally he turned back to her, his face rigid with anger.

"So, witch, what is it? Stay or go?"

She knew then the truth of what her mother had told her, that visions often revealed only what already lay in one's heart.

Her pulse stuttered under Thalgor's icy stare, but her mind was calm and sure. She would cast her lot with him. For now.

"Stay." She heard the three ghostly voices echo in her own.

"Then why run away?"

"To prove to you that you cannot hold me against my will."

"Why choose to stay?" His eyes narrowed. "For revenge?"

She hesitated, and his eyes narrowed more. She wondered, not for the first time, how much his witch blood let him see.

She drew a curtain around her reasons, not sure of them herself.

"You are about to walk into great danger. You will need my help to save yourself and your people."

"Why do you insist on a danger when my scouts can find no sign of it? Do you think they dare lie to me?"

"I think they are men, and men are sometimes stupid."

Rage twisted his face. Before she could move, he wrapped one great hand around her throat. "Do not dare too much, witch."

She could have burned his hand as she'd done before. Instead she simply stared at him until brown eyes fell from blue. He released her throat and stepped back, his face a mask of shame.

She wondered what lay behind that shame, but his mind stayed as closed to her as she hoped hers was to him.

On the ground behind Thalgor, Rygar stirred. Outside birds called. Around them the camp was waking up.

Thalgor waved a hand toward the scullery. "Get water for Gee. Only one jug. We move south today."

She looked at him for a long minute, until she saw the Witch King's face on his, reminding her of her resolve. With a nod, she did as he said.

THALGOR LOVED THE challenge of moving his men into battle, the organizing, the planning, even the fighting itself, if not the killing. On the battlefield he was sure of the warrior he was.

He hated moving camp. Although the organizing and planning were much like preparing for battle, and provided the same lure of the unknown, moving camp only reminded him of his failure as a true leader of his people, of the dream he could not yet see how to make real.

Behind generations of war and wandering, memories of his ancestors burned bright; men who were kings of cities, not leaders of war camps. Men who brought peace and prosperity to their people, not victory and death.

He refused the harsher barbarities of war, too aware of what they cost. How to bring peace he did not know. Every time they moved camp, the not knowing felt more like a weakness that would destroy him and rob his people of the future he dreamed for them.

As they moved south he marched in the second rank of warriors, protected from unexpected attack but ready to lead if one came. Protected, too, from the dust and noise that grew thicker as one moved toward the rear of the long line of people and animals moving south.

His cart was in the middle of the moving mass behind him, so he didn't see the witch all day. Still, now and then he heard her voice echo like a bell in his head—*Danger.*

They made a moving camp that night. After a cold dinner they settled for sleep, Gee and the child in the ox cart, Rygar and the witch on the ground beside it.

Thalgor walked the perimeter to make sure all the guards stood alert at their posts. A moving camp was a vulnerable camp.

As he came back to his ox cart, he heard Rygar and the witch talking softly on the other side of it. A strange fire burned along his bones.

"The second raiding party will be larger than the first?" Rygar asked.

"Not larger, but you will be weakened by the first attack," the witch answered.

Rygar gave a low whistle. "Will they over-run us completely?"

She paused. Taking time to make up more seductive lies, no doubt. Thalgor's bones burned hotter.

"I don't think so," she said finally. "But they will leave many men dead and wounded, so the next battle may be your last."

"When will the next battle be?" Rygar's voice echoed less with fear than loss of hope.

"I cannot see that far. It may never happen." She paused. "Still, if you could persuade Thalgor to move north…"

They both fell silent, but in his mind Thalgor saw the witch touch Rygar in a way that would light the flame of desire that lies shallow in a man so young.

"Yes." He stepped around the cart and dropped down

next to where Rygar sat on the ground. "Tell me what you will do for Rygar if he betrays me for you."

Once seated, he saw that the witch lay on a pallet on the other side of the campfire, not near enough to touch Rygar at all, much less as intimately as he imagined.

"Thalgor…" Rygar warned him in a low tone.

The witch said nothing, but a white flame lit from her fingertips as she cast a line across the fire from where she lay to where the two men sat.

As the cold flame burned near Thalgor, it turned green, then reversed itself and sped back to her hand, where she cupped it into a glowing yellow-green bubble and threw it at him. The bubble burst when it hit him and bathed him in a sulfurous stink.

Rygar gave a snort of laughter and lay down. Within instants he started to snore. The witch turned her back, pulled a blanket around her against the frost. Soon she slept, too.

Thalgor brushed off the green slime and watched the campfire burn down. What had possessed him to take captive a witch who not only healed and saw, as all witches did, but also had the rare gift of flame? A witch who lit fires of jealousy and lust deep inside him, and brought back memories so dark he could not sleep.

CHAPTER FOUR

E RWYN TRUDGED BESIDE the ox cart on the second day, her mind mired in ways they might yet escape the attack she felt draw closer every minute. When Rygar came to walk beside her, she thought he meant to continue the conversation Thalgor had interrupted the night before. She still hoped for the young archer's help, but he walked beside her a long while in silence.

Finally, without looking at her, he said, "The woman I killed…"

"My aunt." Erwyn's voice felt rough with renewed grief. "She cared for me after my parents…died."

He slumped. "I feared she might be your mother, the way you looked at me, but I had hoped to be more wrong than I was."

"She was the only mother the child ever knew."

He looked up at where Felyn rode with Gee on the cart.

"Was your aunt a witch?" A new fear shadowed his voice.

So he knew of the curse that fell on anyone who caused the death of a witch, no matter how innocently.

In spite of herself, Erwyn looked up at the child, too.

"No, she wasn't."

"I didn't aim at her."

"I know. I saw the look on your face when she fell."

He turned away. "I didn't aim at anything."

"Why would you waste an arrow in battle?"

"The battle was over. Thalgor had already killed their leader. Their men no longer stood and fought. I hate the need to kill when the enemy only tries to flee us. That's one reason I became an archer. At least once the battle ends, I can fire a few arrows without the need to aim at anyone."

He hung his head, as if to brace himself against her contempt. When she said nothing, he went on.

"I'm not like Thalgor. He does not like to kill. It grieves him, too. But he knows why we kill. And I know only I am supposed to shoot arrows at men as they run from me."

"Why should it grieve either of you?" Erwyn asked. "All any band does is wander and kill."

"Not our band." He raised his head, eyes alight with a quiet enthusiasm. "Thalgor is not content for us to live like that. He wants to conquer the whole land, end the warfare, and build cities of stone. We were once a great people, you know. His ancestors were our rulers. He wants to bring peace again."

"How can he do that if you kill all the men you defeat?"

The light in Rygar's eyes dimmed. "It is what this band has always done. We never took warriors captive, even before Thalgor…" He stumbled over his words and went on.

"Before Thalgor became our leader. If there is another way to keep our enemies from returning to attack us later, we have no memory of how it might be done."

"At least you do not make slaves of them." She shivered. "My father was no longer the same man after he escaped from slavery in the South."

"Your father was a slave? And escaped?"

Tears filled her eyes. She brushed them impatiently away.

"Death would have been kinder. A quick death—it killed him in the end, in any case."

"I know how it can be. My mother was a slave."

They walked on, both lost in thoughts as uncomfortable and confused as the dust and noise of the moving band around them.

"Rygar!" Thalgor came up behind them and cuffed the younger man on the shoulder. "You're wanted on duty at the head of the march."

"I thought my duty was after midday."

"I have decided it is now."

Erwyn glared as Rygar adjusted the bow and quiver on his back and hurried off. Without looking at Thalgor she made green fire flow down her arm and spun it toward him.

"You see too much, witch," he muttered as he brushed the glowing stench off his cloak and took Rygar's place beside her.

"At least I see a future that will truly happen. Not some old legend brought back to life."

Thalgor jerked his head in the direction Rygar had gone. "He told you about that? What else did he tell you about me?"

"We weren't talking about you." She stepped with more emphasis than was necessary around a steaming pile of fresh ox waste. "We were talking about war."

Thalgor smiled the knowing smile she'd come to hate.

"Rygar's not the man to talk to about battle." His voice held none of the censure his words implied. "He is a poet and a storyteller, that one. He'll tell you many beautiful tales if you become his friend."

"All about you, of course."

"Some about me," Thalgor admitted with more humility than she would have expected. "More about others. If I dream of a different future, a better future for my people, it is because of the stories he has told me. He knows all the legends, all the children's tales."

"Then I will become his friend."

Thalgor strode off again as abruptly as he'd come.

Alone, Erwyn pondered her own words. Could she become friends with the man who had killed her aunt? She'd vowed never to forgive Rygar. And she would never forget. Her heart clenched with pain each time she thought of her aunt's kindness. But what did hatred and vengeance bring but more war and death?

A deeper question—could she live contented with Rygar and the others in Thalgor's band until she found a way to fulfill her promise to take Felyn to the Wise Witches?

To live content hadn't been possible among those who had destroyed her own camp. Her captor's fear of witches had been too intense, her servitude too bitter, her grief at the loss of her home too sharp and deep.

Time had not healed her sorrow so much as softened it. Life with strangers who might be kinder to her, who would let her live free no longer seemed a betrayal of all she had lost.

Still, her duty lay elsewhere. She tried again to imagine ways she might escape to the Wise Witches, but as she grew wearier her thoughts strayed to visions of a life without wandering, without war. The impossible visions that filled Rygar's stories and fed Thalgor's dream.

THE ATTACK CAME on the third day, just before they stopped for the night. Only a small raiding party, but effectively deployed to cut off the last quarter of the march and capture goods, women, and most of the livestock.

At the first cries from the rear, Thalgor sent boys to clamber up trees on each side of the road so he could know exactly where the attack came from.

He moved his men backward in waves so only one rank was left at the front of the march. That kept the attackers from cutting off the rear of the camp, and provided a steady stream of warriors to oppose them.

He moved rearward more quickly than the rest, Rygar at his side. When they came abreast of his ox cart at the center of the line of march, where Gee, the witch, and her child huddled, he turned to the younger man and said, "Guard them, archer."

Rygar nodded and stood over them, an arrow on his string.

Once Thalgor reached the battle, his men sent up a cry. He pulled his sword and held it over his head for all to see before he waded into the nearest skirmish to run the sword through a man who thought to stab one of Gurdek's men from behind. Thalgor pulled the sword free and breathed the acrid smell of death.

The blood lust took him. He hacked and hewed his way through the battle as he searched in the noise and dust for the leader of the raiding party.

He found him by the gold on his breastplate and his size, nearly as tall as Thalgor himself.

Thalgor had almost reached the enemy leader when an arrow slid behind his shield and lodged in his hip. He pulled it out carelessly despite the pain that would come when the blood lust faded, and strode the last paces to his adversary.

"Leader!"

The tall man raised a grizzled head from the now dead man at the other end of his sword. Thalgor recognized the young man, newly a father.

"A challenge," Thalgor called.

Silently the tall man turned to face him.

One of the enemy archers drew his bow, arrow aimed at Thalgor, but the tall man waved him back.

Thalgor smiled. A battle with a man of honor. A worthy death, or a worthy victory.

The battle continued around them, but felt far away, quieter, as Thalgor and the tall man circled, each seeking a weak spot in the other.

Slowly Thalgor edged their duel away from the women and children to create a hole in the battle line through which most of them could flee to safety. If his opponent saw what he did, the man gave no sign, but focused on the search for an opening that would allow him to kill Thalgor and send his warriors into disarray for an easy victory.

The tall man lunged first, but Thalgor easily parried the move. Their circle tightened. Thalgor smelled his opponent's sweat and the blood on the stranger's hands as well as his own. The battle around them became even quieter, even more distant.

Thalgor spotted a vibrant red scar across the tall man's knee and lunged at his legs. The other man moved quickly enough that the stroke missed his knee, but the sword caught the flesh of the man's calf and tore it open.

The stranger took a step back and gave a roar of anger before he charged at Thalgor, sword raised over his head.

In one smooth movement Thalgor raised his shield to

protect his head and thrust his sword upward, but it missed the man's vulnerable belly.

The tall man's sword clanged twice against Thalgor's shield before both men stepped back to catch their breath.

The opponent's eyes were slightly glazed. Thalgor's would be, too, from the pain of his wounds and the blood lust of the battle.

He lunged toward the tall man's heart. His sword met only his enemy's shield, but Thalgor smelled weakness.

The over-eager archer must have sensed his leader's weakness, too, because an arrow sang through the air and lodged at an angle in the leather of Thalgor's breastplate. An answering arrow from among his men felled the archer when he stood.

The tall man took one look at his fallen comrade and spread his arms wide, sword on one side, shield on the other, so his belly and chest were exposed.

An old trick. If Thalgor accepted the invitation the other man's sword would plunge into his neck while his own found only the enemy's shield. He shook his head and saw the tall man smile. A worthy adversary indeed.

The other man lunged again. Thalgor side-stepped him and raised his sword arm across his chest, as if to defend himself. But as his opponent rounded back toward him, he brought his sword back and up. The sharp blade caught the enemy under the breastplate and slid through flesh well into his body.

The tall man gave him an astonished look, then fell dead.

The attackers took one look at their fallen leader, grabbed what goods they could, and fled wildly into the trees along the road.

Gurdek urged their men after the enemy, but Thalgor stood over the tall man's body, breathing hard as the battle lust ebbed. Melancholy took its place.

When he looked up, the witch was at his side.

"Will you kill them all?" She looked past him to where the enemy had fled, his warriors on their heels.

"All we can catch." He sucked in air against the pain from the arrow wound in his hip.

The witch either did not notice his pain, or did not care.

"What about their women and children?"

"They were a raiding party. Either they have none, or the ones they have are safe in some large camp somewhere."

Her hand went unerringly to his wound. Her fingers both measured it and eased the pain.

"Surely some of them were good warriors."

He looked down at the leader he had killed.

"Why all these questions, witch? Your uncle could have told you as much as I."

She took her hand away from his wound. The pain did not return, but his skin felt cold without the warmth of her touch.

"My uncle and I rarely spoke."

Batte came up beside them.

"Are there many wounded?" Thalgor asked him.

"Enough."

"Take me to them," the witch said.

Batte gave her a dark look. "So you can kill those the raiding party left alive?"

"So I can heal them."

"You are a witch and a captive. Why would you heal our warriors?" Batte growled.

"Because it is a law of my power to heal where I can."

"It is the law of witches to lie when they can."

Thalgor held up his blood-stained hand.

"Batte, take her to the wounded. Take the surgeon, the bond-setter, and the herbalist with you. You can watch and see for yourself if she harms or heals."

"But…"

An invisible cloud rose between Thalgor and his old friend. The witch's work. But his wounded men needed her help.

"Batte, do as I say."

THE PAIN OF the wounded flooded over Erwyn as she moved about the battlefield. The surgeon and the bone-setter seemed untouched by it, but the herbalist rubbed his forehead as if it ached. Witch blood, Erwyn thought.

"The worst off first," she told Batte when the small party

was assembled.

The first man was so near death his eyes no longer saw. She closed them with one hand and set the other over his faint heartbeat to let it stop. The man gave a sigh and died.

"I knew you would kill," Batte said with icy venom.

"He was already dead," the herbalist told him. "You could see that. She only made it easier for him."

Batte grunted and led them to the next man.

This one looked unharmed except for an arrow lodged in his neck. The surgeon started to pull the arrow out, but Erwyn stopped him.

"Why leave the weapon in, witch?" Batte reached between the healers and yanked the arrow out. Blood spurted from the open wound faster than Erwyn and the surgeon could stop it, drenching them all. The man quickly died.

Erwyn stood up and took the arrow from the stunned Batte. She broke it in two and threw it at his feet.

"Fool!" Her body shook with rage.

Batte stood, white-faced, over the dead man.

"Here, healer," a young man called.

He led her and the others to a wounded woman, big with child.

"My baby," the woman wailed, her hand clasped to her side where an errant arrow had pierced her womb.

Erwyn laid her hand on the woman's belly and knew at once the child was gone. She whispered instructions to the surgeon on how to treat the woman's wound. Then she told the herbalist to send for the midwife and handed him leaves for a tea to help the woman birth her dead child.

She helped two more fatally wounded men die. The next three had badly broken bones her sight helped the bone-setter repair. The sword cuts and arrow wounds she helped the surgeon clean and closed it with ointment and cobwebs from her bag. Soon the wounds were ones the surgeon could repair, the breaks ones the bone-setter could set on his own.

"Take me to the enemy wounded," she told Batte, who had rejoined them after she saw to the pregnant woman.

"No." He stood in front of her, one hand on his sword.

"I told you. It is a law of my magic to heal."

"Even you cannot heal the dead."

"You killed them all?"

"Did your band not do the same?"

She hung her head, reluctant to admit she'd expected it to be different in Thalgor's camp. Reluctant even to wonder why.

"They attacked us. They deserved to die." Batte's scornful tone compelled her to look up at him.

"Your warriors attacked my camp. Did you deserve to die?"

"We defeated your warriors."

"So it is not attackers who deserve to die, but those who lose the battle?"

"Yes, witch." He rattled his sword in its sheath. "And remember you were among the ones who lost."

She mumbled a few words. He opened his mouth in pain and surprise as a small wound on his arm began to swell and throb.

"Watch yourself," she warned him as she walked away.

Once out of his sight, she eased his pain before she let herself sag with fatigue.

Drained as much in mind as in body, she stumbled through the gathering dark toward the ox cart, where she hoped Gee would have food ready.

Thalgor appeared in front of her. "What of my wound?"

She did not want him to know how close she was to collapse, how unable to protect herself from him.

She pulled the last of the cobwebs and sea-scented oil from her bag and quickly tended the wound. Because it was in his hip, she had to touch him where she would rather not have. Where she would not have earlier either, if she hadn't been compelled by a force she scarcely understood.

His flesh burned and trembled under her fingers, but not from pain.

When she straightened and started to turn away, wobbly with exhaustion, he took her arm with one hand to stop her and with the other hand tipped her face up so he saw the weariness in her eyes. And she saw the desire in his.

"So magic is indeed hard work," he said softly.

He swept her up in his arms like a child and carried her close to his body through the noisy confusion of the camp as it recovered from the attack and began to settle for the night.

He didn't take her back to the ox cart, but away from the camp and toward the dark of the trees nearby.

She saw his intent in his eyes and tried to gather her strength to stop him. But even that small effort exhausted the last of her energy and she sank unwillingly into sleep.

She awoke when he laid her on a bed of fallen leaves, the hood of her cloak pulled over her hair to protect it. She tensed for the attack to come, her magic too weak to stop the inevitable.

But Thalgor turned away and started a small fire.

Once it burned bright he left. Erwyn knew she should flee back to where the others would offer her some protection, but she was so spent she could not pull herself to her feet.

Thalgor came back in a few minutes with a rabbit, which he quickly cleaned and put on a stick to roast over the fire. He propped the spit up with two forked sticks and left again to return with bread and a small jug of water from the camp.

Erwyn half dozed. The rich aroma of the roasted meat tormented her empty stomach too much for true sleep.

But when he silently offered her some of the cooked animal, she shook her head. She dare not let him know she could not sit without trembling. To her surprise, he cut off a piece of the juicy meat, lifted her head and shoulders with his arm, and fed the meal to her, bite by bite, until she could eat no more.

Then he finished the food and banked the fire. Erwyn

thought he would sleep on the other side of it, as he did in the camp, but instead he came and lay down beside her.

Now he would take her. Icy dread swept over her, so deep her breath froze in her chest. She tried to summon the strength she would need to protect herself physically because her magic was entirely spent. To her shame, all she managed was a pitiful, "Please, don't."

Thalgor wrapped his cloak around both of them and pillowed her head on his shoulder. She went so weak with relief her tears flowed and soaked his tunic.

"Sleep, witch," he whispered.

They both woke before dawn. Despite Erwyn's protests, Thalgor swept her up in his arms to carry her back to the ox cart. He moved stealthily, in spite of her weight, so he would not alert the sentries.

As soon as they left the shelter of the trees, Rygar rose up in front of them.

"You are not on guard duty, archer." Thalgor set Erwyn on her feet.

The younger man's eyes searched Erwyn's face. "You told me to guard those who live in your tent."

"Do you think I would harm her?" Thalgor's voice was thick with sadness as well as anger.

"It is all a matter of what you consider harm."

"Do you truly think I would do anything to her anyone would call harm? You know me better than that."

Strangely distressed by the anger between these two men

she sensed loved each other, Erwyn raised her hand.

"He did not touch me, Rygar." She chose to ignore the intimate way they'd slept together. Then she turned to Thalgor. "But if you did not mean to harm me, why take me to the woods so others might suspect you did?"

Thalgor's face flushed red. "I did not expect you to be so helpless."

"Just helpless enough?"

She saw his shame turn in an instant to rage at her half-mocking tone.

"Why don't the two of you stay and talk about it all day?" he growled. "I have work to do, if there is to be a second attack."

Erwyn gave a laugh that startled even her. "So, great man, you have become a believer after all."

Thalgor gave her a look so dark it set her back on her heels. Her heart raced, but she stood her ground.

"Thalgor, you are right," Rygar quickly intervened. "We all have much to do. Where should we start?"

Erwyn turned her back on the two men and walked unsteadily toward the ox cart. A light rain fell, but Gee had fashioned a lean-to from a flap of the tent. As Erwyn approached the makeshift shelter, Felyn gave a cry of joy and ran out into the rain toward her. Erwyn patted the child's head awkwardly and ducked under the lean-to.

"She fretted for you all night," Gee said. "Why did you leave?"

Not, why did she not return until morning.

"I had work to do. She knew that."

The child did know, Erwyn realized. But how? An icy shiver ran through her that had nothing to do with the cold.

"Maybe, but she has lost so much," Gee replied. "She is afraid she will lose you, too."

"Her pain is as strong whether I am here or not." When had their aunt's nearness ever eased Erwyn's pain?

"Perhaps she fears it will grow worse if she loses you."

Grief washed over Erwyn in a rush that crumpled her legs. She fell gracelessly to the ground by the fire. The loss of her aunt just days before had certainly made her pain worse. But at root the child was the cause of it all.

"And how much pain have you caused her?" she heard the Witch King ask, his voice as clear as if Gee had spoken again.

Erwyn pulled herself up to sit with her back against the cart and looked at the child by her side. She nodded, and the girl clambered into her lap. Almost immediately they both fell asleep.

Once the sun rose, and everyone had eaten, Thalgor summoned Erwyn to where his council met. She started to refuse, but a vision of the second attack overrode her anger and pride.

The council crowded around a makeshift table of boards and logs to study the rough map of the area Gurdek had drawn. The men parted to make a place for Erwyn next to

Thalgor.

"Where does the attack come?" he asked her without greeting.

She looked at the map. Before she answered, she took a piece of the charcoal the map had been drawn with and used it to correct the path of a river.

"Here." She indicated a drive from the south. "As the dark time ends, raiding parties from the south will move north in waves. The bands further south have grown stronger and push them toward us. That is why we must move north."

"Enough of moving north, witch," Batte growled. "Tell us about the attack that comes today."

Erwyn realized with a shudder that she'd made a dangerous enemy, one who held Thalgor's trust where she did not.

"They will come from here," she pointed, "but split into two groups at the river, each the size of the raiding party yesterday, but not so well-organized or so well disciplined."

Thalgor gave a grunt of satisfaction as she paused to call the vision to mind again.

"Half will attack the front of our line, half the rear."

"What if we are in a circle, rather than a line?" Thalgor interrupted her.

She closed her eyes. "It depends on whether their scouts see how we are arrayed before they split at the river."

"Gurdek," Thalgor ordered, "take your men and sweep all the land between here and the river. Kill anyone you find."

His lieutenant nodded and headed quickly off.

"A tight circle," Thalgor said. "Even the livestock inside. It will only be for a short time, and the more ranks of warriors around the camp, the less likely the attack will succeed."

Rygar, Batte, and the others nodded and spread out to reorganize the sprawling camp and post their men around it.

"Go back to the ox cart with the others." Thalgor barked the words as if to one of his warriors in battle.

"After the battle we move north?" Erwyn asked.

"After the battle we rest," he replied, his body half turned from her. "Then we move north."

She waited, vainly she knew, for words of apology or gratitude. But she wanted him well aware that she expected them.

They stood frozen until a young man came to say their scouts had already seen the raiding party cross the river and split in two. Thalgor nodded.

"Go, now," he told Erwyn. "You are no good to us dead."

As close to an apology as she was likely to get.

This day's battle went differently. Even though the raiders came sooner than expected, when they did they swooped down on what they thought would be a vulnerable line of march. The heavily guarded circle they found instead sent them into a panic.

Some carried on with the attack, but most turned and ran. The first rank of Thalgor's warriors charged after them.

Erwyn's work as a healer was soon begun and quickly ended. Few of their men were wounded and most of the attackers were dead or dying. Luckily so, as she was still drained from the day before and already exhausted. As she walked wearily across the silent battlefield, it struck her again as wrong that the brave should die as the cowardly fled. Wrong and wasteful.

Thalgor's warriors chased the attackers only as far as the river. When they returned with the swords and shields of those they had killed, Thalgor had the camp spread out again and ordered an ox roasted to celebrate the victory.

While Erwyn and Gee served his council their food, he announced that the next day they would head north. Not even Batte raised any objection.

CHAPTER FIVE

L IFE QUICKLY BECAME routine as they made their way
north. Erwyn helped Gee with the work of the camp by
day, and met with Thalgor and his council by night.

His people did not trust her, so Thalgor never consulted
her openly when the council met to make plans and settle
the petty disputes that arose in the camp. Still, he would
look at her before he made a judgment for a nod or shake of
her head, or a gesture of indecision. She never knew if the
rest of the council saw. She and Thalgor never spoke of it. In
fact, they scarcely spoke at all, except when the council
discussed strategy and needed her second sight.

Rygar, on the other hand, did indeed become her friend.
In the evenings, when the council's work was done, he told
her and the child all the legends of his people, with an
occasional correction from Gee when he didn't tell a tale
quite right.

One thing Erwyn learned from his stories was that Thalgor was a direct descendent of the kings who once ruled the
land. By counting from the family stories Rygar and Gee told
around the campfire, she also calculated that all of Thalgor's

grandparents were of witch blood, except his mother's father. No wonder he could see into her mind at times.

Slowly the child ceased to grieve and began to speak again. Not to Erwyn, whom she avoided now she felt safe, or to Thalgor. But Erwyn heard her sometimes talk softly to Rygar or Gee, or to the other children she'd finally begun to play with.

One or two of the boys teased her at first about her strange eyes, but when she shrugged off their cruel comments, they relented and accepted her as she was.

One evening when Gee was too tired, Erwyn cooked dinner over the campfire while Thalgor played the stone game with the child. Suddenly Felyn stood up and threw the stones at him.

"Don't stare at me," she cried. "Don't stare at my eyes!"

"I'm sorry," Thalgor responded calmly, despite his obvious surprise. "They are lovely eyes."

"No. They're ugly." The child stamped her foot.

"Why do you say that?"

"Because I'm cursed!"

Erwyn dropped the spoon she held and moved to silence the child, but Thalgor held up his hand to stop her.

"Cursed?" he asked gently. "How?"

"I don't know."

"Why don't you know?"

"I don't know that, either. Erwyn knows."

"Did Erwyn curse you?"

"No," they both cried.

The child ran to Erwyn and buried her face in her cloak.

"Is that why you are the way you are with her, because she is cursed?" Thalgor asked Erwyn.

Reluctant to tell him more than he had a right to know, or to upset the child further, Erwyn just shook her head.

But his eyes followed her as she returned to her work.

Another night, when rain drove the camp to set up their makeshift lean-tos and settle for a cold dinner, Gee was the one who broke the glum silence.

"Have you heard, Thalgor, that Dara and Batte are together?"

Erwyn shivered.

"I heard." Thalgor's voice was empty of feeling.

"Is she his woman?" Rygar asked. "Does she tend his fire?"

"Not that one." Gee laughed. "He still lives in the barracks, but she brings him to her mother's fire to eat, and he lets her younger brother care for his sword and armor."

Clearly the news made Thalgor uneasy.

Had he heard the same whispers among his warriors that Erwyn had heard among the women? Rumors that she'd bewitched him so he would lead them all to a certain death in the north. She'd wondered at their source, but now could see they were most likely tales Dara had told Batte, and Batte had spread around the camp.

She shivered again and felt Thalgor's eyes on her. She

looked up to find him appraising her as if he, too, wondered if the rumors were true. An unexpected pain made her look away.

Sometimes, late at night after an especially acrimonious council or a rainy day that covered everything with mud, when the child whined and Thalgor barked, she prepared herself to leave and go on to the Sea Mountains alone.

But the Witch King's face would appear in the fire, or hover over the child as she slept, or shine in Thalgor's eyes, and she stayed.

One night, the urge to leave was so strong she slipped away from the others and walked along the stream where they were camped. The steady gurgle of the water—a thin echo of the sea, mother of all witches—brought her peace.

The night was quiet. Only the occasional hoot of an owl or the rustle of mice in the leaves disturbed her thoughts. Even the call of a panther on the prowl could not disrupt the calm.

She sat on a rock in sight of the warriors who guarded the camp and lost herself in dreams of a life for the child freed of her curse, a home for herself as a Sea Witch, a future without wandering and war. Thalgor's dreams, as well as her own.

A sound interrupted her reverie. Her heart jumped. Thalgor.

"Do you follow me, great man?"

"Do you flee me, witch?"

"No."

"But you want to." It was not a question.

"Yes."

"Why? Why this need to go to the Sea Mountains?"

Half an honest answer was better than none. "To find a home there."

"Have you not a home in my camp?"

"No."

The air between them crackled. Her denial hurt him, she realized with surprise.

"Will the Sea Witches give your child a home as well?" His voice was brittle because he knew the answer. "You mean to leave her with Gee?"

"Yes. It would be cruel to uproot her again."

"And not cruel to abandon her?"

"It is complicated."

"You do not love your child. The reason may be complicated, but the fact is simple."

Unable to bear the contempt in his voice, she stood and turned to face him in the silver light of the full moon.

"She is not my child."

She sank back on the rock and braced herself for whatever came next.

"But she looks…" He stopped. "Your sister?"

Erwyn nodded.

"But not a witch?"

"My father was captured and sold as a slave five years

before she was born."

Thalgor was silent for a long time. "This uncle you seldom spoke to?"

She nodded.

"And he carried no witch blood."

She nodded again.

"But still, to be so cold to a mere child, your mother's child…"

"The cause of my mother's death." She stood again to face him. "And my father's."

Thalgor frowned.

"My father escaped from slavery, but a different man. What he endured had turned his strength to raw cruelty. Perhaps that was necessary for him to survive. In any case, when he found our camp and saw my mother with an infant, he killed her with one stroke of his sword, then turned the sword on himself."

"You saw this?"

"I grabbed the child from my mother's arms and shielded it with my body so he would not kill her, too." Tears streamed down her face but she ignored them.

"He did not kill you."

She shrugged and refused to take any comfort in the fact.

"The curse on the child comes from this?"

"Yes." She turned half away to wipe the dampness from her face on her cloak.

"And you go to the Sea Mountains to have the curse removed."

"To ask. Even the Wise Witches may not be able to do that."

"Your mother cursed the child for eternity?"

"No! The curse comes from causing my mother's death."

She heard him move closer in the darkness and shrank back in reaction. The false promise of comfort he brought made the now familiar torment of his nearness more powerful.

"Your mother deserved her fate."

Erwyn tamped down an angry denial. A man would think that.

"She said not. She told me she knew a special magic to keep my father's seed alive in her body. Only when she could no longer touch his mind with hers and was certain he was dead did she allow the child to be conceived. Or so she said. She did not know that madness, not death, had broken the bond between them."

"And you think the Wise Witches can tell you if she spoke the truth."

"Yes." The single word rang with the pain of her doubt.

He moved quickly and took her hand in his. A flow of heat shot up her arms, then sank more slowly down through her body.

"You blame the child for your parents' deaths?"

She nodded, unable to trust her voice.

"Your parents did not die because of her," he said gently.

"They died because one of them made a tragic mistake. But you don't know which one. It wasn't the child's fault, in any case. It took me many years to learn that simple thing."

Puzzled, she looked up at him, but saw nothing in his face but pain. Her free hand reached up to smooth the tension away.

She never knew what might have happened next if at that moment one of the guards had not come up to them.

He held a bedraggled man tightly by the arm and carried the stranger's sword in his other hand. The guard pushed the man roughly toward Thalgor, so he fell at the leader's feet. The guard handed Thalgor the sword, then left without a word.

Batte's man, Erwyn thought as she pulled her hand back.

Thalgor inspected the well-worn sword while the stranger righted himself to kneel on one leg at the large man's feet.

"I ask to become part of your band," the man, no longer young, said in a tone of resignation.

Thalgor lowered the sword toward him. "Yes?"

"My band was small…"

"Marauders?"

"Yes." The stranger hung his head. "We became too few to feed ourselves, so we turned marauders. A raiding party found us ten days ago. They killed all the other men and took what little we had—women, children, our few goods and tents. I was badly wounded and left for dead but, to my regret, the wound healed. It was too late to save my family. I have no wish to be a renegade, so I ask to join your band."

The man slumped, as if this speech exhausted him.

Thalgor turned to Erwyn, who looked into the man's heart.

"I see a good man, brave, and loyal," she said quietly.

Thalgor grunted. After a moment's thought, he turned the sword in his hand and offered its hilt to the man at his feet.

"Welcome, comrade."

The man stood. The lines of weariness and grief etched in his face eased a bit, but he only nodded and took the sword.

"I follow you now." He held the sword across his chest.

Thalgor motioned to the nearest guard to take the man into the camp and find him food and fresh clothes. The guard, one of Gurdek's men Erwyn guessed, greeted the newcomer with a smile.

When they were gone, Thalgor turned to Erwyn. He placed one hand on her shoulder. Shivers of sensation rushed through her.

"Forgive me," he said.

"For what?" She hated the breathlessness of her own voice, hated that she made no move to push his hand away.

"For what I have thought of you."

"I let you think it. Wanted you to think it."

"Why?"

"I thought motherhood might protect me."

She smelled the leather of his breastplate, the subtle aroma of maleness that surrounded him. She smelled and savored, and hated herself for that as well.

"Protect you from what?"

She pulled free and sat back on the rock. "From you."

He walked away and stood with his back to her.

"You know I cannot take you by force."

"I did not want you even to think of me that way."

He gave a low laugh. "As if I would take captive a witch and her child if I did not think of her that way."

"But I have been useful to you."

"Very useful," he acknowledged, turning back toward her. "But I am not certain it has been worth the trouble you cause."

"The trouble I cause?" She stood to face him. "I made an enemy of Batte, I know. But you can handle Batte. Otherwise I see no trouble I have caused you."

He took her by the shoulders.

The delicate trembling in her body began again. The moon behind him shadowed his face so she saw only the movement of his head as he lowered it toward hers.

"No." She pushed him away. "Never."

She fled back to the camp, pursued not by Thalgor but by the Witch King's voice saying, "Yes. Forever."

THALGOR SAT ON the rock Erwyn had abandoned and laughed.

Not caused him trouble! The witch had done nothing else since he first set eyes on her.

She only troubled his body at first. Badly. So badly he could scarcely think of anything else, could scarcely sleep, could scarcely look at her without being awash in lust.

The lust had finally overwhelmed all that was sacred to him, even the memory of his mother's suffering. His need to take doubled by the battle lust that day, he'd carried her off to the woods with every intention of breaking the only vow he ever took.

But she had been so vulnerable, so empty not only of her power, but almost of herself. Empty because she worked to save his wounded men, warriors who would not have been wounded if he'd listened to her warning.

The need to take had died when she fell asleep in his arms. In its place had grown something he could not name at first, but now knew was tenderness. A strange and unexpected thing, that tenderness.

Not that the lust went away. Once the witch was whole again, it returned double. And grew each day.

So he avoided her when he could and cursed his weakness for her when he couldn't.

Tonight she had confided in him, allowed herself to weep, and he thought perhaps...

She had never been with a man, he realized with a sudden certainty.

His body was swept with waves of lust, tenderness, and a need to protect that fragile body with its great powers.

The Sea Witches gathered their strength from the sea and from their total devotion. She could not become one of them if she surrendered to her desire for him.

He never doubted her desire. He had witch blood enough to see it in her eyes, smell it in the air around her, feel it in her touch. That would have to be enough. For now.

Rygar waited when he reached the edge of the camp.

"Trouble?" Thalgor's hand went to his sword.

The younger man shook his head. "Erwyn left the camp. You followed her. She returned alone. I came to make sure she didn't turn you into a toad."

Thalgor laughed. "Witches can't do that. At least not ordinary witches."

The two of them fell into step, walking parallel to the edge of the camp as if on guard duty.

"I know," Rygar replied. "But it might be a good idea."

"Why? So you can be leader of the band?" Thalgor joked.

Rygar laughed and shook his head. "I have no desire to lead. Only to help you be a better leader."

"And to be turned into a toad would do that?"

Rygar sobered. "It might keep you from hurting Erwyn."

Thalgor wanted to tell him he would never hurt Erwyn, but they both knew that was a vow he could neither make nor keep.

"You care so much for her yourself?" Thalgor's heart paused as he waited for the answer.

He and Rygar shared much. But to share that tenderness...

Rygar laughed again.

"Erwyn is my friend. A sister, perhaps. But to be her man would be to live a life of constant battle."

"Doesn't that excite you?"

The other man caught his involuntary confession and whistled softly between his teeth. "Not as it apparently excites you."

"Don't presume too much, archer."

Rygar shook his head. "I'd sooner have Dara than Erwyn. Dara only wants your body. Erwyn would demand a man's soul."

"I know that all too well."

In spite of his words, a sense of relief swept over Thalgor now that he had told Rygar what was inside him.

"You will be good together." The younger man clapped him on the shoulder as they turned to enter the camp.

ERWYN WENT BACK to the ox cart, told the child a story to put her to sleep and fell into a restless sleep herself.

Thalgor haunted her dreams at first, then they shifted. She saw her father as he once was, his love for her and her mother in his every look. That same love was on her mother's face as she cradled her second daughter. Nor did it ever falter when she looked at Erwyn, even when her older daughter accused her of the worst kind of betrayal.

Her father's image returned, broken in body and mind by his enslavement.

"No," she screamed against the dream. "No!"

Then she saw herself, holding the child, bathed in her parents' blood.

She woke up in tears.

Three days later she could smell the sea. The scent spread a peace through her she had not known since her father's capture over ten years before. But the sea's nearness also brought a restlessness, fed by Thalgor's now more open looks of desire.

The next day she heard a seagull cry and peace passed into joy. The restlessness became plans, plans to leave within hours instead of days.

She expected visions of the Witch King that night to tell her she must not go, but she slept dreamlessly.

Perhaps the warnings were only to keep her in Thalgor's camp until he brought her safe this far. And now she was free for her destiny.

During the day she slid whatever food she could take into the bag she always carried at her waist. When they stopped for the night, she ate as much as she could bear.

She silently blessed the child as she put her to bed, and

Gee, who slept beside her. She touched Rygar's head lightly as she passed where he slept to bless him as well.

She lay down, but didn't sleep. She waited for Thalgor to return from gambling with Gurdek and his second two fires away.

Finally he came back and extinguished their fire last of all in the camp, as he always did. She watched through half-closed eyes as he lay down beside Rygar.

When he snored, she filled a basket with food and, reluctant to steal an ox, tied it across her back. Then she left the camp.

She walked through the night. After a cold breakfast at dawn, she crawled to the center of a thicket to sleep.

A drizzling rain woke her in mid-afternoon. She walked the road openly now, certain Thalgor could be no closer than half a day behind her. If he followed her at all.

After he complained about how much trouble she caused him, she began to think he might let her go. He knew now why she needed to reach the Sea Mountains, and his desire for her was perhaps not enough for him to keep her from them. Or enough to make it worth the trouble to follow her.

That possibility caused her more pain than it should have.

She walked until the moon set, then slept beneath some bushes by the road. In the morning she found the bushes were heavy with tangy ripe berries and ate her fill.

She walked in daylight now, mind alert for renegades

more than followers from Thalgor's camp.

As her store of food dwindled, she ate less each day, except when she found more early berries to gorge herself on.

The hunger grew until she began to have waking dreams, always the same. A woman very like her mother stood by a fire. Erwyn could smell the rich aroma of the meat she cooked. The woman beckoned her onward, but never smiled.

The mountains on each side of the river she followed grew closer together. The road finally climbed half-way up the mountainside to keep from disappearing under the roaring water.

She found the climb hard in her weakened state, but the vision of food, now even more than the nearness of the sea, pulled her onward.

She ate the last of the dried fruit she'd brought as sunset colored the fog that crept in at the end of the sixth day. She huddled by a bush on the treeless mountain for shelter. Birds had already eaten the ripe berries. She was still hungry enough to taste the green ones, but their bitterness turned her empty stomach to pure bile.

She vomited them up, then turned greedy eyes to the white rush of water in the river below. But it would be folly to try to climb down through the rocks and slag to drink and bathe. Impossible to climb back up.

She lifted her eyes and for the first time saw a thin line of blue and gold shimmer in the sunset under the fog on the horizon.

The sea. Reconciled to dying within sight of her goal, she slept.

When she found herself still alive the next morning she trudged on through gray mist, only to be rewarded with a clear mountain stream around the next bend in the road.

She drank and washed, calm and joyful despite her hunger. Not only was the sea within sight, but a damp breeze ruffled her hair. Two more bends of the road and it all lay before her.

The sea stretched endlessly to the horizon, blue in the distance, gray-green near the shore, curling white waves on the beach. The fog had floated away to become a cloud. The beach sand was more golden than river sand, and she knew it would be finer.

Except for the mouth of the river where some great ancient cataclysm has split the wall of rock, the sea roared right up to the mountains that lined the shore on both sides as far as she could see. In some places rocks jutted out into the water, drenched with the spray sent up by the waves that crashed against them. Gulls landed, then soared away again from the tide.

The road wound down the mountainside until it crossed the river where it formed a great shallow fan on the beach. Half-way up the mountain opposite her was a great stone citadel half carved from, half build upon, the solid rock.

She had never seen a stone building before, only tumbled

rocks where they had once stood. She marveled that human hands could make anything so ageless and beautiful, even with the help of the Wise Witches who lived there.

She hesitated before she followed the road to the beach, aware her every move could be seen from the citadel. No wonder it still stood. Even without the power of the Wise Witches to protect it, the great stone tower would be impervious to attack.

She found going down the road to the sea almost as hard as the climb behind her. Soon her calves ached. But she focused on the fresh water of the river and ignored both the steep climb up to the citadel ahead of her and her growling, empty stomach.

When she reached the river she followed it upstream to a wide, deep pool sheltered beneath low-hanging trees. She drank the cool, sweet water, then bathed. Afterward she floated on her back to ease her sore legs before she dried herself and dressed.

When she returned to the roadside to gather up her cloak and bag, a woman stood beside them. The unsmiling woman of her dreams.

"I am Mafern." She was no longer young but not yet old, about the age Erwyn's mother was at her death. "I am the youngest of the Sea Witches."

Erwyn's heart sank. If this was a young Sea Witch...

"I brought food." Mafern held out a bag that smelled of fresh bread and fruit.

Erwyn managed to control her hunger enough to say "Thank you" and wait until Mafern handed her the bag, but then she sat down on the spot and greedily ate every bite. Mafern watched her with the same unsmiling face that had haunted Erwyn's dreams.

"Come now," Mafern said when Erwyn had eaten all the food.

Erwyn stood and immediately fell down again. Her legs didn't simply ache. They would no longer hold her.

"Ah." Mafern dropped to the ground beside her and pulled Erwyn's gown up to her knees, then reached for the bag she wore at her belt and pulled out a vial of red ointment. Expertly she spread it on Erwyn's legs and massaged them as she chanted softly.

The spice-scented potion and the Sea Witch's touch healed more than Erwyn's legs. All the weariness of the journey melted away with the pain. When she felt whole again, she nodded.

Mafern put her ointment away and held a hand out to help Erwyn stand. "Come now."

The walk to the citadel was much less arduous than Erwyn had feared. A full stomach and a companion, however silent, made light work of the climb.

Still, the fog rose and the sun set behind them before they neared the great door of the citadel.

Mafern turned off the road and led Erwyn into a cave in what had seemed from across the river to be a solid wall of rock.

"You will sleep here tonight." Mafern showed her a bed by a small, cheerful fire. "Do you need more food?"

"No, thank you." Sleep already dimmed Erwyn's senses.

"I will bring breakfast, then take you to the Wise Witches."

Erwyn nodded and collapsed into a deep, dreamless sleep.

Mafern woke her with milk, a bowl of berries, and more fresh bread. Then she led Erwyn into the citadel.

They followed long, twisted passages through dark, empty rooms and climbed well-worn stairs. Their steps echoed against the ancient stone walls. At each landing were two windows. One looked out over the sea, the other across the river toward the road.

As they climbed, Erwyn noticed someone come down the road, a mere speck from this distance. Slowly she was able to make out a man and an ox with baskets on each side of its back. A servant who brought food to the citadel, perhaps. She turned to cross the next empty room and climb the next long flight of stairs.

They emerged at last on what should have been the roof of the citadel. But rather than the stone and mortar Erwyn expected, she found herself surrounded by the perfume of a thousand flowers, the sweet scent of fruit-bearing trees, and the music of scores of singing birds.

Water leapt down a stone bridge from the mountainside

to form a stream that meandered through the garden before it crossed another stone bridge to flow down the mountainside again.

Mafern let her stand there and absorb the healing power of the joyful sounds and sweet smells.

Erwyn had wondered why anyone with all the power the Wise Witches had would live in the drab, cold tower she'd walked through. Now she saw that they lived not there but here, in the perpetual warm time created by an invisible magic tent that sheltered this roof from fog, wind, and rain, letting only the sun and its warmth shine through.

"Welcome to the garden of the Wise Witches," Mafern said.

CHAPTER SIX

T HEY WALKED THROUGH the lush foliage to a small stone table. Seated around it were three very old women. Each glowed slightly with colored light—one red, one blue, one green.

The likeness to a council in Thalgor's camp brought the unwelcome sting of tears to Erwyn's eyes.

The three Wise Witches stood and smiled kindly at her.

"A visitor, how lovely," said the one who would be Fire.

"Did you have a hard journey?" asked Air with a small frown.

"You must be hungry," commented Earth, one hand on her own round belly.

Erwyn's knees wobbled. She could barely manage a smile in the presence of so much power and wisdom.

"I'm fine, thank you." Her voice came out thin and shaky.

"Then we will start," Fire declared and all three sat down.

"Why have you come here?" Air began with a look that was sharp and deep, but not unkind.

"I came to know if my mother spoke the truth."

"You doubt your mother's word?" Earth asked in obvious surprise, her kind smile fading.

"She had reason to lie."

"Tell us what she said," Fire suggested.

So Erwyn repeated the story of Felyn's birth.

"You wish to know if witches do have the power to keep a man's seed alive in their bodies until they choose to conceive?" Air asked.

Erwyn nodded.

"Some do, some don't." Earth told her with a shrug.

"The answer to your true question," Fire added gently, "is written in your heart."

Erwyn stood silently for a moment, stunned that they would deny her the truth she has come all this way to hear. But to protest or plead would clearly be useless.

"Why have you come here?" Air asked again.

"To learn the nature of the child's curse and how it might be lifted." The words were pulled from her more than said.

"What are the signs of her curse?" Earth asked with a frown.

"Her eyes. The black is a slit in the green, not round."

"Nothing else?" Fire peered more closely at Erwyn.

"She is only a child."

"The answer to your question is written in the child's heart," Air told her kindly.

Again disappointment settled on Erwyn like a dark weight.

Before she had fully absorbed the impact, Earth asked again, "Why have you come here?"

This time Erwyn spoke the words she meant to say all along. "To become a Sea Witch."

Fire smiled and shook her head. "It is not your fate." She made a swirling motion in the air and the face of the Witch King appeared above the table.

"Is...is he my fate?" Erwyn's voice shook with dread.

Air waved her hand to make the vision disappear. "Your fate is written in the heart of another."

Erwyn's ears rang with the need to deny their words. Her eyes stung.

But the Wise Witches stood and Earth made a kind, but definite gesture of dismissal. Erwyn had no choice but to go.

Mafern led her in silence back down the citadel and to the door they had entered through, then finally to the road. She handed Erwyn a bag of food, then raised her hand above her head.

"Blessings, sister witch," she said solemnly before she left Erwyn alone.

Unable to hold the pain inside any longer, Erwyn ran down the road toward the sea. Her rage swirled the air around her into tiny cyclones of dust.

How could they treat her so, like a child? She'd came so far, suffered so much, lost so much...

"Lost what?" a voice asked her. The Witch King's voice.

The question only made her run all the faster. Blinded by tears, she felt her feet leave the road for the soft sand of the beach, but she ran on.

"Mother!" she was surprised to hear herself cry. "Mother!"

When the first wave hit her feet with a shock of icy cold, she opened her eyes. She stepped back on the hard, damp sand at the water's edge. Ahead of her was one of the rocky points that jutted into the ocean.

Overwhelmed by a sudden, soul-deep need to be as close as possible to the source of power, to the place where the Mother Sea crashed and swirled, she dropped the bag of food and her cloak in the sand, closed the distance to the rocks, and began to climb them.

Once on the flat, pitted top, slick with sea plants and water, she made her way to the farthest point. Hurt and anger melted like the fog in morning. Every wave that broke below her drew her onward, until their roar filled her mind completely.

She went to the very end of the rocks. The waves crashed on three sides of her now and wrapped her in a fine, salty mist.

The mist parted and her mother walked toward her across the water, her face smiling and serene.

"Mother!" Erwyn opened her arms to the vision.

But her mother shook her head as she rose slowly into

the air and disappeared into the clouds.

Erwyn raised her arms after the vanishing illusion, then lowered them in submission.

To be a Sea Witch was not her fate. So be it.

The weight of disappointment lifted. In its place came a lightness in her heart, as if she were freed from a burden she never knew she carried. Flooded with joy, she lifted her hands to the sky in praise.

The waves crashed higher around her, as if to welcome her. Their rhythm quickened to match the rush of her heart. The world shrunk to this one moment of dizzying exhilaration.

And power. She felt as if she made the water rise and fall.

Here, she was free. Here, in the thundering tides, was her fate. She leaned forward to fly into the crashing surf below her, to become fully one with the Mother Sea forever.

"Erwyn." The Witch King's voice?

"Erwyn!" Closer. From the land, not the sea. Thalgor's voice.

She turned to see him clamber across the rocks toward her on all fours like the crabs that scurried away from him.

She looked back at the sea and suddenly saw the lure of oblivion for what it was—cowardice. An escape from the Wise Witches' judgment.

She started back across the slippery rocks toward Thalgor, toward the future.

A great wave crashed over her and knocked her to her

knees. If she still stood at the very edge, it would have washed her into the sea.

Thalgor reached her as the water rushed away. He pulled her to her feet and held her at arms' length to look at her.

She'd never seen fear in his eyes before.

She let him guide her, drenched and shivering, back to the sand. Her cloak lay where she'd dropped it. He wrapped her in it, cursing under his breath.

She pushed him away. "Leave me, if I caused you too much trouble again."

"After I came so far to find you? You cause me nothing but trouble, witch, but you'll not get rid of me so easily."

He cursed again and leaned his forehead against hers.

"I thought the sea would take you." He shuddered. "I never saw anything like it. As wide as the sky, but alive. Alive and dangerous. Yet you danced with it! Are you mad, witch?"

The fear was back in his eyes. His hands trembled and for a moment she saw the frightened child inside the great warrior.

"The sea is our mother." Her teeth chattered as she spoke.

"A mother who can take life as well as give it." His voice was tight with unaccustomed fear. "A witch mother."

She put one icy hand on his face to comfort him, but he shook the gesture off. The frightened child disappeared again.

"Come." He took her hand. "I made a camp by the pool. There's a fire laid and a lean-to out of the wind."

She nodded, too cold to refuse his offer of shelter.

"How did you get a lean-to here?" Then she saw the ox that grazed on the grass by the river and waved the question away.

Once they reached the makeshift camp he hunkered down with his back to her to start the fire while she pulled off her sodden clothes.

"There's another gown in one of the baskets," he told her without turning around. "Gee thought you might need it. But I didn't bring another cloak. We'll have to hang everything on some bushes to dry."

She found the gown and quickly slipped it on, then hung her clothes on the bushes. She took both of their cloaks to the edge of the beach and spread them on the rocks.

"The rocks are hot from the sun. They'll dry faster," she explained in answer to Thalgor's frown when she got back.

"Do you never do what you're told, witch?" He sighed. "Come here, closer to the fire. You're still shivering."

"Why did you follow me?" she asked when her teeth stopped chattering.

"I wasn't going to. You were always going to go to the Sea Witches. We found a place to camp for the warm time."

He sat across the fire from her, but through the pale daytime flames she could see a look of pain cross his face.

"Then I dreamed of my father. He told me to come after

you. He said it was not your fate to be a Sea Witch."

Witch blood, father and son.

"How is the child?" she asked.

"Content. But she clings to Gee. I think she feels safer when you are there. Perhaps because you are a witch."

Thalgor got up and searched through the baskets.

"I have food." She pointed to the bag Mafern had given her.

"You see too much," Thalgor grumbled as he brought the damp bag to the fire.

The bread inside was too wet to eat, but he rinsed the salt water from the fruit in the pool.

"Why does it annoy you if I know what you want?" she asked.

"If you knew what I truly wanted, you would not sit there so calmly, witch."

A flash of what he wanted blazed through her mind and skittered down her spine. Witch blood to witch blood.

She made the image go away.

"The Sea Witches gave you enough for two," he commented quietly as he handed her the larger portion of food.

"Did you think no one from the citadel saw you come down the road? Even I saw you, though I did not know it was you."

He laughed. "And who else would come alone and unarmed to the stronghold of the Sea Witches with a laden ox?"

They ate in silence as the small fire burned low.

She started to stand. "I'll get more wood."

Thalgor shook his head. "I'll go. You rest."

She was still surprised how willingly he and Rygar did the women's work her uncle, even her father, would never have touched.

She must have fallen asleep as she stared into the flames because the next thing she knew she lay on the bed in the lean-to, where Thalgor had carried her.

That he had made only one bed should have frightened her, but the shiver that ran through her body was hot.

Thalgor had banked the fire and was swimming in the pool of clear river water.

Suddenly the salt and sand that still clung to her skin under the clean gown became unbearable. She pulled the gown over her head and walked into the water.

It was cold. Colder even than the sea. But sweet and clean.

She drove under the surface, unbraided her hair, and ran her hands through it, reveling in the feel of it as it floated free.

When she came up for air, waist deep in the shallows, she saw Thalgor in the center of the pool treading water. The wonder on his face as he looked at her body melted something deep inside her.

She wanted to see his body with a yearning so sharp it made her gasp.

She plunged into the water and swam toward him, but

he swam away to the rocks at the upstream end of the pool. He climbed up to sit on one of them, his beautiful, scarred body on glorious display. She wanted to hear the story behind every scar, to kiss and smooth away all the pain they'd ever caused him.

She wanted to touch the unfamiliar maleness of him. She wanted him to touch her, wanted with a terrible urgency for him to caress all the soft, aching parts of her she'd never known existed before.

She walked as close as she could with her feet still on the sand and stared.

"Stay away, witch." He covered himself too late with his hands. "Don't look at me."

Confused by the rebuff when she thought he invited her stare, she swam back to the camp and waded ashore.

A loud splash behind her was all the warning she had.

Thalgor grabbed her from behind by the shoulders and spun her around to face him. "Do you want me, witch?"

She looked into his face. Joy filled her the way light fills the sky at dawn. "Yes."

"Man to woman, woman to man?"

Woman and man, not witch and warrior, not anything but what they simply were, now, together. "Yes."

"To keep my tent and bear my children."

A new thrill of joy flowed through her at the thought. "Yes."

"Me," he pulled her against the hardening of his body.

"Only me."

"Only you, Thalgor."

Then the sweetest words of all. "Only you, Erwyn."

She reached her arms up around his neck and rubbed her body against his in an enticement as old as time. He claimed her mouth with a moan, swept her up into his arms and carried her back to the lean-to.

"Only one bed," she said with a smile as he laid her on it.

He gave a lazy shrug and lay beside her. "I could have slept outside."

Then he gently kissed her. His touch was gentle, too, as his hands explored her damp, cool flesh.

She wasn't cold. His touch lit a fire in her skin that swirled through her to pool at her core.

As of their own will, her fingers played along the muscles and scars of his body, lingered where her touch made him moan. Brazenly she eased lower, toward the maleness pressed against her softening belly.

His hands on her breasts made her cry out. His thumbs on her nipples made her hands fly away from him to grasp the blanket at her side. He slid his body down hers and took her nipple in his mouth. The swirl of fire became an inferno of need. She grasped his head to her breast and let the desire carry her on its roaring, searing flight.

His hand found the heat at her center. Gentle here, too, but the more tantalizing for it, he opened and explored the secrets hidden there.

Suddenly she was consumed entirely. She called his name as she soared to a place she'd never imagined.

With a cry he entered her, the pain no more than she could erase with the tiny part of her mind not drowned by desire.

He lay still upon her as they both savored the shudders of delight that flowed now from her to him, buried inside her.

He brushed his lips against her cheek. "So precious."

His arms trembled with restrained need as he held himself over her. She answered his unasked question by lifting her hips to claim him more fully. He moved against her, slowly at first, then faster, until she arced again beneath him. He caught her cry with his mouth and gave one more great thrust before the raging flames consumed them both.

She lingered in the bliss, her only reality the strength and heat of his body over hers. Their hearts beat to the same rhythm as the cloud of pleasure slowly ebbed.

She dozed until she felt Thalgor leave her. Through half-closed eyes she watched as he brought a bowl of fresh water. He turned her gently, then dabbed a bit of cloth in the water and wiped her legs clean of the blood she had shed.

Then he poured the water reverently back into the pool, lay down beside her and wrapped his arms around her.

She slept again, afloat on the sea of his tenderness.

THALGOR AWOKE TO find Erwyn sitting on the bed beside him, fully dressed. Before he could act on the need to have her naked beneath him again, she proffered the clothes she must have collected from the side of the pool where he left them. She didn't look at him.

Reluctantly he sat up and dressed. Then he put his hand on her chin to turn her face toward him. She didn't resist but kept her eyes downcast.

"You will not look at me. Do you regret what you said, what we did?" For the second time that day his heart froze in his chest as it hadn't since he was a boy.

"No. But it grows dark and cold. If I look at you, we will freeze and starve and lose our ox."

Delight sprang him to his feet. He pulled her up, wrapped his arms around her, and spun her in a circle.

"You are truly my woman now." He set her down. "You have begun to nag me."

"I nagged you before." She pulled her dry clothes from the bushes, shook off the salt and sand, and folded them into one of the baskets.

"Then you nagged me as a witch used to having her own way. Now you nag me as a woman who cares if I am warm and fed."

She opened her mouth to argue but he kissed her soundly. She laughed. The sound sang in his heart as he went to find their ox and tether it.

In the night, between sweet dreams, he taught her the joy

of long, slow pleasure. As he plunged into her one last time, he thought, *My woman.*

And heard her voice in his mind, half-mocking, "Your witch."

THE NEXT MORNING Erwyn woke at sunrise and went to the edge of the sea. She watched as the fog lifted and day colored the water. Icy little waves washed over her toes.

When Thalgor came to stand close behind her, she felt him tremble.

"The sea is truly the mother of all witches," he whispered as if the water could hear. "It is so vast, so powerful, so unpredictable. Like any woman. But even more like a witch. I know now why no men live near the sea." He put one arm protectively around her. "How do you fight something so huge? How do you protect what is yours from its power?"

His fear of the sea surprised her. He was a brave man. More than brave.

And now the sea was tranquil, shining. Erwyn loved it like a mother. Loved the sound of the waves, the smell of the salt, the feel of sand and fog. She could live in this place forever and never tire of it or be afraid.

"Let's go." Thalgor's voice was still heavy with fear.

THE THREE DAYS it took to reach Thalgor's new camp were like floating in honey. The warm time was almost upon them. Between the food Gee had sent, the sun-warm berries they picked along the way, and the meat Thalgor brought back from hunting each night, they ate lavishly. Each evening they swam together in the river or a pool in one of the creeks that fed it.

They celebrated their delight in each other every sunrise, every night. More than once, when they stopped to eat at midday, Thalgor let the puzzled ox roam and pulled Erwyn down on a patch of flowers or shady grass to love her yet again.

She'd always thought of her body as something she used, like words or magic, to get things done. Like words, or magic, it sometimes didn't work exactly as she wanted, sometimes caused her pain, but by and large she knew its limits and enjoyed using it well and efficiently.

With Thalgor as her teacher she learned that her body held a whole world of its own. A world of sensation, of pleasure, of sheer joy.

To know Thalgor's body gave him the same wants, the same bliss seemed to double all the hidden possibilities of her own. Man to woman, woman to man.

She wondered at times, as they trod along at the end of the day, dusty and tired, if he knew the same bliss with Dara, with others. But she knew better than to ask. She could only be grateful his bliss was with her for now.

They arrived at the camp mid-morning on the fifth day.

Thalgor hadn't told her how close they were, but made love to her with even more than the usual intensity when they first awoke, then joined her in the river, where he bathed her tenderly, kissing all of her body's most secret places.

Unaware their time alone was at an end, she trudged up a steep hill and suddenly saw the camp spread out below her.

A warm time camp. Warriors patrolled the perimeter, but the other men and older boys prepared the ground for planting food crops on three sides of the cluster of tents. On the fourth side shepherds sheared the sheep. Their bleats of protest floated lazily on the air. Closer to where they stood, the younger boys watched the oxen graze, new-born calves small and white among the gray cows.

The camp itself was much as she first saw it, except quieter. The great fires needed for warmth and light in the dark time were gone. In their place stood looms, dozens of them, circled in groups among the tents. The women sat in the morning sun and talked while they wove. Young girls carded wool at their feet, and the older ones spun. The littlest children played all around them under their mothers' watchful eyes.

The memory of her mother weaving while she spun filled Erwyn's eyes with tears.

"Do you weep to return to my camp, or at the end of our time alone?" Thalgor asked.

"I weep for the home I lost."

"Ah." He looked up to the sky. "I lost a home once, too."

"Is this not your camp?"

"Now it is." He turned away. "And yours, as well."

She reached up to caress his shoulder, not sure why she felt the need to comfort him.

He took her other hand in his. "Shall we go?"

As they came nearer to the camp, word spread of their arrival. Boys appeared to free the ox of its burden and carried the baskets to Thalgor's tent. Women left their looms, warriors their posts to welcome them back.

Batte and Gurdek met them just inside camp.

"Has all been quiet?" Thalgor asked.

They gave him their report as the three of them walked together toward his tent.

Erwyn fell a few steps behind. No one seemed to notice her in the excitement over Thalgor's return. Only Dara glared at her from the door to her mother's tent.

And Rygar greeted her with a handful of flowers when he met them half-way through the camp.

"I'm glad Thalgor persuaded you to come back."

Persuaded, she thought with a shiver of pleasure, is not quite the right word. But she let Rygar think the warmth of her smile was all for him.

"The child has missed you," he went on. "Gee missed your help. And I missed your company."

"Rygar," Thalgor called gruffly.

The younger man sighed, kissed Erwyn's cheek, and went to see what his leader wanted.

Felyn appeared in his place, her cursed eyes wide and questioning. For a moment Erwyn felt again the terrible loss of the Wise Witches' refusal. And knew the child felt it, too.

She drew Felyn to her side, gave her Rygar's flowers, and rubbed her shoulder for comfort, as she had done that night in the forest when Thalgor found them.

Gee lumbered up to them, her hands stained from dying wool.

"We're low on water," she told Erwyn cheerfully.

Rygar had set up the loom Gee was too old to use in hopes of Erwyn's return. After lunch, while the old woman cooked a celebration dinner, Erwyn began to lay the warp.

While the others were outside finishing their dinner that night, she moved the few things she called hers from the alcove she shared with Felyn to the one on the opposite side of the tent where Thalgor slept.

By unspoken agreement they waited until the others were asleep before going together to his bed. He smiled when he saw her clothes and bags of herbs in his sleeping chamber.

"Welcome." He drew her into his arms.

When she emerged from his side of the tent the next morning, the child looked up at her and nodded, as if in approval, but the others pretended not to notice she now slept in Thalgor's bed. To Erwyn's great relief, no one said anything about it.

EVERYONE, THALGOR FOUND, had something to say about the fact that he has taken Erwyn as his woman at last.

Batte spat, "The witch?" in disbelief.

Gurdek only shrugged, but he began to shoot Thalgor nervous glances, as if he expected a curse to fall on his leader at any moment.

The second morning, before the others were awake, Gee quietly asked him, "Are you certain it is wise to give your child to a witch?"

The idea of making Erwyn pregnant flooded him with a desire so intense he almost rushed to their bed to ravish her with that intent right then. As if she would have allowed it when the others might hear.

"Time will tell," he told Gee through teeth gritted against the sudden ache in his loins.

Later the same day Rygar caught him staring at the witch as she sat at the loom among the other women. The others chatted gaily, but Erwyn was intent on her work. She paused only now and then to smile at something someone else said or to speak softly to Felyn, who carded wool at her feet.

"Being a witch will always come first for her." His second shook his head.

"Being a warrior and leader of this band will always come

first for me." Thalgor turned away from the peaceful scene before them.

"Then you are well suited, aren't you?" A mocking tone haunted the younger man's words.

Well-suited? Thalgor thought as he went to check on how the planting went. Was that the word for the peace that filled him at the sight of Erwyn weaving? The lust that filled him at the thought of her carrying his child? For a moment he was not even certain the answer he had given Rygar was true.

Even the child, who still rarely spoke to him, had something to say.

That evening, when Erwyn got up on some errand from where they sat side by side, she patted his thigh with casual intimacy.

The child took her place next to him, patted his thigh with childish intimacy and said, "Nice."

He gaped at her and swallowed hard, but she scampered away before he could respond.

CHAPTER SEVEN

A NOTHER MADE A comment in her own way.

Late one night as Thalgor lay sated, Erwyn's body draped across his, he heard voices outside the tent.

He gently edged away from his sleeping woman, threw on his tunic, and slipped to the drape that covered the door between the scullery and the cooking fire outside. He opened it a small crack and saw clearly in the firelight what he suspected he was meant to see.

Rygar sat reciting poetry to Dara. He seemed not to notice how close she sat to him, or how her hand rested on his thigh and moved slowly but inexorably toward his manhood.

Thalgor could tell the exact moment Dara's hand found its target because Rygar fell silent and pushed the hand away. While he still seemed to be figuring out what had happened, she drew him to her and began to kiss him.

Rygar brought his hands to her shoulders and tried to free himself, but she opened her mouth so wide even Thalgor could see from his hiding place. Then she pulled her intended victim tightly against her again.

Thalgor held his breath. He did not want Dara for himself, nor did he fear Batte's reaction if she should abandon him for Rygar. As Erwyn had said, Thalgor could handle Batte. But he did not want Rygar to take the lover who was once his.

People would talk. And some might remember…

Rygar was more to him than any other man. He would kill whatever hurt his second. But he did not know how to protect him from Dara.

When Rygar broke free of her embrace and stood up, Thalgor let out his breath with a low hiss.

"No." Rygar wiped his mouth with the back of his hand.

Dara stood and linked her arms around his neck.

"Why stop?" she pouted, jutting her breasts into his chest.

"I…I am due on guard duty."

"No one will know if you don't go. The guards sleep all night, in any case."

She tried to kiss him again, but he pushed her away.

"No." His voice was stronger this time.

"Why not?"

"You are with Batte."

"Only so long as it pleases me. Right now, you please me more." She swayed against him.

"You were Thalgor's."

"But no longer."

"This is his tent."

"We could go to the woods," she suggested in a husky

voice.

"At night? Are you a fool as well as a wanton? Did you not hear the panther scream only a few moments ago?"

But Rygar's words didn't deter her.

"Maybe after the next battle." She ran her hand up his arm. "You're an archer, aren't you? Swordsmen like Batte are always so tired after a battle."

"Not after the next battle." Rygar stepped away. "Not ever. I do not want you. And you do not want me. You only want revenge on Thalgor because he chose another."

"Revenge is not such a bad thing. Watch out for it yourself, archer." Dara stomped off into the dark.

Thalgor let the drapes fall shut and returned to his bed, both relieved and disturbed.

LARGE BANDS RARELY fought battles in the warm time, but marauders and raiding parties were a constant threat. Thalgor wasn't surprised when he was awakened later the same night by Batte's second because marauders had tried to steal an ox.

"You wake me for a single ox?" he grumbled to the man.

"Not the ox. The argument."

Thalgor ran a hand down his face. "What argument?"

"Batte wants his men to kill the marauders, but Rygar and your men won't let them."

Thalgor sighed. He knew this day would come. Perhaps not in this exact form, but the conflict between his lieutenant and his second, the one too blood thirsty, the other perhaps not blood thirsty enough for the role Thalgor had forced on him.

As Thalgor strapped on his sword he asked Batte's second, "What do you think?"

"It is hard to kill men who cannot fight back."

Thalgor grunted agreement and followed him into the night.

They reached the knot of warriors on the far side of the camp where Rygar and Batte silently faced each other, their men arrayed behind each of them.

Thalgor walked past them to survey the enemy they encircled. The prisoners were a pitiful sight. Ten of them, dirty, dressed in rags, half-starved. But they stood proud and tall even as they faced almost certain death. Only one kept looking behind them toward the woods.

Thalgor looked at the weapons his men took from them. Four swords, two bows with a handful of arrows, three knives, and one slingshot between the ten of them. He shook his head, then turned his attention to the discord in his own ranks.

He stood between Rygar and Batte, and waited.

Batte spoke first. "They are marauders. They tried to steal from us. Perhaps they have stolen from us before."

Thalgor glanced over his shoulder at the prisoners. "Not

recently, from the looks of them."

Rygar seized the advantage. "We cannot kill them as if they were oxen themselves. What threat are ten men to us?"

"There must be others hidden in the woods. Why else risk stealing an ox when five rabbits would do?" Batte replied.

His men nodded in agreement. All but his second.

"What if the others are women and children?" Rygar asked.

Batte snorted. "Then they deserve to starve for entrusting themselves to this motley bunch of weaklings."

Several of the prisoners stepped forward at the insult, but their fellows held them back.

"Fetch the witch," Thalgor whispered to one of his men.

"So, Thalgor, what say you?" Batte asked in the ritual demand for a judgment.

"I say we give these men some food and water before they die of their own accord and render the whole discussion moot." Thalgor turned to Batte's second. "Can you find food for them?"

Batte grumbled but waved his second on his way. He gave Thalgor a dark look, then sat on the only nearby rock so his leader and Rygar were left to stand.

Thalgor accepted the subtle insult as a fair return. He waited until a soft scent on the air told him Erwyn was near. He went to meet her a little distance from where they stood.

The women who had come with food and water for the

prisoners served to distract his men. The marauders fell on the cold meal like wolves, all except the one who kept looking into the woods. He ate little and seemed to have trouble with even that.

"What do you see?" Thalgor asked Erwyn.

He positioned himself so Batte and the others could not easily see her, but she could look into the circle of prisoners.

"Hunger," she told him quietly, "and bravery."

"Even the one who keeps looking back at the woods, as if he sought a way to escape?"

She didn't answer right away, but closed her eyes to see more clearly.

"His fear has nothing to do with you or your men. They would all be good warriors, except perhaps the one who thinks himself a leader."

As Thalgor nodded his thanks, a plan formed in his mind. A plan, he realized as he walked away from her, that the witch planted there. He turned to look back at her. She smiled and gave a small shrug.

When Batte saw Erwyn, he frowned and stood.

"What say you, Thalgor?" he intoned again.

"I say that if they will lead us to their camp, and the others with them are indeed only their women and children, we will allow them to join our band, if they wish it. If we find more warriors, we will kill them all in battle, not slaughter them like oxen."

Rygar nodded in immediate agreement, but Batte

frowned.

"What if they will not lead us to the others?"

"They seem wiser than that." Thalgor spoke with more certainty than he felt. The witch's certainty, he realized again and shuddered.

She was too much in his mind, but he knew no way to keep her out of his thoughts when she shared his bed, and no way to live just now without the solace of her body.

He, Batte, and Rygar went to the prisoners, who were done with their meal and bravely awaited their fate.

"Take us to your camp," Thalgor asked the one who presented himself as their leader. The one Erwyn was unsure of.

"Never." The other man crossed his arms over his emaciated chest.

"You might live if you do."

"Live at what cost?"

The other prisoners stood solidly behind him.

"We will not take your women and children," Rygar said.

"Are you so sure we have only women and children at our camp?" the leader asked.

"That is what we want to know," Batte growled.

"You ask us to trust you?"

"I ask you to save your own lives and perhaps those of your women and children," Thalgor said. "They will easily be captured by others once you are dead, if they do not starve first."

Some of the prisoners began to mumble among themselves. The leader turned back to silence them, but the talk continued.

"Ask your warriors what they choose," Thalgor suggested.

"I am the leader." The other man wheeled back to face him as if he had a weapon in his hand.

"Do you have a witch?" a prisoner called out into the tense silence. The one who kept looking into the woods.

Thalgor didn't even look at Erwyn.

"Why would you think we do?"

"You listened to her." The man pointed at Erwyn as he moved around his leader to speak directly to Thalgor. "You do not strike me as a man who listens to women. And," he looked away, "I have witch blood. I can feel her in my mind."

The leader of the bedraggled group stepped toward the man, fist raised, but Rygar grabbed him by the elbows.

The man who spoke looked from his leader to Thalgor, then to Erwyn. "I will take you to our camp, if you bring the witch."

"Why?" Batte asked, his hand on his sword.

"My woman gives birth. It has been three days. The witch may be able to save her, if not the child."

"Bring them all." Thalgor gestured Erwyn to his side.

Rygar had to tie the leader's hands but the others came without protest as Erwyn, Thalgor, and his warriors followed the man whose wife was giving birth into the woods.

They thrashed about in the darkness for a while, but slowly day turned the dark shadows into gray, dream-like mist. Through the mist came the scream of someone already half-dead.

The men froze, but Erwyn leapt forward to follow the sound. Thalgor found his bearings first and went after her, leaving his men to follow with the prisoners.

A second piteous scream and they were in the camp.

Not even a camp. One tent, a few scattered lean-to's, and one small fire. As soon as Thalgor appeared the women who stood about outside the single tent tried to gather their children and flee, but his men already encircled them. Then the women saw the prisoners and fell upon them, weeping.

Erwyn moved calmly through the chaos. A third scream rent the air and the laboring woman's man ran after the witch. Both of them disappeared into the tent.

"Rygar, you and your men stay here and bring those in the tent to our camp when Erwyn is ready," Thalgor ordered. "Batte, you and your men will escort the others back now. Send one man ahead so there is food and water for the women and children."

Batte glared at him, then began to organize the move.

Thalgor headed back to camp ahead of everyone else. He hoped for some sleep before what promised to be a hard day.

ERWYN ENTERED THE small, dark tent afraid she might be too late. But the woman giving birth still lived, her breath ragged, her mind half demented with pain.

Her man gave an anguished gasp when he saw her.

Erwyn didn't need to worry about him, too. "Sit behind her. Let her sit up so she leans back against you. Now, wrap your arms around her between belly and breasts."

Erwyn felt the next contraction come, but the woman didn't scream. Instead she wept silently and grasped her man's hands, as if his presence made her stronger.

As the contraction eased, Erwyn put her hands on each side of the woman's belly.

"Your child lives," she was able to tell them. But she knew the child, like its mother, was tired and weak.

"Warm water," she said to the woman who was probably the midwife.

When a cup appeared, Erwyn sprinkled pungent herbs into it.

"Drink it all," she directed the birthing woman.

The woman started to object, but her man took the cup from Erwyn and held it to the woman's lips. She drank and fell asleep so fast the cup dropped to the ground.

"Stay with her," Erwyn told the man. "She will sleep for a while, but the laboring will go on. When she wakes, she may be able to birth the baby."

"And if she cannot?" he whispered, as if his woman might hear him in her sleep.

"You will have to choose. I do not have a magic that will save them both."

"Why would I want a child without my woman?"

Erwyn nodded, then went to where Rygar waited at the door of the tent.

"By midday, if all goes well," she told him. "See if your men can kill a rabbit or two. I'll ask the midwife to cook whatever other food they may have so you and your men can eat."

Rygar gestured toward the couple in the tent. "Don't expect Thalgor to hold you like that when you give birth."

"One expects a fish to swim. Only a fool expects the eagle who eats fish to swim, too."

"You are a wise woman," Rygar laughed, "or a woman in love."

"I am a witch who knows her fate."

The midwife left to cook for Rygar's men. The birthing woman's man slept. Erwyn gathered pillows to lay down, too.

Before she fell asleep she had time to wonder if Thalgor would make the same choice as this man, would choose her life over that of his child. The obvious answer chilled her.

She thought it was the smell of roasting meat that woke her, but then she heard the second wail. The wail of a newborn.

The midwife had wrapped the child and handed it to its mother, still in her man's arms, both of them lit by a glow of love that turned the small, dingy tent into a place of joy.

Erwyn slipped out unnoticed and ate a hurried breakfast while Rygar's men turned one of the lean-to's into a travois to pull the woman and her child to Thalgor's camp.

The midwife came and sat beside her as the men dismantled her tent. "That herb…"

Erwyn answered her unasked question. "Works without my magic, but less well. I will show you where to find it. It grows only in the darkest part of the woods on the longest day of the warm time."

The midwife nodded and offered her a piece of dried fruit she had pulled from some secret pocket in her gown.

Erwyn took it with a smile of thanks.

The sun was low in the sky before they reached Thalgor's camp, slowed by the makeshift travois.

The rest of the marauders were still held prisoner at the near edge of the camp. Erwyn wondered why until she saw the midwife go to their leader and realized she was his woman.

As the captive women gathered around the new mother and her child, a warrior went to tell Thalgor of their arrival.

When he strode up a short while later, Thalgor gestured for Erwyn to stand behind him as he faced the prisoners. He made the same speech to them as he had to those captured from the camp where Erwyn had been enslaved, then added that each of the men could choose to fight with his band, or take one weapon and leave with their families in peace.

Batte, who followed him, growled his disapproval and left, but his second and their men stayed to watch with Rygar's men.

As each of the captured men pledged to follow Thalgor, Erwyn looked into them and saw the wholeness there. Each time she tapped Thalgor lightly on his back, by his heart, and he nodded his acceptance until only the leader remained.

"I will follow you as your lieutenant," he told Thalgor.

Batte's second stifled a laugh. Rygar, his friend from childhood, gave him a small kick in the leg.

Erwyn saw in the leader the thirst for power she'd warned Thalgor of before. She tapped his back on the right, away from his heart. Thalgor shook his head.

"Then I will leave." The marauder defiantly took both a sword and a bow from the pile of their weapons, and all the arrows. Then he motioned for the midwife and the two half-grown children who stood with her to follow him, but she shook her head and stayed where she was.

He moved closer as he spoke a few harsh, quiet words. The midwife pushed the children behind her and shook her head again.

When he reached around her as if to grab the boy, both he and his sister fled to where the others from their camp stood and watched.

The man spoke to the midwife again in the same hushed, violent tone. When she still refused to move, he struck her with a backhand across the face so hard she fell to the ground, then he walked off into the forest.

Those around them had stood frozen, but when the woman fell everyone burst into action. The captured women rushed to the aid of their midwife and comforted her frightened children. Their men reclaimed the weapons that remained in the pile and gathered around Rygar, obviously eager to join his patrol.

Women appeared from Thalgor's camp with food and tents for the newcomers. His warriors went back for their dinners.

Thalgor and Erwyn headed toward their tent as well.

"So you saved the child and the mother both."

Erwyn nodded, amused by what might have been a note of pride in Thalgor's voice.

"Boy or girl?"

"A boy. Can you guess what they named him?"

"Thalgor?"

She smiled up at him and shook her head. "Rygar."

For a moment he frowned. She held her breath, suddenly afraid she might have misjudged him.

Then he laughed. "Well-named, I'd say."

Something shifted in her heart at his words.

THE FIRST HARVEST had just begun when one of his men woke Thalgor in the middle of the night to tell him Gurdek had caught marauders after the crops they had gathered the day before.

As Thalgor girded on his sword, Erwyn appeared at his side.

"There will be wounded," she said, and he nodded.

They arrived as the skirmish ended, the last of the marauders found and disarmed. Erwyn moved at once to Gurdek's wounded, followed by the surgeon, the bone-setter and the herbalist, who had come with them from the camp.

Thalgor got a report from Gurdek–none of their men dead, no marauders escaped–and looked over the men they had captured.

They had been twenty. Two were dead, one nearly so, several others wounded. But a dozen stood untouched, fear in their eyes.

Thalgor sighed. To kill them all, as he would have done a short while before without a second thought, now seemed wrong.

He looked over at Erwyn, who helped the surgeon sever a man's badly mangled foot.

Did she bewitch him? Was that why what had been normal was now unthinkable and what was unheard of–to take defeated men into his band–now seemed the most reasonable thing to do?

He turned to Gurdek, the question of what to do unasked. But his lieutenant nodded, as if the same question filled his mind.

"They fought well. Clearly they have women hidden somewhere to prepare the food for winter storage. Their leader is among the dead." He thumped his chest. "My sword found his heart."

It crossed Thalgor's mind that Gurdek, who lost his woman to sickness in the last dark time, now spent much of his free time with the midwife whose man had been the leader of the last group of marauders. Thalgor had even seen his lieutenant teaching her son to use a sword.

Rygar and now Gurdek. Erwyn didn't need to bewitch them. She put a thought in their minds, and their whole lives changed. His, as well, Thalgor admitted reluctantly.

Batte appeared from the woods, followed by his men and the marauders' women and children.

"I thought they might be a raiding party," Batte said in a tone of disgust. "So I went to see if there were more. But all I found was a miserable camp and a bunch of weeping women."

The woman of one of the dead men sent up a wail.

"Silence her!" Batte growled at one of his men, but Thalgor held up his hand to stop him.

"Surely you do not mean to allow these marauders into our band as you did the others?" Batte asked in disbelief. "The others were pitiful and few. These are strong, and almost fifty in all," he gauged with a glance at the families huddled now around the captured men.

"More reason to take them in, if they are willing," Gurdek responded. "We can use the extra hands for the harvest and in battle. They will only make us stronger."

"Your men captured them easily enough."

"With more warriors and better arms. And we took them by surprise. Your men could not defeat us under those conditions."

Thalgor stepped between his lieutenants.

"We will take those who wish to be of us," he said in a tone that allowed for no dissent. "And we will not speak ill of any of our own men," he added sharply to Gurdek.

The two men went off in opposite directions, both grumbling.

But Batte soon returned, eyes ablaze with anger.

"The witch!" He pointed to where Erwyn and the herbalist conferred over a wounded man. "She heals the enemy!"

Thalgor sighed and asked one of his men to fetch Erwyn.

She looked up at the messenger, then went back to her work.

After what seemed to Thalgor to be a long time while he listened to Batte mumble curses, she finished her instructions to the herbalist and walked over to them at a leisurely pace.

"Why do you heal the enemy?" Batte demanded.

"Do you intend to kill them all?" she asked Thalgor.

"No." Thalgor couldn't help but wish he'd captured a more compliant witch. If there was such a thing.

"Then I must heal. It is a rule of my power."

"Don't speak to me of rules," Batte told her. "You do as

you please, witch. Even if it helps those who would destroy us as we destroyed your band."

"Do you do as you wish in battle?" she asked him.

"I do what I must do to win."

"I do what I must do to heal. And what I must do is save any life I can. A world where witches do not follow such a rule would soon be a world with only witches and no men."

For a moment an image of the Wise Witches' invincible citadel filled Thalgor's mind. He shook his head to clear it.

"Or only men and no witches," Batte said thoughtfully.

Erwyn nodded. "Perhaps. Is it not better to have both?"

"Perhaps," Batte echoed. "Or perhaps not. It is of no importance so long as you have Thalgor's protection. But beware if ever he should come to prefer another."

Thalgor stepped forward at that. "Enough, Batte. Tell your men to help Gurdek's organize the prisoners so we can see who of them chooses to join us."

Batte muttered to himself as he walked away.

"He is a good man," Erwyn said, "but he thinks being strong and courageous, and winning in battle is all a leader need do."

A strange prickle crept up Thalgor's spine when he remembered his lieutenant was now Dara's lover.

His warriors brought the prisoners. Erwyn stood behind him as before. Two men he would have liked to add to his band chose to walk away, but none of the men Erwyn was unsure of chose to stay. Most were men he would not have trusted either. Only one, a man with an open face and strong arm, seemed a good warrior to him. When he asked her later why she warned him against that one she shuddered.

"He is a good warrior because he finds joy in killing and causing pain."

Thalgor remembered that no woman left with the man and shuddered in his turn.

"You are tired from healing," he told Erwyn. "Let us return to the tent so you may sleep."

EVER SINCE ERWYN had saved the marauder's woman and her baby, the band's midwives sent for her whenever they had a difficult birth. Some women still died, and some babies, but fewer than before.

They most often sent for her in the middle of the night, and healing always tired her, especially when she could not save both lives. Many days she was too weary to help Gee with the work of the tent.

Finally the old woman brought the third daughter of a family with too many children to the tent and set the girl to the work Erwyn used to do. Thalgor and Rygar exchanged raised eyebrows, but nothing was said.

The girl, Tya, moved into the sleeping chamber with Gee and Felyn, who was soon her constant shadow.

But Erwyn's weariness and late night wakings were a

burden on Thalgor as well. One night she returned to the tent to find him pacing the small space of their sleeping chamber.

"You no longer fetch water, or weave, or cook," he complained. "I have an extra mouth to feed, and I must suffer through Rygar's agonies as he discovers he is in love."

"Rygar in love? With that girl?"

Tya was lovely, with long brown hair, deep honey-colored eyes, and a body that would be rounded and soft when she was grown. But she was not yet grown.

"Yes. That girl." Thalgor sighed. "She is too young to take as his woman, so he suffers. And I suffer."

"Why?"

"That is not the point! What do I have to do to keep you in my bed at night?"

Worn and irritated, Erwyn threw up her hands.

"Batte does not want me to heal our enemies. You don't want me to help with births unless it is convenient for you. Why do either of you think you can control my power?"

"Batte has nothing to do with it. I control your power because you are my witch."

She dredged up the last of her energy and pulled herself tall, although that meant she only reached his shoulder.

"I may be your woman, but I am not your witch."

"So be it. But if you are my woman, you will do as I say."

"Will I?" She stood defiantly with hands on her hips, but a familiar heat burned low in her belly.

He reached out and took her hands in his.

"Do I have to tie you to my bed?" His voice was no longer angry, but thick with passion.

Her heart beat with unexpected excitement. "Try it."

In one swift warrior's move Thalgor had her on her back underneath him, both her hands held above her head in one of his. He looked down at her for a moment in the glow of the single lantern. Erwyn saw the mixture of anger and need in his eyes shift to pure want. The heat of his desire pressed hard against her body, followed by a familiar, sweet quivering deep inside her.

He kissed her then, deep and wild. Her body strained against his, half in protest, half in need.

He lifted his mouth and gave a low laugh. He slid his free hand between them to pull up her gown, then stroked her breast until she moaned. With a growl, he pressed her legs open with his and entered her in one thrust.

They both froze, stunned by the intensity of the flow of heat and craving between them.

As one they melted. His hands came to frame her face, hers to encircle his neck as they kissed with a passion beyond any they had known.

They finished their loving tenderly, even at the end when he caught his name on her lips as she sank into the sea of pleasure.

When he called her name as he joined her there, Erwyn knew she now freely chose the man she had seen before as her fate.

CHAPTER EIGHT

THREE NIGHTS LATER a dark dream startled Erwyn awake. She shook Thalgor's shoulder. He snorted in his sleep and rolled away from her.

"Thalgor." She shook him again. "Thalgor."

"What?" He sat up, still half asleep. "A battle?"

"No." She stroked his arm to soothe him. "A dream."

Suddenly he was fully awake, and angry.

"You woke me for a dream? Are you a child who cannot know it is a dream and go back to sleep on your own?"

"A dream. A vision."

"Of what?"

"I don't know."

"Witch, it is too late at night for riddles. Go to sleep and leave me alone." He lay down and turned his back to her.

Why did everything have to be a struggle with this man?

"Thalgor, I must go into the woods."

"I hope you find it pleasant there in the middle of the night," he grumbled, but sat up. "Tell me."

"For several days I have felt danger, but too far away for me to see it clearly. In my dream, the Witch King…"

He drew a sharp breath. "The what?"

"The Witch King. He comes to me often in my dreams."

She felt him shiver. "All your life?"

"Only since you captured me. Why?"

He unshuttered the lantern and looked at her intently. A strange mixture of fear and tenderness flowed through her at the look on his face. She was not sure she wanted to hear what he was about to say.

"Think, witch. A Witch King? What can that mean? There are no kings, and only women can be witches."

Erwyn shrugged. "I've become used to it. He says that is who, what he is. And I feel…I feel I can trust him."

Thalgor nodded and said, "Me, too."

"You've seen him?" she gasped in surprise.

"He sent me after you when you went to the Sea Witches."

"You told me it was your father."

His eyes fell to the rumpled bed clothes between them.

"He is very much like my father. And I thought you might think a Witch King a false vision."

They both sat in silence. She wondered how two could have the same vision, even a witch and her man.

And she wondered what Thalgor thought as he sat beside her, his mind cut off from her–by what?

"What did the Witch King tell you?" he finally asked her.

"That danger is close and I must fly to be able to see it."

"Fly?"

"Come with me into the woods, and you will learn."

"Why do you not go alone?"

"You threatened to tie me to your bed," she reminded him with mock innocence, then her smile faded. "My body is vulnerable when I fly. If a panther or a renegade should find me..."

"And this must be done in the dark of night."

He stood to pull on his tunic and picked up his sword.

"Of course." She rose, put the herbs she would need into her bag, and threw on her cloak.

He stepped out of the tent first, to make certain no one was around, and they disappeared together into the night.

THEY WALKED IN silence.

Thalgor was half asleep on his feet before Erwyn stopped at the edge of a clearing that formed a perfect circle deep in the woods.

The full moon filled the glade with eerie light. No bird or animal stirred. A rainbow of flowers covered the ground and filled the still air with their sweetness. Had he been less of a man, he might have fallen to his knees in awe at the beauty of the place.

"Make a fire." Erwyn spoke in equally awe-struck tones and pointed to a flat rock in the center of the circle, its top already black from earlier fires. How many fires, over how many years? he wondered.

As he gathered wood, Erwyn took leaves from the trees around the clearing and mixed them with herbs she'd brought.

When a small fire burned, she motioned him to the edge of the clearing and laid the herbs and leaves on the flames. The fire almost went out, then began to burn with a thick white smoke that rose up straight in the still air.

Erwyn dropped the cloak she wore and all thought was wiped from his mind.

She wore nothing underneath it. She stood naked in the moonlight, her body only a gray shadow. The sense of wonder he always felt at the beauty of her bare flesh deepened into reverence.

She held her hands open in front of her in a gesture of supplication and began to chant. As she chanted, her body grew whiter, began to glow. Her hands lifted toward the moon.

Thalgor stepped deeper into the shadows at the edge of the clearing, overwhelmed by the power he felt course through that slender body, at once so familiar and so unknown.

Finally she fell silent and went to the fire. She circled it three times in each direction, then stepped across it.

He started to stop her, to keep her from burning herself, but the flames were buried under the leaves.

She walked through the column of pungent smoke four times, north to south, south to north, then east to west, west to east, where the moon stood. He saw her breathe in the smoke, but despite its thickness she did not cough. Instead her face became more ethereal and serene.

He half expected her to soar off on her upraised arms like a great silver bird, but she walked to where her cloak lay on the ground instead and collapsed with the small cry of a lover.

He rushed to her side. His heart pounded with dread.

"She flies," said the voice of the Witch King. "Wait."

Thalgor looked around him in a panic, but saw nothing. He covered Erwyn's inert body with his cloak, then took one of her hands in his and cursed the day he ever captured a witch.

The fire didn't burn down the way a normal fire would. Nor did it give off any heat. Only a dim light and the column of smoke showed that it burned at all.

He shivered in the night for a long time, half-hypnotized by the flame and the pungent smoke, practicing a patience that was far from easy for him.

He listened for the usual sounds of birds and small animals in the woods, but the silence was complete, the stillness total.

Suddenly the smoke vanished. Only a pile of smoldering ash was left on the rock. Erwyn stirred. She opened her eyes and began to tremble. He held her until the shaking stopped.

When it eased, he started to ask what she saw, but she gestured for him to remain silent. Slowly she got to her feet.

She was so weak she needed to lean on him as they made their way slowly back to the camp. The sky began to grow lighter. An owl hooted nearby, warning of sunrise.

When they neared the edge of the woods Erwyn, still very pale, mumbled a few words and swirled her arms around herself. Then she was gone. Thalgor blinked twice, stunned.

A familiar hand tugged at his and he realized she was still there but invisible.

If a leader reconnoitered before daybreak, he was a brave and dedicated warrior. If the same man returned from the woods with a woman, even his own, at the same hour he could easily be suspected of acts so obscene they had to be hidden from the others in his tent. And if the woman wearily leaned on him…

He almost laughed at her wisdom, but merely nodded at the sentries as he tried not to tread on Erwyn's unseen feet.

She reappeared as they neared their tent in the sleeping camp, her face a mask of worry and exhaustion. By the time they reached their chamber, she could scarcely stagger.

He pulled off the cloak, and she fell into the bed, barely strong enough to say, "Call a council for midday" before she fell asleep.

"HOW COULD SHE see far enough to know this is true?" Gurdek scratched his head in sincere puzzlement.

"Why should we trust a witch?" Batte glared at Erwyn.

"It is full harvest. To keep our men ready for battle will mean less food for the dark time," Gurdek's second pointed out.

"If the raiding party Erwyn saw catches us off guard, it might mean no food for the dark time," Rygar replied. "Or worse."

"Surely our scouts will see them in time," Batte's second objected.

"Not if they come in many small groups, the way the witch says they will," Batte replied.

Thalgor let the others have their say, as he usually did. He didn't need to defend Erwyn. His men knew the truth of her visions, as much as Gurdek feared her and Batte resented her.

Today his lieutenants were driven by contrary impulses. Batte's to distrust and to do battle, Gurdek's to protect and to manage the camp's food supply. Even Rygar was caught between his desire not to kill and his faith in Erwyn's magic.

To think two ways at once was good practice for the day when one of them, probably Batte, became leader of this band in Thalgor's place, or of his own band when this one grew too large and needed to become two. A day that would come soon.

Erwyn sat silent once she told what she saw when she

flew. Neither of them mentioned the special nature of her vision. It was a gift few knew witches had, she told him, only those entrusted to care for them when they carried out the ritual and no second witch could do so. Her trust weighed on him more than he would have liked.

The conversation ebbed. Gurdek's second was sent to Gee to bring food. When he returned Thalgor finally spoke.

"Gurdek is right," he began with deference to the older man. "We cannot have all our men ready for battle at the peak of the harvest, even if the women and children help. But we won't need all our men unless all of the enemy's small parties make it to the rallying point on time and without any desertions or loss to marauders. Which is unlikely."

His men nodded. Erwyn glared, but remained silent, wary as always of appearing to have too much power over him.

She would speak her mind fully enough, he knew, after the others left.

"Gurdek, your men will continue to harvest. You will also enlist the women, the older children, and anyone else who doesn't have more important duties. Celebrations will be curtailed until the harvest is in, the danger past."

Gurdek's second began to protest, but Thalgor stopped him.

"You may inform the women that the men will help them preserve the food after the harvest is complete, so they will still be able to make their other preparations for the dark time."

The man looked at Gurdek. Both nodded their agreement.

"Batte, you and I will keep your men and half of mine ready for battle at all times. Double the scouts, sentries, and guards. Gather the young men almost ready to be warriors. Let the men train them in the ways of battle, both in case they are needed and to pass the time while we wait. Rygar, when the battle begins, you and the other half of our men will go to the hill behind the camp and wait there until the tide of battle shifts."

"I don't want any of those marauders you've taken on in the half of your men who fight with mine," Batte said darkly.

"No. They will harvest with Gurdek's men nearest the point where Erwyn saw the attackers come and keep their weapons at hand. If more of the enemy makes it as far as the attack than I expect, they will be ready on our flank."

Rygar, Batte, and his second all nodded.

"Do not alarm the camp. We have fought off many raiding parties. There is no need for everyone to know how many Erwyn saw in her vision or that the outcome of the battle was not clear." Gee appeared with the food. "Eat. We have much to do."

Soon a new problem appeared. A few of Thalgor's men and some of Batte's were reluctant to leave the harvest for a possible battle based only on Erwyn's word. Thalgor, Batte, and Gurdek were discussing what to do when the leader of the marauders who had recently joined Gurdek's men approached.

"We hear some of those chosen to fight prefer to harvest."

Thalgor and Gurdek nodded.

"Go on," Batte growled.

"We will fight with Rygar and the other marauders. Your men who wish to can have our places among Gurdek's men."

"A reserve all of marauders new to our camp?" Batte eyed the man suspiciously.

"We owe you our lives." The leader stood straighter. "And we know you will care for our women and children if we are killed."

Batte looked him up and down, then nodded slowly. "We will settle this easily, without Rygar's reserve, in any case." With those words he turned and walked away.

"Done." Thalgor suppressed a sigh of relief and sent for Rygar to explain the change.

Thalgor ate dinner with the warriors and talked with them about the battle until late. The tent was dark and silent when he returned. When he slipped quietly into his sleeping chamber, he expected to find Erwyn either asleep or in a rage that he had discounted some of the danger she warned of.

He found her weeping instead. The solemn sound tore at him.

When he slid into bed beside her, she turned into his

arms and wept more wildly. He held her and stroked her head, surprised at the power of his touch to ease her tears.

Finally she fell silent and rolled onto her back. He waited for her to explain why she cried, but she said nothing.

"Tell me," he urged gently.

To his surprise she started to cry again and rolled back into his arms for comfort. But still she said nothing.

They fell asleep like that, her tear-drenched face buried in his shoulder, her arms clinging to him while his sheltered her.

He woke before dawn, troubled as much by her silence as by her tears.

As soon as he stirred, she woke, too, and stretched a little against the awkwardness of the way she'd slept.

"Have you seen more?" he asked, his mind clear now. "Have you seen me die? Or Rygar?" No other warrior's death would make her weep so.

He heard the rustle of her hair on their pillow when she shook her head. But no words came.

"Tell me," he said again. "Please."

"I was with child." He barely recognized the hollow voice. "Barely. I should have known, but I didn't." She turned toward him. "I swear to you, I didn't know."

With child. His mind was frozen on those words. Then another word crept in.

Was. Was with child.

Now he understood her silence.

There were no words for the shock and pain beyond those three.

He took her in his arms again. They lay locked in time, together yet alone with their loss.

"What happened?" he asked even though he feared no answer would comfort him.

She rolled to her back again.

"I didn't know," she repeated in the same empty voice. "I can't say what I would have done if I knew, but I didn't."

"Thalgor," Rygar called from the door to the chamber. "We meet with Batte."

"Go without me," Thalgor told him. "Tell him I am unwell. I will be along when Erwyn has given me some of her herbs."

Disbelief radiated through the fabric that separated them.

He heard Rygar sigh. "I will tell him."

None of the others dared distrust his word.

Thalgor turned toward Erwyn. "Tell me what happened."

"The magic." Her body trembled as she struggled to give voice to the black grief. "Magic is dangerous. For anyone. But especially for the unborn. That is why the Sea Witches must live without men. We are all told never to use our magic when we carry a child. The power is too much. Flying takes almost all the power I have. And the smoke has its own power. The child was so new it had no chance to survive."

She turned to face him, eyes wet. "I didn't know."

He wrapped her in his arms as she wept, his mind whirling.

If she could not use her magic…He was not so reliant on her second sight and her wisdom that he could not lead without it, but he also knew he led better with it.

"Thalgor," Batte called from the other side of the curtain that hid them. "You are not ill. I don't know why you are still abed with your witch, but you are never ill."

Erwyn went stiff. Thalgor eased away from her and sat up, rubbing his face, surprised his friend would challenge him so.

"A moment, Batte."

"Don't bother yourself. I just didn't want you to think me a fool." Batte stomped angrily away.

Thalgor looked down and stroked Erwyn's tear-stained face. "I must go."

She held his hand on her cheek. "I understand."

"I don't blame you." His heart was full of other words, words he did not know how to say.

"I know," she said.

He started to stand, but she looked at him as if he were her only shelter in the midst of a raging storm. It unnerved him to see her as only a woman. A grieving woman.

Would she grieve for him so? He pushed the question away.

"Thalgor." Her voice was wet. "What am I going to do?"

Her pain was too raw for him to bear any longer. His

helplessness in its face brought searing memories of his mother's suffering, and his own when she was unable to protect him. Both fed this new, wordless grief.

"Not get with child again," he told Erwyn and stood.

Her eyes clouded, then flashed with hurt and anger. She sat up, fully the witch again.

"Very practical advice." Her voice was clear and icy.

There's no telling with a witch, he thought as he pulled on a fresh tunic. Batte's anger at least he understood.

TO WAIT FOR an attack was hard. And the longer they waited, the more likely it was the whole raiding party Erwyn had seen would gather. But their scouts found no sign of them.

To make things worse, the days were growing shorter, the nights colder. They had to burn large fires in the camp at night so the women could weave after they worked on the harvest.

Erwyn wove late, too, and listened to the night birds, owls, and the other creatures that warbled, hunted, and scurried nearby without a thought of the cares of those inside the camp.

The other women were too tired to gossip, too worried to sing. When the patrols changed, the women followed their men home to bed, all of them too weary to do more than fall into a dreamless sleep and start all over again the next day.

Thalgor slept each night near the patrol on duty. Their bed felt empty without him, but it allowed Erwyn to practice the ritual of mourning she had learned from her mother when she thought Erwyn's father dead.

That he still lived but had become a different person, a dangerous one, was as much to be grieved as his death, Erwyn realized for the first time.

The child she lost would have been male, so she performed the ritual for both of them together and gave the unborn child her father's name.

One night as the candles burned low and their exotic scent filled the air, when the ancient words flowed from her tongue, Felyn appeared at the door of the sleeping chamber.

The child stood and watched silently with her cursed eyes. When Erwyn paused, Felyn spoke the name of her dead father, the lost baby. Erwyn looked at the sad little face and began the ritual again, patiently teaching it to the girl, as she had been taught.

That Felyn would mourn the madness of the man who killed their mother made a sort of sense, whether that man was her father or not. If Felyn proved to be a witch, she would need to know the ritual. If not, Erwyn was certain the girl would never reveal the secrets of the ancient magic.

The girl stayed to sleep with her. Erwyn fell into troubled dreams she couldn't remember, then woke with a sense of dreadful loss. But not the loss of the unborn child. A future loss.

She fell back asleep at last, but wasn't surprised when the sounds of a camp under attack woke them.

Gee came to take Felyn to the center of the camp with the other women and children. Erwyn moved swiftly through the organized panic to the hill where Rygar and his reserves were to meet. From there they could see the freshly harvested crops the raiders came to steal.

Rygar frowned when he saw her. "Thalgor would want you safe."

"I am a witch. That is safe enough."

He shook his head and lifted her to a low branch of a tree, then posted a man to guard her.

She allowed him to do it because she could see the battle more clearly from the tree.

And because it hid her from Dara, who watched the men fight from a rock a little away from Rygar and his patrol of marauders, as if she found them unclean.

Thalgor, Batte, and their men were already engaged with the enemy. Not as many as in her vision, but many more than most raiding parties. Gurdek and a few of his warriors stood back while they waited for the rest of his men to return with their weapons, all but those left behind with the old men and boys to protect the women and children huddled in the center of the camp.

Erwyn spotted Batte in the turmoil first. He was not as

large as Thalgor, but his battle cries carried in the crisp morning air and he swung his sword two-handed over his head so it shone in the early sun, until it became clouded with the blood of their enemies.

She finally saw Thalgor closer to the center of the battle, where movements as broad as Batte's would have resulted in having his arms severed by the mass of swords on all sides or a hail of arrows.

Thalgor fought with a cool, clear precision she knew hid an icy rage. Short, powerful strokes killed and maimed as he moved with his men toward the leader of the raiding party.

She saw that one, too, flailing and shouting as Batte did. He was not large, but a kind of malevolent energy flowed from him as he fought. Witch blood. She shuddered with the knowledge.

Why the enemy's leader stood so far from the center of the fighting became clearer when she saw a fresh wave of his men pour into the battle so they half encircled Thalgor's men.

"Rygar!" she called.

But he was already leading his men in a headlong charge down the hill, bow across his back, sword held high in the air.

They attacked the fresh wave of enemy so close to the hill that she heard the arrows fly and the clank of sword on shield, heard the cries of triumph and death, smelled the blood.

Nausea roiled through her, but still she watched, now Rygar, now Batte, now Thalgor as they appeared among their men, Thalgor always closer to the leader of the raiding party. He reached him just as Gurdek's men ran into the battle with a single roar.

The sudden onslaught distracted the enemy's leader enough for Thalgor to run his sword past the man's shield and clear through his body. The man raised his sword one last time.

Time stopped. Nothing existed for Erwyn but those two men, the dying enemy and Thalgor with the sword hanging over his head.

The other man fell. The sword dropped harmless to the earth.

Thalgor stared at it for a moment, then looked up toward the hill, but Erwyn doubted he could see her hidden in the tree. He would only see Dara, who watched the battle avidly.

He looked away, to the dead man at his feet. He placed one foot on the man's chest and pulled his sword free from the corpse. Then he bent to pick up the sword that had almost killed him. He carried both with him as he walked calmly through the chaotic remains of the battle.

Their leader dead, the raiding party's lieutenants tried to regroup their men, but their only real choice was flight or slaughter. Most wisely chose flight.

As they had agreed, only Batte's men pursued them. The

rest of those alive and unhurt returned to the harvest.

The man set to guard her had charged with the rest, so Erwyn slid out of the tree and walked carefully down the steep side of the hill to the battlefield.

There would be wounded to care for.

And Thalgor still lived.

They took no prisoners this time. It grieved Erwyn to have wounded men killed she might have saved, but she knew it was necessary. Drained from death and healing, she returned late to the tent with Thalgor. One of Rygar's men stood outside.

"Tell Rygar there is a council at midday," Thalgor said.

"He is here."

A chill crept up Erwyn's back but her mind was too weary to focus on its cause.

"In my tent?" Thalgor asked, as exhausted as she.

"We thought the woman Gee could care for him."

"What is wrong?" Thalgor brushed past the man, who followed him into the tent.

Erwyn entered more slowly. She knew now what they would find and doubted whether she had the strength to help.

CHAPTER NINE

R YGAR LAY ASLEEP, or unconscious, on a pallet on one side of the tent. Blood seeped through the blanket that covered him. Gee sat by his side, asleep, her hand resting tenderly on his chest.

"Why did you not call the witch?" Thalgor asked the man who met them at the tent door.

Erwyn heard the anger he controlled in order to be able to speak at all. Luckily the man seemed not to notice.

"As an enemy fell, his sword pierced Rygar's thigh," he explained calmly. "The sword broke off in the wound. The surgeon removed the metal and bound the cut. The herbalist gave him tea to make him sleep. The surgeon said there was no need to call the witch from tending men with more serious wounds."

Thalgor looked at Erwyn. Rage boiled behind the mask his face had become.

She knelt beside Rygar and laid her hands near the wound. He slept. The wound had begun to heal. It didn't feel right, but in her weariness she couldn't tell whether it was a piece of the sword still lodged there or something more sinister.

Thalgor helped her stand.

"I am tired, but all seems well," she told him. "Gee can fetch me in an instant if he grows worse."

"You may go," Thalgor told the man, who immediately left. "And the surgeon may live."

"Each of us does our best," she reminded him.

"Go to bed, woman. Council at midday."

He stared down at Rygar's sleeping form with the look of a father worried about his child. If she had been less weary, she might have wondered about that.

Thalgor woke her at dawn.

When she started to protest, he said, "Rygar is awake and in great pain."

She went to her friend at once, a bag of herbs in her hand.

While Gee brewed the tea to let him sleep again, Erwyn started to lift the blood-stained blanket. Rygar held it in place, his face red.

"The wound has been bound," he reminded her. "It hurts, but why would it not? It is very high on my leg, almost as if the enemy meant to unman me as he fell."

A chill ran again up Erwyn's spine, then prickled her scalp, but no definite danger took shape in her mind. She was still weak from the day before.

Rygar's face was cool. No sign of fever.

She smiled at him as Gee returned with the tea. "Drink.

You will sleep and tomorrow the pain will ease."

He smiled back at her and drank, then fell asleep at once.

"The wound?" Thalgor asked when she touched it through the blanket.

"Heals."

Something was still wrong, but she could not say what. Her mind would be clearer by evening when Rygar woke again. Maybe she could coax him into letting her look at the wound then.

The council was quiet, the usual disputes tempered by the sleeping presence of the wounded man.

"If Rygar did not lead the charge when he did..." Batte stopped and shook his head.

"Well done," Gurdek agreed, "for an archer. But if the marauders hadn't followed him and fought so valiantly..."

Erwyn watched pride and honesty struggle on Batte's face.

"Thalgor was right," he finally admitted. "It was better to let them join our band than to kill them."

Rygar and I were right, she silently corrected him.

Gurdek and Thalgor looked at her as if they expected her to protest, but she said nothing. It didn't matter whose idea it was, only that the decision was wise. Still, the insult rankled.

The council soon finished what needed to be done in the aftermath of battle. Then Erwyn made a quick visit to where the wounded were gathered to make sure each progressed as he should. With these men she could easily see what caused every flicker of wrongness she sensed.

Why should it be different with Rygar? Was her mind clouded by the witch blood he might have carried, or by her own fondness for the man who was her friend?

He slept when she checked on him and, still exhausted, she told Gee to wake her when Rygar stirred, then lay down to rest.

It was full dark when Thalgor woke her.

"What?" she asked, her mind filled with sorrow.

"Rygar." Thalgor's face was white with worry.

She went to the wounded man's side. With something like panic she saw he was unconscious, not asleep. When she touched his face, it burned with fever. The air smelled of death.

She threw off the blanket that covered him and gasped. Thalgor, at her side, swore more violently than she'd ever heard him swear before.

The wound was swollen, red, and festering. But worse, much worse, great red branches of sickness reached down his leg and up his body, almost as far as his heart.

Chilled without the blanket, Rygar opened his eyes, squinting against the light.

"Water," he whispered through cracked lips.

Erwyn was still too stunned by what she saw to move.

Thalgor knelt to hold the cup for him. Rygar took a few slips then lay back, exhausted.

"Erwyn will heal you," Thalgor told him in a husky voice.

"I'm afraid it's too late for that," the other man said with a weak smile. "I'm dying. I hope the child will remember some of the stories I've told her and pass them on someday."

"The witch will heal you." Anger reddened Thalgor's face.

Rygar shook his head and fell unconscious again.

Finally Erwyn stirred herself.

"The wound was unclean. Gee thought he was asleep and didn't wake me. Now it has gone so far I may not be able to save him." She focused on what she knew instead of the pain that gripped her heart. "It is a slow and painful way to die, Thalgor. The treatment is worse. It would be kindest to grant him a quick and easy death."

"Heal him," Thalgor thundered.

She wiped away the tears that had begun to fall. "Didn't you hear me? It may be too late. He will suffer."

"He must live."

"But if he only suffers and dies?" The tears were a flood now, so she let them flow.

"He must not die," Thalgor repeated, more solemnly, as if it were a vow.

"Think of Rygar, not of yourself."

"I made a promise." The words were barely breathed.

He turned to face her as both of them knelt by Rygar's bed.

"Please. If you never do another thing for me, if you ever owed me anything, if you ever cared for me, save Rygar."

She put one hand on Thalgor's powerful chest. His heart pounded with a fear she doubted he ever felt in battle. Tears glistened in his eyes. She never thought she would ever see him so, except perhaps over his own child. Certainly never over her.

"What if I fail?" she asked.

"You cannot fail."

Erwyn reached with her mind to see if he was right, but the haze of pain made it hard to see. She glanced up to find Tya, the girl who now helped Gee, watching them. The one Thalgor had said Rygar loved. The girl's eyes were wide with sadness. And with a love for Rygar beyond her years. A sign. Perhaps an answer.

"Fetch the surgeon," Erwyn told her.

"Thank you." Thalgor took her hand and kissed it.

She sighed. "If I am to put him through this, I will need to know why."

"I will tell you."

"Get me my bag. We will talk later."

The surgeon was appalled when he saw the festering wound. And so afraid of Thalgor that his hands shook when he reached to touch the ugly red lines on Rygar's belly.

A surgeon whose hands shook was a bad surgeon. Erwyn cast Thalgor a meaningful look. He put his hand on the surgeon's shoulder. The man jumped as if he expected a blow.

"I know it was no one's fault," Thalgor said with truth in his voice as he glanced at Erwyn. "Even the enemy who struck him did so only as he fell. Still, that he should die the first time he led in battle…"

The surgeon heaved a visible sigh of relief. With calmer hands he heated a knife in the brazier Erwyn brought near.

"Keep Gee and Tya away," Erwyn whispered to Thalgor.

"Gee and the child sleep. Tya was left to watch him. I will send her home to her family."

When the knife cooled from red hot, the surgeon opened the ugly wound. Rygar, half unconscious, cried out in pain.

"Can you do nothing to make it easier for him?" Thalgor groaned to Erwyn.

Since she could be no help until the surgeon finished his grisly work, she moved to Rygar's head. She cradled it in her hands to let oblivion flow from her mind to his with a quiet chant. Rygar stilled and slept.

When the surgeon was done he hurried away as if still uncertain of Thalgor's temper.

"Hold his head," Erwyn told Thalgor. "Your witch blood might help keep him under my spell while I work."

And at his head Thalgor would see less of the gruesome work she needed to do.

Her herbs and oils ready, she carefully cleaned the reopened wound.

Rygar stirred and shifted, but remained asleep.

She coated the wound with sea-scented oil and packed it with herbs while she intoned age-old chants. Time crawled by.

"You leave it open?" Thalgor asked, tall enough to see what she did even while he held Rygar's head.

She cast him a look, then finished the ritual. Finally she bound the open wound loosely with cobwebs and sat wearily back on her heels.

"It is not only a matter of the wound now." She rolled her sore shoulders. "The herbs are to clear the illness from his whole body. Once that is done, the wound can be closed."

Thalgor grunted in understanding.

"I must rest. If you can stay as you are it may help ease his pain. But you cannot recreate my spell, only sustain it."

"I will stay here until sunrise."

She knew he was weary, too, but it was pointless to argue, so she went alone to their bed.

She woke as the camp first stirred, before dawn. In the main room of the tent Thalgor slept where he sat, Rygar's head cradled in his hands. The wounded man's cheek was still hot, but not dangerously so. She shook Thalgor awake.

"Help me repack the wound, then you may rest."

"I will stay here."

Stubborn man. "As you wish."

Removing the spent herbs would be painful, replacing them with fresh ones more so. She laid her hands on Rygar's forehead and flooded his mind again with oblivion, then set to work.

He cried out and struggled more this time. A sign he was stronger.

But it meant Thalgor had to leave his post to hold the wounded leg so she could do what she needed to do.

Rygar was fully conscious and in agony by the time she finished.

When Thalgor left to chase away Gee and the child, awakened by the cries, Rygar reached down and grabbed Erwyn's hand.

"Let me die, witch," he pleaded, his lips dry and cracked.

She freed her hand and offered him water, which he drank greedily. Another good sign.

"Thalgor orders me to save you."

"Does Thalgor think he orders the sun to rise as well?"

"Sometimes."

Rygar managed a thin smile.

"And another wishes you to live." Erwyn nodded toward Tya, who had appeared at the door. "If she could choose she would stay by your side as he does."

"She is too young." Rygar closed his eyes in pain.

"Her heart is older than her years."

He smiled again and slept.

Thalgor brought back food for the two of them and hot water so she could make a tea to ease Rygar's pain. When she woke him, he drank only a little, then vomited it up again. She cleaned him and eased him back to sleep with her mind.

"I must see to my men," Thalgor said as they finished a meal both ate with grim reluctance.

She put a hand on his arm to stop him. "You need rest."

"I need to be busy about something."

"You owe me a story."

"Later, witch."

Erwyn covered Rygar, then let Gee, Tya, and Felyn come to see that he lived and to stroke, each in her own way, his hands and face. When they left, she laid her hands on the wound and chanted a healing chant, but she felt no answer from Rygar's weak and weary body.

Thalgor returned with food at midday. He saw at once that Rygar was no better.

"Does your magic fail, witch?"

She knew he spoke to hide his fear, but the words cut. "I told you it might."

"Have I entrusted my people to a false witch?"

She pulled herself to her feet and faced him.

"I am a true witch, but I am not all-powerful."

"You are my woman. Can you not save the one I love most?"

Stunned and hurt by his words, she sat again by Rygar's side. His hot, gray flesh stirred when she laid her hand on him.

"Tell me now," she said.

Calmer, Thalgor sat opposite her.

"Why does it cause him so much agony?"

She uncovered the wound. "Think of it as a battle between the illness and his body. My magic can fight on his side, but the enemy has a strong foothold and is hard to ferret out from all its hiding places. Sometimes one side gains the advantage, sometimes the other. But his strength wanes through it all."

"Erwyn."

She looked at him. He seldom said her name.

His eyes were soft with tears again. "When you know for certain you cannot save him, give him an easy death."

She didn't tell him that moment had come and gone more than once already. Saving Rygar for Thalgor's sake had become more important than saving him for his own sake. That was a sin against her magic and she would not make the same mistake again.

"He is my mother's son," Thalgor said.

Her first impulse was to ask why that did not make Rygar his brother. Then she remembered her mother's daughter she did not call a sister. She remained silent and waited.

"His father captured us when I was a boy. He raped and beat my mother more times than I could count. He finally beat her to death when Rygar was a small child because he was ill and she could not make him stop crying. Before she died, I promised her I would keep him safe." He stopped and stroked Rygar's gaunt cheek. "Her murderer gave Rygar to his mother to raise." He looked up at Erwyn, eyes damp.

"Gee. He kept me around as a kind of whipping boy, but she protected me from him when she could. Better, perhaps, than my mother had." His fists clenched and unclenched on his legs. "That brute was the first man I killed. When I grew to be as tall and was nearly as strong as he was, he ceased to hit me. One night, after a raid that went badly, he knocked Rygar, still a child, across the tent. Gee intervened, and he threw her to the ground and kicked her senseless. I picked up the sword he'd left by the door and ran it through his throat. He died slowly, drowning in his own blood, while Rygar and I watched."

The silence vibrated with emotion, but neither spoke.

Most men would have bragged of such a feat, but Erwyn heard in Thalgor's voice the echo of the boy still struck numb by the horror of what he had done. She wanted to cry for that boy, but the man would not welcome her tears.

Rygar's eyes fluttered open. "Water."

Erwyn handed him a cup of the cold tea. He drank it, then fell back with a sigh.

He was able to keep the tea in his stomach this time and soon closed his eyes.

His wound needed to be cleaned and repacked again, but she would wait until he was fully asleep.

"Why keep your closeness a secret?" she asked Thalgor.

"Long tradition makes us enemies. I killed his father and eventually took his place as leader of this band. People may not understand he is all I have left of my mother and our band. It is best they forget we are brothers."

She nodded. Rygar slept peacefully. She uncovered his wound and began to clean it.

As THE MOON rose, Thalgor made his rounds of the camp to check on the sentries and talk briefly with Gurdek, who had the night command.

The whole camp seemed subdued by Rygar's illness, even in the rush of final harvest. Everyone he spoke to asked about him. Many were eager to assure Thalgor his second would recover under the witch's care. Perhaps people had not forgotten they were brothers after all.

He returned late to the dark tent, lit only by a shuttered lantern next to Rygar's makeshift bed. Erwyn had fallen asleep, her inert body spread across Rygar's chest. One of his arms had come up as if to hold her.

There was a time, perhaps only days ago, when such a sight would have filled Thalgor with jealous rage.

Tonight he felt only worry. He knelt and brushed Rygar's cheek with his hand. The skin felt cool. Its color was almost normal, even in the dim light. The battle was won.

Thalgor wanted to shout in celebration. Instead he silently let the relief and joy run through him. And the gratitude.

Tenderly he moved his brother's arm and picked Erwyn up.

She settled against his chest before her eyes flew open.

"Rygar?" she whispered.

Thalgor laid his forehead on hers. "His fever has broken."

She smiled and closed her eyes.

Thalgor carried her to bed, then went to cover Rygar. Gee padded in from the chamber she shared with Felyn.

"He will soon be well," Thalgor told her.

She gave him a fierce hug and sat by Rygar's bed.

Weary, Thalgor went to his own bed and lay beside Erwyn. He would have awakened her to find comfort in her body, but it was too soon after losing their child. A life lost, a life won.

He remembered a chant he had learned from his witch grandmothers as a boy. A song of the dead and the cycles of life.

He intoned it softly to himself, grateful that he had been able to keep his promise to his mother and the cycle of Rygar's life had not ended. He needed his brother's stories and the memories he kept alive.

The chant done, he wrapped himself around his woman's body and slept with a peace he hadn't known in years.

As Rygar's wound recovered, the days became ever more filled with the preparations for the wanderings of the dark time.

But the nights were filled with a new wonder for Erwyn. Thalgor, always an ardent and attentive lover, was now a tender one as well. The sense of floating in honey returned every evening and left only with each busy day's dawn.

He never seemed to notice when the midwives woke her in the night to help with difficult births. Perhaps because Gee relied more and more on Tya, and on Rygar as he grew stronger, to do the work the old woman no longer could.

One day, as the camp got ready for the final feast before the wanderings, Thalgor called his council and laid the map out on the great table to choose a route south.

"There has been little rain," Gurdek noted. "We must stay well away from the arid moors."

"Less rain in the warm time means heavier rain in the dark time. We must not be too near the rivers," Batte added.

"What do you see, Erwyn?" Rygar asked. He still limped, but was strong enough to return to battle as an archer and had returned to his place as Thalgor's second on the council.

Erwyn had waited for this day to come with hope and dread.

"I cannot see. I cannot look."

Six pairs of eyes turned to stare at her, but she saw only Thalgor's, brown and hard as when he first captured her.

"A witch who cannot see?" Gurdek's second asked in surprise.

"She is with child," Thalgor explained.

His tone was so empty of emotion that Batte's second asked, "Your child, Thalgor?"

Thalgor wrapped both hands around the man's throat before Batte and Rygar could move between them.

"You think otherwise, fool?" Thalgor roared as the man struggled vainly to pull his leader's hands away.

"She is a witch," he gasped.

"She is my woman."

Thalgor gave the man a little shake before he released him and calmly turned to Batte.

"Your second speaks his mind without fear. You chose well."

Batte nodded, his face red with an anger he dared not express with Thalgor in such a mood. Rygar slipped away to bring the half-strangled man, who still choked and coughed, some water. Gurdek and his second pretended great interest in the map. None of them dared even cast a glance at Erwyn.

She willed her heart to beat more slowly. She could not look, but for just a moment she had seen her own neck in Thalgor's huge fists. A neck so slender, she knew, that he could crush it in an instant if he chose. Instinctively her hands flew to protect the baby that grew in her womb, despite her certainty Thalgor would die rather than see either of them harmed.

Gurdek stabbed a finger randomly at the map. "If we go here," he said too loudly in the stunned silence around him.

He, his second, and Batte began again to discuss the options. Batte's second joined in more slowly, his voice raw. Rygar threw in an occasional comment, but he also kept looking back and forth from Erwyn to Thalgor, who stared silently over all of their heads at the blank wall of the tent.

Erwyn watched Thalgor from lowered eyes. She knew him well enough that she didn't need magic to read most of what he felt. Surprise, anger, worry, maybe a little pride. She watched as worry slowly overcame anger and began to hope.

But there was no sign of the tenderness, joy and love she felt as soon as she discovered she was with child again. Perhaps that would come with time.

Or perhaps not, she reminded herself with fierce honesty.

It didn't matter. This child had a mother who wanted it and already loved it with all her heart.

Erwyn sensed it was a girl. And with Thalgor's blood, her daughter would be a witch.

A route south finally determined, Thalgor called for food. They ate in uneasy silence. When the meal was done, Gurdek, Batte, and their seconds quickly made their escape.

Rygar lingered to talk with Tya, as he did at every opportunity. Felyn had wandered in while they ate and now napped with her head on Erwyn's lap, face against the spot where the child who might be her niece also slept.

Erwyn felt like taking a nap herself, something she now had to do most days. But Thalgor turned to her at last. He waited in silence while Gee and Tya cleared the food away.

When they were alone, he asked, "Why did you not tell

me?"

Erwyn could not quite look him in the eye.

"You told me not to get with child again."

"And you thought it would be easier for me to learn of it in front of my men?"

Her face went hot. "Perhaps I thought it would be safer."

"Safer!" He looked at the child who slept in her lap and repeated more quietly, "Safer? You thought I might harm you?"

"You dare not." She lifted her eyes to his. "I was afraid to hear what you might say, since you didn't want my child."

"And you want it so much you would defy me."

His voice was rough, caught between anger and tenderness.

Erwyn felt her face grow more red as she looked away. "It was not exactly my choice, but you...we..." She cleared her throat. "The magic I use takes thought and attention, and when we...when it must be used so often..."

He laughed. The warmth of the sound melted the ice of worry in her heart.

"Never was a man so flattered by his woman's failure to obey him, so charmed." He frowned. "Do you charm me, witch?"

Felyn stirred in her lap and laid a hand on Erwyn's belly. Then she smiled and went back to sleep. Strangely reassured by the innocent gesture, Erwyn looked back up at Thalgor.

"You are my man."

He sighed and nodded in agreement.

THE TRIP SOUTH was uneventful. A small skirmish with a badly outnumbered raiding party was the only battle.

The stress of travel, harder as a band grew larger, led to more conflict among their own people. Thalgor spent much of his time settling petty disputes and talking with his men. The former marauders were still distrusted by some, despite the victory they made possible. In times like this he had to listen even to minor complaints before they became major ones, and to reassure his people in myriad small ways of his leadership.

Some called the yearly move south the birthing time because of all the children born one birth cycle from the cold of the dark time. Each birth meant a halt in their progress. Two or three together meant a halt long enough to pitch tents. The warriors without birthing women grumbled and quarreled with those already stressed by new or impending fatherhood.

As always, some of the birthing mothers died and some of the babies. Now Erwyn could no longer use her magic to save any of them, the bereaved muttered against her. They were angry to lose their babies to protect hers, as they saw it, and easily forgot the lives her herbs saved, the births they eased, even without her magic.

Thalgor listened to the one or two grieved or angry enough to complain about her to him, and knew they spoke for many more less brave. This small core encouraged those who still saw the band endangered by the marauders to blame their presence in the camp on Erwyn as well. Her inability to heal the few wounded in the single skirmish created another pocket of resentment. Added to the usual distrust of witches and the rumors Dara and Batte still spread, Thalgor knew he had been right to wish she carried a child at another time of the year.

But he could not be sorry she carried his child now. Even after she told him, a little tremulously, it was a girl, every thought of that tiny life filled him with a joy and wonder he could never have imagined. He stroked her belly each night with a kind of awe, and was struck speechless the first time he felt a tiny foot tap against his palm as he cradled the mound of flesh in his hands.

Erwyn, for her part, glowed with a serenity and strength that stunned him. Not for the first time, and likely not for the last, he wondered what madness led him to take a witch for his woman.

CHAPTER TEN

T HALGOR SAT AT council one day, preoccupied with his woman's lush new body while his lieutenants argued over how to divide sentry duties for another prolonged halt for three births, when Erwyn appeared beside him, a dark frown on her face.

"A council?" she asked with raised eyebrows. "Why was I not told?"

"Do you care how we divide up the watch?"

"I was always told in the warm time camp. Even if the council only met about sentry duty."

"But you didn't carry a child then," he explained patiently.

The others stopped their argument to listen. Erwyn tossed them a thoughtful look before she turned back to him.

"What does the child I carry have to do with whether I am called to council?"

Thalgor sighed. So far she had not shown the strange emotions other men complained of when their women were with child. She made up now for the delay, he supposed, by having this argument in front of his men. He exchanged a look of forbearance with them.

"You cannot use your magic when you carry a child."

"I am well aware of that."

She broadened the stance of her still slender body as a man might when a brawl beckoned.

"So what use are you at council?" he finished with a shrug.

The angry red that flooded her face quickly became a white mask of rage. He was glad she could not use her magic to exact the painful penalty he could almost see form itself in her mind. She opened and closed her mouth twice, like a fish, before she found the air to speak.

"I only sat at your council because of my magic?"

She asked the question with a calm air of wounded dignity that surprised him even more than the anger that had preceded it.

"When you cannot see, why would I call you to council?"

"Have I never advised you except about what I saw?"

Again, both her question and her tone surprised him.

Surprised him enough he stopped to think about what she had said in the council in the past. All of it wise, in one degree or another, despite her ignorance of battle. Some of it based on what she saw with her magic. But all of it? Possibly not, but he remembered nothing in particular. Just the confidence he felt about a decision when she agreed with it. And no major decision had been made since they chose a route south the day she told them she carried a child.

He glanced again at his men. Rygar and Gurdek looked as surprised and confused as he. Batte and the others merely looked impatient.

Clearly none of them wished to become involved in what they saw as a dispute between their leader and his woman. Best to cut the whole thing short.

"Women do not sit at council," he told her. "Your magic has been helpful, but without it I see no reason to include you in our deliberations. Please tell Gee we would like to eat now."

Erwyn opened and closed her mouth one more time, then strode away in the opposite direction from Gee's campfire.

Rygar quickly got up to ask for the food, and the argument among the others continued where it had left off.

That, Thalgor thought with relief, is the end of that.

That, of course, was not the end of that. Thalgor first realized his error when the dinner Gee served him that night consisted only of dry bread, water, and cold meat, while the others ate a hot, savory-smelling venison stew.

But the coldness of his meal was nothing compared to the coldness of the back Erwyn turned to him when he came to bed.

He was wise enough in the ways of women not to fondle her and see what followed, as he did most nights and very much wanted to do this night as well. He could see all too easily what would follow, and it would not be pleasant. But he also refused to deny himself the warmth of her body completely.

He curled himself carefully around that cold back and encircled her round belly with one arm. Erwyn ignored him.

But someone else did not. Tiny feet battered his hand and arm with a strange intensity, until he pulled away with the eerie sense that his child was as angry as her mother.

He rolled on his back and faced a hard truth he had managed to ignore until now.

His daughter would be a witch. She would belong to her mother, not only as every daughter did, but in a way he could never understand.

He remembered the envy that flooded him as a child when his grandmothers spoke together. Worse, he remembered the same envy on his parents' faces as they watched the bond their mothers shared with each other and could not share with them, his father because he was a man, his mother because her father carried no witch blood.

The vision of a future shut out of the life Erwyn and their daughter would share compounded the pain of being shut out of his woman's warmth, her body tonight.

Are you certain you want to give your child to a witch?

When Gee asked him that question he had only thought of the physical act that would give her his child. Now he understood what the old woman truly meant. His daughter, their daughter, would be stronger than he was, wiser than he was, in ways he could only imagine. As was Erwyn.

He was roused from an uneasy sleep by Rygar.

"Marauders after our livestock."

"Whose men are on duty?" he asked his second sleepily.

"Batte's. They have them surrounded."

The two of them made their way quickly to where Batte stood toe-to-toe with a man almost as tall as Thalgor, but darker and several years older, half his face scarred by fire.

Before Thalgor could get a full report from Batte's second, an arrow flew from a nearby tree and the second fell dead.

Instantly Rygar stepped between Thalgor and the stand of trees the arrow came from. He notched an arrow and lifted his bow in a single movement. A leaf moved in the still night air and he let loose. With a cry the hidden archer fell from the tree, as dead as his victim.

Rygar turned to Thalgor as he slid his bow to his back.

"The arrow was aimed at you," he said.

Thalgor looked at the good man who lay dead at his feet. "I know." He looked up at the frozen stars in the dark-time sky.

Batte had pulled his sword as soon as his second fell, but Gurdek grabbed his arm. The two of them now struggled silently, strength against strength. The tall man who would die if Batte won the silent battle watched with stoic calm.

Batte must have noticed the man's courage because he finally lowered the sword.

"I'll tell his woman," he said in a hollow voice.

When he was gone, Thalgor clapped Rygar on the back, then repeated the gesture with Gurdek before he took Batte's place across from the dark man.

"Your men are brave," he said to the stranger. "Why let them die without need?"

"Your lieutenant wanted our women and children."

"You misunderstood. We would welcome all of you who agree into our band. But you must lead us to your camp, or we have no proof you are not a raiding party that would betray us to their band at the first opportunity."

The other man's eyes narrowed. "Are there others with whom you have struck such an unusual bargain?"

Thalgor narrowed his eyes in return. These men were well-fed and well-armed. Either they were very good at surviving under the harsh conditions of a marauder's life, or they were indeed a raiding party from some large band. Strange Batte did not assume the latter in the first place and kill them all.

Then Thalgor made out in the darkness what his lieutenant had probably seen more clearly during the skirmish. Fully a third of the would-be thieves were boys, not men. Large, armed boys, but boys all the same. That explained their surrender. Their leader hoped yet to save the boys' lives.

"We made such a bargain," one of the former marauders said. "Our women and children are safe. You can believe this man."

The tall man nodded. But rather than agree at once, he

did next what Thalgor would have done—he turned to talk in whispers with the two men who stood behind him. Each of them, in turn, spoke quietly to a few of the others.

Only when his seconds had reported back to their leader did he say, "All but the brother of the dead archer will join you. He has no woman or child. Just the brother your archer killed."

Thalgor nodded. One of the younger marauders knelt by the dead man's body, threw it awkwardly across his back, and staggered into the night with his sad burden.

"I am Sett." The tall man held out his hand to Thalgor. "I will lead you to our camp."

"My warriors will hold the rest of your men here."

"If the boys can come with me? Their mothers…"

Thalgor nodded and followed Sett and the boys into the woods with Rygar and their men.

Batte added the marauders to his men, but stayed in his tent to mourn his fallen second the next day. Thalgor called no council in deference to his loss.

If he thought the gesture might make his night less cold and lonely, however, he had misjudged Erwyn. Her back still greeted him when he came to bed. Even during the day she stayed away from him and denied him the chance to feel his child move inside her.

The next night, he caught her staring at him with those unforgiving eyes and that lush body, and knew he could take her at will without her magic to protect her. For the first time he almost understood what drove the man who became Rygar's father.

But unlike that brute, Thalgor hated himself for the thought.

They moved on, but soon had to stop and pitch their tents because some of the children fell ill, including Felyn. The illness was not serious for the older ones, but two babies died before Erwyn and the herbalist found the herbs to save them.

One day, as Erwyn and her helpers brewed tea and instructed the women on how much to give to their sick children, Batte came to Thalgor's tent with Sett at his side.

"We should call a council," Batte said without preamble. "Too many men have sick children for the usual rotation of sentries. We need to discuss how to make up for the gaps."

Thalgor, who had been thinking the same thing, nodded. He stood to carry Felyn, who napped on his lap, to her bed. The child was better now, but still clung to him when none of the others were around.

Gurdek soon arrived, followed by his second, Rygar and, to Thalgor's consternation, Erwyn. He gave Rygar a sharp look as she walked in, but his second shrugged his innocence.

Felyn came back into the room, placed her hand in Erwyn's, and smiled. Erwyn didn't respond, all her energy seemingly focused on staring at Thalgor so hard his head began to ache.

Although Erwyn doubted Felyn was a witch, Thalgor

was long convinced she must be. Her return now only confirmed his belief.

The thought of a life with three witches once his daughter was born made him shudder as Erwyn calmly took her usual place at the table next to him.

If any of his men thought to object to her presence, one small dose of that stare silenced them. Only Sett whispered a question to Batte, who merely shook his head. Sett nodded, and they all turned their attention to the business at hand.

"I have chosen a new second," Batte began.

"The marauder?" Gurdek's second asked in surprise.

"He is a brave man, experienced as a leader and in battle. He knows what we have given him."

"Good choice," Gurdek agreed solemnly.

His second echoed him, as did Rygar.

Thalgor was surprised when he hesitated, then chagrined at the reassurance he felt when Erwyn gave a small nod of approval. Why should her opinion carry such weight for him without her magic? He quickly turned his mind against the obvious answer.

"Agreed," he said. "Now about the sentry duty…"

"How long will the illness among the children last?" Gurdek interrupted him to ask Erwyn.

Thalgor cast him a dark look, but none of the others objected to the question he asked of a woman who should not have been there at all.

"From how quickly the first ones sick recovered, with the

herbal tea, four or five days," she explained.

"So here is what I propose…" Thalgor began again.

The meeting went on as usual from there, but he heard little of it, his thoughts on the woman beside him.

"Anything else?" he asked when the sentries were organized.

Batte and Sett exchanged looks, then Batte spoke.

"Sett and his men say another large band moves south on a path parallel to ours. Right now they have pitched their tents half a day's journey from here. They may have sickness, too, as they have been there several days. Sett's men didn't try to steal their oxen because they have so few they keep them very close to their camp. Yesterday Sett and his men scouted the camp again. They have less than half as many warriors as we do, but many tents and ox carts. I propose we attack their camp."

"How many warriors exactly?" Gurdek asked.

"We saw perhaps thirty," Sett replied. "Some may have been ill. From the number of tents, as many as sixty or seventy, but no sign of that many men. And too few oxen for so many."

"That seems strange," Rygar commented.

Batte, always eager for battle, frowned. "You all agreed to take Sett into our council. Rygar, you are the champion of the marauders. Why question Sett's report?"

Rygar looked at Erwyn, who nodded.

"It isn't a matter of questioning his report," Rygar said.

"But few or many warriors means the difference between victory and defeat. The number of tents is more certain than the number of men who can be seen at a given time. Seventy warriors who defend their women and children would make for a hard fight. The few oxen bother me, too."

"Illness, perhaps," Batte replied. "If in a day or two we send all the men without sick children, and leave those who have them to guard the camp, we can find the true numbers in battle, and retreat if we are outmatched."

"We did not know of this other camp," Erwyn said quietly.

"Because we have no useful witch," Batte snapped.

"But how do we know they are unaware of us?" she went on. "I agree with Rygar that it seems strange. Perhaps we should send out more scouts to see if they spy on us."

"Do you see some danger?" Gurdek's second asked uneasily.

"No."

"Do you doubt Sett's report?" Gurdek asked.

"It's not his report, as Rygar said."

"Perhaps a raiding party would be better than a full battle," Gurdek suggested thoughtfully. "We could take food, livestock, and some of their tents."

"You raid for crops or oxen," Batte sneered. "To take tents or food stores is a full battle in any case."

The others nodded.

"Something does not feel right," Erwyn protested.

"Perhaps it is the child in your belly," Batte grumbled.

Thalgor had had enough of all of them. He stood and leaned forward over the table, wickedly gratified when the other men, even Rygar, leaned back away from him.

"I will consider it. I want full numbers of men available for a war party, sick children or no."

"A full war party?" Gurdek was brave enough to ask.

"I said I would consider it. In the meantime, order your men to bring the camp tighter together, tent by tent, so it can be more easily defended. Council is over."

He knew Batte, Sett, Gurdek and his second would continue to talk among themselves about the possibility of going to battle. He would talk it through more with Rygar, too, to see if his second's objections stood on their own or relied on Erwyn's worry about Sett's report.

But all of that would be easier when he wasn't distracted by the woman herself, by his inexplicable need to have her support if he went to battle, by the scent of her body. Now he knew why women were not usually allowed at council meetings—not because they were weak but because men were.

She lay on her back awake when he came to bed.

"Do you plan to go to battle?" She stared up at the roof of the tent.

"Do you plan to let me touch you?"

"Will my answer change yours?"

"Will my answer change yours?" he echoed.

"No."

Resigned, he turned away from her. Then he felt her start a little as the baby kicked. He rolled on his back again.

"Can I at least touch my child?" He hated the need in his voice even more than he hated his need for her.

"If you can do it without touching me."

He worked to wrap his tongue around the unfamiliar word and managed to say "Please."

She gave a brief nod, then turned her face away from him.

He lightly placed one hand on her belly. Nothing. He slid his other hand under where her flesh protruded beyond her hips and held a firmness there that was clearly one end or the other of their child. A sharp kick to the first hand told him the second cradled the baby's head. He smiled to himself as he felt it kick and wiggle and even gently punch where his arm rested on the belly that sheltered it.

Erwyn sighed.

"Do I keep you awake?" he asked gently.

"She keeps me awake. You keep her awake."

"You are so sure it is a girl?"

"You don't mind that it is not a son?"

"That our first-born is not a son, no. But a life with a tent full of witches, well, it would not be my choice."

Erwyn sighed again. The baby fell still.

"I miss you," he heard himself say.

"You miss my body." She brushed his hands away and rolled to her side. "Perhaps you miss feeling your child inside me."

"I miss your warmth," he confessed. "I miss your smile. I miss your company in life."

"But not in council."

"Did I keep you out today? Even with a new man there?"

"Could you?"

He didn't know the answer to that question, so instead he shifted toward her and curled his body close against her back.

He wrapped one arm around her and kissed her neck. "At least keep me warm."

She said nothing, but he sensed her smile in the darkness.

SLOWLY OVER THE next two days Sett convinced Gurdek, then Rygar that what he and his men reported was true. Erwyn did not think they lied, but she could not believe what they said.

She hated being powerless to find out for herself or to stop his lieutenants from convincing Thalgor to do something she thought unwise. She developed new respect for women who lived all their lives with this lack of certainty, this lack of power.

She became gentler with Gee, whose age made the cold of the dark time especially hard. Tya did almost all the cooking now, and most of the work. Often Rygar appeared, to no one's surprise, to help her carry the heavy jugs of water.

He had spoken to Tya's father, and so they only waited until she was old enough to become his woman. If the delay weighed on Rygar, he showed no sign. Only the buoyant joy of a man who loved and was loved.

Thalgor and Erwyn were talking about Rygar's happiness the night of the third day when she found the courage to ask, "Would you risk his future to fight an enemy none of your men has seen?"

To her relief, he kept his temper. "Sett and his men are now my men."

"But not men you have fought with, who know your warriors and what they can do in a full battle."

"So they probably underestimate our strength."

She bowed her head to the wisdom of that. If only she knew why she did not trust what they reported.

"My men are restless. Life is hard in the dark time. They have been cooped up with sick children and fretful women. A battle, a small victory, and life will be easier for everyone. If the enemy are too many, we need only retreat."

A shudder ran through Erwyn, but she could not say why.

Thalgor cleared his throat. "We leave at full light."

"You held a council?" She stiffened with the old hurt.

"A war council. Your views are known. Could you have said anything that has not already been said?"

She shook her head.

"Rygar will lead those who remain to guard the camp."

"That is best, with his wound still so recent."

"Will you let me touch you before I leave?"

She nodded again. But afterward, as he slept, she lay beside him a long time, even the child inside her still. She wept and felt as if the child inside her wept, too.

THALGOR LOWERED HIMSELF wearily into bed the next night, careful not to wake Erwyn. She would have worried the day away and needed her sleep.

She was right to worry. Right to oppose the battle plan.

When Sett and his men guided them to the enemy camp, they found almost a hundred warriors. Thalgor, with more experience of life in a large band than Sett, had realized at once that when the marauders scouted the camp the majority of the warriors had been off chasing a raiding party that had taken most of their oxen.

Their numbers were evenly matched, but Thalgor never attacked men who protected their women and children without a sizeable advantage. So they returned to camp without doing battle. And, if he was lucky, without even being seen.

His lieutenants had agreed, but some of the younger men grumbled about the wasted effort and blamed it on Erwyn's distrust of the plan. Thalgor grumbled not a little himself, but he never began a battle he wasn't certain he could win.

The alarm came at dawn. The warriors they meant to attack had followed them back, camped the night just out of sight, and at first light fell on Rygar's dozing guards, on duty a full day and night by then.

Quickly the rest of their men banded to support them, but they had no time to plan, no time to think beyond the need to keep the battle away from the luckily compacted camp where their women and children already huddled around freshly lit fires.

Thalgor found his second in the middle of the battle, intent on defending one of their fallen men. Rygar was gray with exhaustion and drenched in sweat with the unaccustomed exertion, but he called orders and rallied their men as he kept an enemy, intent on the kill, at bay. An unexpected wave of pride almost stopped Thalgor in his tracks.

He reached Rygar's side and dispatched the enemy with a single blow to his belly. Rygar lowered his sword and knelt at his fallen man's side, only to find him already dead.

"Give me your report, then fall back," Thalgor told him as he helped his second stand again on his weakened legs. "When you are able, we can use your good bow arm."

Rygar nodded and wiped a mixture of tears and sweat from his face. He gave his report and walked calmly to the rear, swinging his sword now and then to fend off attacks from the few enemies who had managed to get past their first line of defense.

Thalgor fought just behind the first line and scanned the enemy ranks for their leader. His sword arm was already weary before he saw a large man in the enemy's second rank who was clearly in command. Thalgor made his way toward the man, but with their warriors so evenly matched he made slow progress.

He sent a man to Gurdek, whose duty was to hold back and keep a view of the whole battle, to ask his lieutenant to send any free men to reinforce the line so Thalgor could engage the enemy leader as soon as possible. Once he killed him, it would be easier to draw the attackers away from the camp.

In a scant moment of quiet, he looked back to where Gurdek talked with his second and the messenger. While Thalgor watched, three arrows struck the side the second had turned toward the enemy. The man fell dead at Gurdek's feet. The pain on his old friend's face cut through Thalgor like an enemy sword.

A slow, cold rain had begun to fall. The smell of mud mixed with gore and hot metal filled the misty air. Men easily slipped in the muck to their death. Unfortunately, the enemy held more of the rocky ground, Thalgor's warriors more of the bare earth below it.

The man he sent to Gurdek returned with an arrow in his shoulder and an expression of near panic.

"All our men already fight, except the few who stand

guard around the camp," he reported. "Gurdek has sent for them, but that will leave only old men and boys in their place."

A wave of utter blackness swept over Thalgor, as devastating as it was unexpected.

With an effort, he kept his face free of emotion as he nodded at the messenger and told him to find the surgeon to tend to his wound. When the man was gone, Thalgor looked up and down the battlefield and saw what he had missed in his focus on finding the enemy leader.

Gurdek's men, to his right, were holding their own, but they made no headway against the enemy. The line of Batte and Sett's men on his left had broken. The enemy had gotten through in places and now battled some of their men from two sides. As the guards began to arrive from the camp, Gurdek sent them to close the broken line, but they were too few, too late.

Soon, Thalgor saw, the line would break entirely and they would be surrounded. Defeat was inevitable. His daughter would be born, live, and die some other man's slave.

If they allowed Erwyn to live at all.

And he could do nothing to protect her. He could only continue to fight in the cold, mud and rain, killing and grieving now with equal passion and equal despair.

The enemy's leader made his way toward him, but Thalgor doubted killing him would do more now than slow the tide of defeat.

But kill him he would.

The two leaders raised swords against each other. Their men moved away from where they stood, some out of deference to their strength and valor, some simply out of fear.

The enemy glanced away for just a moment to appraise his men's advantage.

Now. Thalgor brought his sword down hard, but it struck only his opponent's shield, as his sword stuck only Thalgor's.

They fought on that way, blow for blow, until Thalgor's arms grew numb, his breath hot and tight in his chest.

Just when he began to doubt he could ever kill this man who would soon take from him all he loved, a stir ran through the warriors on all sides. Both leaders froze and looked as their men did at a rocky outcropping just to one side of the battlefield.

A man stood on the highest point in a shimmering silver robe. The Witch King.

Beside him stood Erwyn.

CHAPTER ELEVEN

H IS WOMAN'S PREGNANT body made a perfect target. Thalgor vowed to kill this Witch King with his own hands, vision or not, for putting her in such danger. Before he finished the thought, an arrow flew from the enemy ranks and pierced the shimmering vision, which immediately disappeared. Without her companion Erwyn, in her dark cloak, all but disappeared as well.

Thalgor sighed with relief as his opponent's sword swished past his right ear.

Without having to think, he took advantage of the near miss to thrust his sword up under the man's shield. He struck him deep below the ribs. The sword that had barely missed his ear came back down and knocked Thalgor's shield into the mud as the enemy leader fell to the ground with a terrible crash.

No. The crash was thunder. Thunder in the dark time?

Again the battlefield stilled. Most of the men on both sides looked at the sky. Thalgor looked at Erwyn.

She circled her hands in the air to create another ball of glowing white light. When she threw it to the sky, thunder rocked the air again and the rain became a downpour. Then she raised both arms and fire shot from her hands to strike the ground like lightening between the two lines of warriors locked in battle.

Some fought on despite the bolts of white heat. Some stood still. Some on both sides ran.

One of the lieutenants of the leader Thalgor had just killed rushed toward him, sword raised. Thalgor prepared himself for the blow, his shield lost in the mud, his own sword still stuck deep in the dead leader's body.

As he prepared himself for death, Erwyn cast a flash of light and fire at the attacker's feet.

The man jumped back from the lightening, slipped in the mud, and fell on the sword of one of his own fallen men. It must have lodged near his heart because a fountain of blood sprang from the wound, then stopped.

Thalgor freed his sword and dug about in the mud for his shield. As the word spread among his men that Erwyn was the source of the flashes of light, they ceased to run and began again to fight.

The enemy, for their part, began to run in earnest.

"Should we follow?" Batte appeared at Thalgor's side.

"No. We've lost enough men for one day."

He looked up to find Erwyn gone.

It was late before he could return to his tent. He had plans to set, wounded to visit, new widows to console, weary men to assure of their bravery even without a victory.

The tent was silent as he entered and crossed toward the chamber he shared with Erwyn.

Gee appeared from the dark and blocked his path.

"She is exhausted," the old woman told him in a hushed voice. "And she bleeds."

"She was wounded?" His heart pounded with terror.

Gee shook her head.

The full horror of the old woman's words hit home.

She bleeds.

"No!" An anguish he never expected coursed through him like the lightening Erwyn had created that day. He took a step toward the sleeping chamber, intent on punishing her in a thousand ways for the crushing pain she'd caused him, but Gee still blocked his way.

"Out of my way, old woman."

He was barely able to keep from putting his hands on her to move her from his path.

"I saw being leader of this band turn my own son into a brute," Gee said. "I'll die before I let it do the same to you."

"No!" He held his hands up in impotent rage. "No!"

He ran blindly from the tent to the battlefield. The rain had stopped, but the enemy dead lay covered with mud. In the light of the half-full moon, he pulled his sword and began to hack his way through the inert bodies, blow upon blow upon blow, until he was covered in blood and filth. Finally, beyond exhaustion, he stumbled to a patch of clean grass and slept.

An icy chill woke him at dawn. Someone had covered him with a cloak. Rygar sat on a rock nearby, half asleep. He'd brought Thalgor fresh clothes and water to wash.

When he was clean and dressed, Thalgor put a hand on the younger man's shoulder. "Nothing to say, Brother?"

"There are no words to name the grief I feel, Brother."

They stood like that a while, both weeping silently.

Finally Rygar said, "There will be others."

"Other women?"

They turned to walk back to the camp.

"Other children for you and Erwyn."

"No. I will give no more of my children to the witch. She is too careless of them."

"What was she to do, Thalgor? Let us all die?"

"You defend her?"

"I defend your love for her."

Thalgor swore violently. "You know what I once saw, what I once endured, what I once did. Do not speak to me of love."

"Thalgor…"

"Or of the witch. She killed my babies with her magic. How can I touch her after that, much less love her?"

"Thalgor…" Rygar tried again, but his brother gave him a look so dark he fell silent.

ERWYN KNEW WHEN Thalgor returned to the camp because her head began to throb so badly she thought it might split open. By the time he reached the tent Gee was already packing food in a basket for her.

When she saw him, Erwyn wished fervently for the ignorance she had lived in for the last few months so she could not read his thoughts so clearly.

"Leave my tent," Thalgor said, then added to Rygar's obvious surprise, "The archer will provide another."

"There's no need." Erwyn managed to keep the quaver out of her voice. "I go to the forest to recover and to grieve."

"Alone?"

"I will take the child with me."

"How will a child be of any use?" he asked in a tone that sent Felyn scurrying to hide in the folds of Gee's gown.

"She will keep me company. She can tell Tya when we need more food."

His frown deepened. "Why can you not recover in camp?"

"I need peace. Here there is too much anger against me."

"I have a right to be angry!" He took a step toward her.

The pain in her head doubled and her stomach twisted.

"Not only your anger. Some blame me for not seeing what would happen. Some blame Sett and his men, and blame me for encouraging you to take marauders into the band. Some blame me for not ending the battle sooner. Some blame me for not healing in its aftermath. I have no more magic, Thalgor, only enough second sight to make peace impossible for me here."

"Am I supposed to keep my people camped here until you decide we can move on?"

"Whether you will abandon me and the child in the dark time is something only you can decide." Nothing in his face answered the unspoken question in her words, so she went on. "I do what I must do to care for myself and my magic."

He sighed. "We will need to stay here, in any case, until we have regrouped from the battle and our wounded are healed. Let us hope you recover no more slowly than they."

The pain that split her head was met with a pain that all but split her heart. She managed not to cry out.

"I grieve, too, Thalgor."

He narrowed his eyes. "Stay out of my mind, witch. And stay out of my tent. A witch's grief means nothing to me."

He turned away from her and left.

But later, as she wrapped her cloak around her, Gee handed her a dagger.

"From Thalgor," the old woman said. "For protection."

The knife felt alive in her hand. She wanted to throw it—and the omen it brought—away from her, as she would a snake.

But she heard the Witch King's voice in her head say, "It is his heart."

She wrapped her hand around the hilt of the dagger and slid it up the sleeve of her gown, then tied the hilt to her wrist with a cord. The metal, strangely warm, pulsed against her flesh.

Her body still protested the loss of the life it once sheltered. She and Felyn were barely out of sight of the camp when Erwyn needed to stop and rest.

She lowered herself to the ground and leaned back against a tree. She used the resting time to sew a small, narrow pouch in the sleeve of her gown to hold the dagger near her hand.

By the time it was done she felt strong enough to move on. She called Felyn from where she'd crouched down to sort through the leaves the tree had shed before the dark time came. The child brought an especially beautiful red one and handed it shyly to Erwyn.

Although the attempt to cheer her up only made her grief more clear, she put the leaf in the pocket with Thalgor's knife and told the girl, "It's beautiful. Thank you."

Erwyn rose awkwardly to her feet. A fallen branch lay nearby, the perfect size for her hand. She broke off both ends to make it the right length to carve into a staff with the dagger. One gift from the child, one from Thalgor. Would there be a third?

The thought buoyed her a bit. With that lightness and the stick, she climbed the hill to see the forest in the valley below, the trees spread so no part of it was completely dark, almost as if planted that way on purpose. Halfway down the hill, Felyn waited, singing softly to herself.

They made slow progress, but as the dark of the day became the dark of night, they were well into the forest. They found a fallen tree near a stream to shelter them. Erwyn made a small fire and they shared a meal of the food Gee had sent with them.

Erwyn's body ached from tiredness and from its loss, but the long walk made it so she could sleep, her cloak wrapped around both of them for warmth.

In the night she woke from dreams of the battle. Her mind flooded with memories of the pain that grasped her as she stumbled back to the camp, the soul-wrenching despair when she realized her loss. She wept silently until dawn, careful not to wake the child huddled next to her.

When Felyn woke, they ate a cold meal, then Erwyn, who still ached too much to walk far, sent the girl to find the witch's circle that should lie in the midst of any forest.

While she was gone, Erwyn peeled the bark from her staff. The dark honey color and fine texture of the wood reminded her of the way Thalgor's hair spread across their pillow while he slept, patches of bark the brown of his agate-colored eyes.

She took the knife and began to carve, not his face, but the face of the Witch King.

She would grieve the loss of Thalgor when the deeper wound had healed. He was not an innocent, and he was never hers.

Felyn came back at midday to share another cold meal

and lead Erwyn to the circle she had found, uncertain whether it was made by witches or not.

Erwyn entered the circle reverently and found the flat, half-hidden stone in the center that proved it was what she'd sought. She cleared the grass and weeds away from the stone and lit a fire.

Felyn hovered at the edge of the circle, perhaps aware of how sacred this place was, perhaps unsure of Erwyn's mood. Or both. Erwyn summoned the girl to her side.

"Do you remember the ritual for the dead we did before?"

Felyn nodded, eyes wide.

"Can you help me again this time?"

Rather than nod, the girl slipped a small hand into hers.

"I wish to give the girl child I lost my mother's name. Because she was your mother, too, you must agree."

Felyn replied in a voice rusty with disuse, "I agree."

Erwyn could not stop the tears that began to flow at those reedy words. Felyn threw her arms around her waist and began to cry, too. They stood there a long time in shared sorrow.

Finally Erwyn noticed the fire was dying. She stepped gently from the girl's embrace and asked her to add more wood. Felyn wiped her face with the edge of her cloak and did so, while Erwyn opened the bag of herbs she'd brought.

The ritual, often interrupted by tears, lasted until the thin dark-time daylight was gone. Erwyn lit a long piece of wood from the fire to serve as a torch so they could find their way back to the fallen tree, then used it to start a fire for warmth and to keep animals away. Too tired to cook, they ate another cold meal and rolled up together in Erwyn's cloak.

Felyn slept at once, but Erwyn's eyes refused to stay closed. She'd expected the ritual to ease her grief. Instead it made her loss more real, just as the name she had given her lost child made her more real. Worse, the ritual forced her to acknowledge that she would not, could not, have acted differently, even if she had known for certain the child would not survive.

As the Witch King had said as he led her to the battle-field, she'd risked one life for many. Not to save Thalgor or Rygar or their band, but to save Thalgor's vision of a world where none would wander, where no more battles would be fought.

She drifted into sleep as the green line of dawn began to form in the east. She dreamed again of the image with the half-formed face that had appeared with her mother and the Witch King the night she tried to flee from Thalgor's camp in the last dark time. This time she knew at once who it was.

"Forgive me." She could not look the apparition in its eerie face.

"It was my fate," the vision said. "As Thalgor is yours."

"No!" The word spoken aloud shocked her awake and frightened Felyn so much she began to weep.

Erwyn made a hot breakfast for them, then carved some more on her staff while Felyn played among the trees. They were almost out of food, so as the sun warmed the day they headed out of the forest in the direction of Thalgor's camp.

They moved more quickly this time. Erwyn's staff made it easier for her to walk, and her body was slowly healing, even if her heart was not. She stopped at the same tree just out of sight of the camp and sent Felyn to bring Tya with the food.

The two returned together soon after midday. Tya brought not only a basket of food, but also a warm meal.

"Thank you." With an effort, Erwyn pulled herself out of the melancholy she had sunken into while she waited.

"No, I should thank you." Tya smiled and offered Erwyn some of the meat she brought. "A day away from the tent is a gift."

"Why? What's wrong?"

"Better to ask what's right. Thalgor rages at everyone and everything. His suffering distracts Rygar so he barely remembers to smile at me, and grieves Gee so she relies on me more than ever to do the work for them all. Gurdek and Batte argue endlessly, so the whole camp is upset. There are still many wounded from the battle, which casts a gloom over everything. This is the most quiet I have known since you left."

"Is Thalgor well?" Erwyn asked in spite of herself.

"He eats little and sits up most of the night to stare into

the fire. But he is strong. Gee worries more about his temper than his health." Tya paused, then cleared her throat and looked away. "The woman called Dara visited him yesterday."

"Oh," Erwyn squeezed past the pain that threatened to strangle her. "Did she stay long?"

"No. Like everyone else, she managed to have him quickly in a rage. But I thought you should know."

"Why?" Erwyn asked, as casually as she could.

"You are his woman."

"Were you not there when he asked me to leave his tent? Dara may have him, if she wishes. It is no concern of mine."

Tya looked as if she believed the brave words as little as Erwyn did, but she said nothing.

They finished the meal in silence. When it was gone, Tya stood with a heavy sigh. "Nothing to do for it but go back."

"It will get better."

Tya reddened. "I suppose it was wrong of me to complain to you when you..."

"I will get better, too." Again she hoped the words sounded more certain to Tya than they did to her.

Erwyn pulled herself awkwardly to her feet with her staff.

"It's Rygar," Tya exclaimed when she saw the face Erwyn had carved in the wood.

"Is it?" She had meant to carve the Witch King.

Tya looked closer, and even Felyn came to peer up at the face in the wood.

"No," Tya said slowly. "You're right. It's not. But if he had a brother…"

Erwyn almost told her he did have a brother, but that was Rygar's story to share with the woman he loved, not hers.

They both jumped when Felyn said solemnly, "Thalgor."

Tya looked closely at the carving again.

"She's right. It could be Thalgor, too. But I don't think it is. Did you carve it yourself?"

"It keeps my hands busy when I rest. It's not finished."

"Strange how it could be Thalgor or Rygar, but isn't."

Erwyn merely nodded. It was a familiar puzzle to her.

Tya returned to the camp, Erwyn and Felyn to the fallen tree, where they ate a warm dinner and sat by the fire until Felyn fell asleep with her head in Erwyn's lap.

Perhaps it was a mistake to give the lost child our mother's name, Erwyn thought as the moon sank behind the trees. This new grief may not end until I know the truth behind her death. And that I may never know.

To think this pain might never end was unbearable, yet she could not wish the child unnamed.

She vowed to try the ritual again and, if that failed to ease her grief, to take an ox from Thalgor's camp and return to the Wise Witches to beg them again for their help. Even if they refused a second time to give her the answers she needed, she could leave Felyn in their care.

Then she would be free to finish the deadly dance with

the sea Thalgor had once interrupted. With the possibility of that end to her sorrow her only comfort, she finally slept.

They ate a cold meal at dawn, then went to the circle to repeat the ritual.

Felyn dragged her feet, her small face an endless, silent complaint. When she refused to enter the circle, Erwyn sighed and told her to play nearby until the ritual was done.

A wise child. Without Felyn to distract her, Erwyn was able to concentrate more fully on her loss and its place in the cycles of the world. The ritual was slower as she took in the full meaning of every word, every gesture, until she felt as if she had finally done what she must do for the lost child.

But the aching sorrow remained.

She walked the whole perimeter of the circle, but saw no sign of Felyn. Weary from the ritual, she used her staff to half drag herself along the path to their small camp.

The girl was not there, but someone, or something, had eaten most of their food and left their things strewn on the cold ground like leaves after a storm.

Too tired for the alarm that tried to skitter along her nerves, Erwyn numbly packed what could be salvaged in the one basket that remained whole. Then she lowered herself to the ground and leaned back against the fallen tree to wait for Felyn.

She woke to the feel of a man's hand on her breast.

Caught in dreams of Thalgor, she pulled away with a murmur of protest.

Then the stench hit her. Her eyes flew open.

Within inches of her nose was a face that seemed vaguely familiar but was so caked with dirt she couldn't be certain. The stench that woke her came not only from the man's unwashed body, but also from the blackened teeth that filled his grim smile.

"It is you," he hissed. "I could not be certain until I saw those blue witch's eyes."

Erwyn tried to pull away, but he sat astride her.

A sound drew her attention to where Felyn lay beside them, arms tied behind her, a filthy rag stuffed in her mouth.

Erwyn started to scream but the man held up a knife.

"Don't try it." He laughed at her terror. "Where is your magic now, witch? Or that giant man of yours? Both gone or I would already be dead. Gone the way my band and my wife and my children are gone. Because you bewitched them away from me."

Through the blind panic that swept around her like a whirlwind Erwyn recognized the marauder whose woman had been the midwife who now cooked for Gurdek.

The renegade squeezed her breast so hard she gasped, then touched its point with the knife.

"So many choices. Do I rape you, or make you watch me rape the girl? Untouched she might bring me the worth of an ox when I sell her as a slave in the South. You I will kill, of course, for fear your magic might return. But I will not kill you quickly, not quickly at all."

The knife pricked through her cloak and gown to cut the tender skin, but she knew better than to give any sign of pain.

"Brave or petrified with fear?" The man laughed again as a small spot of blood flowered on the fabric over the wound.

The pain cleared Erwyn's head. Thalgor's dagger throbbed against her wrist. Slowly, so the renegade could not see, she felt for the dagger's handle and edged it out of its pocket.

Thalgor had given it to her for just such a moment, but he could not have remembered what it would cost her to use it.

If she killed, she would lose her magic. No longer Thalgor's woman, what would she be if she was not a witch?

While she shifted the dagger in her hand, unsure what to do, Felyn wriggled around enough to give the man a solid kick in the leg.

He cursed wildly, dropped the knife, and wrapped his blackened fingers around the girl's throat. "If you were not worth so much…"

He had turned his body, so Erwyn might not be able to kill him with a single blow. If he moved closer again, she could thrust the knife up under his ribs, straight into his heart.

Could, but would she? Not to kill was so much a part of what she had learned from her mother that even to think of thrusting the dagger home felt like a betrayal of her mother's love. But to let Felyn be taken felt like a betrayal of herself.

The child ceased to struggle and went limp in the man's hands.

The renegade threw her unconscious form to one side and stood up. He bent to try to pull Erwyn up by the shoulders.

Thoughts tumbled through her mind. Kill this man and lose her power, or abandon Felyn to her fate? Both were unthinkable.

A calmer inner voice told her she had less chance to find his heart if they stood.

She wriggled free of his grasp and fell to the ground. Somehow she managed to kick his knife away in the process.

"Get up!" His foot found her ribs with a vicious blow.

"I am ill," she wheezed. "You must help me get up."

Time stretched as the man cursed viciously again and bent toward her, closer, closer.

She tensed the arm that held the dagger and braced her body against the ground so she could thrust with greater force. Closer he came, almost within reach.

She heard Felyn gasp for air. In that moment she knew the renegade was a dead man.

But before she could act, a noise came from behind them. The man cried out, straightened, then froze.

Thrrr. Thonk! Erwyn heard the sounds clearly this time.

The man opened his mouth in a silent scream before he fell forward across her body, dead. His weight pushed all the air out of her. Two arrows still quivered in his back.

"Rygar!" she called.

But it was Thalgor's face that floated in front of her as the terror swallowed her.

Thalgor. She let the blackness take her.

WHEN HER MIND cleared, the renegade's body was gone. Someone was gently washing her face with warm water, but she was too weak to turn her head to see who it was.

"How?" she managed.

A man's hands offered her a cup of broth, but she ignored it.

"How?" she asked again.

"I dreamed of the Witch King."

Her breath caught. An answer only Thalgor could give. She closed her eyes against the flood of emotions that threatened to overwhelm her again.

"The Witch King sent me to you." His voice was as gentle as his hands. "And who do you think taught Rygar how to shoot an arrow?"

She smiled. When he touched the cup of broth to her lips this time she opened her eyes and drank.

"I saw to Felyn first," he explained as she sipped the welcome liquid. "She was hurt, but not badly. You seemed only to have fainted. The cut is minor, but I cleaned it for you."

She reddened at the thought that he touched her bare breast.

He gave a small laugh. "I have seen it before."

The broth gone, Erwyn sat up and shook her head to clear it. What had just happened came back to her in an icy rush. A chill filled her body.

She would have killed! All her mother taught her meant nothing. She'd let her babies die, one knowingly, and now she would have murdered.

She turned the dagger in her hand, but Thalgor saw the movement and took it from her.

"One blow clean up through here." She struck her chest just below the left ribs.

Thalgor slid the dagger into its holder on his belt. "In his heart, or yours?"

"Witch blood!" she hissed. "Stay out of my mind."

"It is not a pleasant place to be just now. Nor is mine."

"So go back to your camp and worry about your own thoughts."

She struggled to her feet, but the earth swayed under her. She stumbled a few steps, then fell to her knees and emptied her stomach.

Thalgor held her shoulders as the tremors ran through her. When they stopped, he lifted her face to wipe it clean again.

"You are ill."

She stood slowly and squared her shoulders. "No, I

grieve."

"For our lost child?"

She shook her head. The gesture made her so dizzy she sat down hard on the ground at his feet.

"Because I asked you to leave my tent?"

He picked her up, carried her back to the fallen tree, and laid her down gently.

"I grieve for myself."

With those words what she had almost done hit full force, a soul pain so deep she felt it in her body, so unbearable she could only be grateful when the blackness took her again.

CHAPTER TWELVE

WHEN ERWYN FOUGHT her way back into this world, half against her will, Thalgor's rich baritone mixed with Felyn's piping laughter somewhere nearby.

The weight of her grief was still so great she could scarcely stay conscious long enough to drink the broth Thalgor brought her when he saw she was awake. Then she slept.

"Enough." Her mother's face hovered over her in a dream. Tears of unbearable longing flowed down Erwyn's face.

"Enough," the vision said again, as her mother had long ago when Erwyn had grieved too long after her so-beloved father had first been captured. "Leave it go. Live, child! It is all we have, this life."

"No!" Erwyn struggled awake.

She looked up at cloth and thought for a moment she was in Thalgor's tent. That the whole ordeal had been only a dreadful nightmare.

Then she heard raindrops and felt a cold breeze. Thalgor had built a lean-to to protect her from the icy rain.

It was full night. Felyn slept curled up beside her for

warmth, but Thalgor sat by the fire and stared into the flames.

A strange sweetness filled her. She wanted this life. This man. Grief and pain remained, but she no longer wished to die.

Carefully she sat up. Her head remained clear. She licked cracked lips.

"Thalgor," she whispered.

He looked over from where he sat and said softly, "So you've decided to live."

She shrugged. "I'm hungry."

"Too wet to cook or hunt. Of course you are hungry now," he grumbled, but she saw the relief in his eyes.

He rummaged about in one of the baskets and handed her a piece of bread. She ate it eagerly, then drank the rainwater he caught for her in a cup.

"Thank you for staying here to care for us."

It was his turn to shrug. "What was I supposed to do?"

"Go back to your camp and send Tya?"

"And have Rygar at my throat because I deprive him of her company? No, thank you."

"Send him as well."

"And have Tya's father at my throat? Think, woman!"

She laughed, a strange, rusty sound.

"How is Felyn?"

He came and sat beside her, but didn't touch her.

"Thoroughly tired of this place. As am I."

"No harm from...from the renegade?"

Erwyn shuddered at the memory of what the man did. And what she had almost done.

"A nightmare. She hasn't said much, but that is how the child is."

Yet Erwyn had heard the child laugh with him.

"Why are you here?" she asked.

"I told you, the Witch King sent me after you."

"I meant, why are you still here?"

"I told you that, too."

"You told me some story. I want the real answer."

He shifted so their legs touched. She did not move away.

"A man thinks many things when he isn't sure he will arrive in time to save his woman's life. Isn't even sure she wants it to be saved."

"Am I your woman still?" she asked, almost against her will.

"Would I care so for a stranger?"

A tiny crack broke through the pain and grief that was still frozen around her heart like ice on late-ripening fruit.

"Tya said Dara visited you." Another unbidden question.

He gave a puff of laughter. "She tried to tell me you had killed our child on purpose, as you had helped her rid herself of Batte's. I knew it was a lie as soon as the words left her mouth. And I knew then that, in my grief, I had wronged you."

"You grieved, too," she acknowledged. "But even then

you did not come to find me."

"No. I thought the words could wait until you came back. Then the Witch King warned me you might never return."

She nodded again and laid her head on his shoulder.

"I am tired. Will you keep me warm while I sleep?"

He pulled his cloak around them and gathered her to his chest as she pulled Felyn to hers.

She woke at midday, or what would have been midday if the rain hadn't turned the dark-time sun into the gloom of evening.

Thalgor had made a small fire beyond the edge of the lean-to and sat by it, shivering as he heated battle gruel.

When he saw Erwyn was awake, he brought her some broth and tea. She drank both apprehensively, but like the bread the night before they warmed her and settled comfortably in her belly.

After they ate, Thalgor cleared away the small meal, then came to sit beside her. Felyn huddled on her other side.

The three of them sat in silence for a long time as they watched the fire burn in the shadowy afternoon.

Words would be nicer, Erwyn knew, but words were also more dangerous. Better just to sit with the feel of Thalgor's body near hers once again.

"Is there enough food?" she finally stirred herself to ask.

"I will kill another rabbit when it stops raining, and Felyn has gotten quite good at finding nuts. I think this was an orchard once."

Erwyn looked around and noticed for the first time the trees around them were all fruit- or nut-bearing kinds. "Our ancestors must have planted them."

"Which means there might be ruins nearby. I plan to look for them while I hunt, now that I can search farther away."

"How long will we stay here?"

A memory of their journey back from the sea flittered unbidden through her mind and she smiled.

"We will stay until you are well enough to walk all the way back to camp."

"Are you not needed there?"

"To stay away might be better now. Batte blames Sett for the failure of our raid and our losses in the battle that followed. He wanted him and those who came with him forced from the band. Gurdek saw more clearly the fault that lay with the enemy leader, who took a risk no leader should, even if they were almost victorious. So he took Sett as his second." He shook his head. "Councils have become nothing but a battleground between the two of them, with Sett and Batte's new second, a solid man named Tynor, trying to stay out of the way and Rygar trying to make peace until he loses his temper with them all."

"So Tya told me."

"We cannot even reach a decision about which way to move south." He sighed. "While I am gone, no one will expect a decision, and perhaps Batte and Gurdek will learn how to work together again. At least I don't have to listen to them argue."

"What if Batte decides to take his men and leave the band?"

"He might have, if they argued so before the last battle. But we lost so many men there are no longer enough warriors to defend two camps, and Batte has no desire to live as a marauder. He wants to lead a great band."

"He will not try to take your place while you are gone?"

"Not with Rygar and Gurdek there. And Sett."

THE NEXT DAY dawned clear and cold.

Thalgor hunted while Erwyn and Felyn stayed close to the fire. When he returned with a rabbit, Erwyn made a thick stew. She was weary when she finished, but it felt good to be able to carry out even that simple task.

"I found the ruins," Thalgor announced while they ate. "They're at the southern edge of this grove. Nothing is left but huge cut stones thrown about, as if by some angry giant."

Angry witches, more likely. But Erwyn dared not say so.

"I'm sorry. I know you hoped for more."

After a long silence, he said, "I found the witch's circle, too. You used it recently."

"To perform the ritual for the dead." She took a deep breath and looked out among the trees. "I gave the child my mother's name."

Thalgor nodded. "That is good. She was a witch."

Erwyn made soup from the remains of the stew for their dinner.

"You are stronger?" Thalgor asked her when he returned from scouting the woods to find her cooking.

"Yes, but not yet strong enough to walk all the way to the camp."

"If they have not moved on without us," he commented glumly.

"You said they would not."

He hunkered down beside the fire. "Who knows what men will do during the dark time? The wandering is hard. But to stay in one place is to invite attack from all the other bands as they wander, and gives us almost no chance to make raids of our own."

"Why do you need to raid? You take no slaves to sell."

"For livestock, goods, and food. For women, children and old men to help with the work of the band."

"But then the band grows too large and must divide." Erwyn shook her head. "It doesn't make sense, Thalgor."

"It never makes sense to kill. But it is what we have always done. And to sit during the dark time and wait to be attacked is harder on my men than the wandering."

Erwyn took the handle of the spoon she'd used to stir the

soup and drew a circle in the dry dirt under the lean-to.

"What if you did not have to worry about attacks? What if your men could spend the dark time hunting and tanning hides and making weapons and doing all the other work that interferes with planting and tending crops in the warm time?"

"How would that be possible?"

She traced the same circle. "Inside a stone wall."

He looked at the circle she drew and traced it with his finger. "The stones from the ruins. Four high would be taller than a man. And they are wide enough for a man to stand on."

They talked about the whys and hows through dinner and until late in the night, both more excited as each part of the plan fell into place like the stones with which they would build their new way of living.

Finally the fire burned low and they curled up together by Felyn, well-fed and contented as lambs in the warm time sun.

"The hard part," Thalgor said as they ate at midday the next day, "will be convincing the others. Batte sees himself as a warrior first, which means he is certain to object. Gurdek likes safety and a full belly. He and Sett will be easier to convince."

"And Rygar. He will have the whole dark time to tell his stories and help the children learn them."

Thalgor smiled. "I will go to the ruins today to see about

a water source and find a site that can easily be defended."

"We could move the stones, if need be."

"No. Or not far. They are too large. It would take more oxen and men than we have. The camp would be left without enough warriors to protect it."

He returned later with the hopeful news that two springs fed the stream that ran by the ruins and the flat ground around them would be easier to defend than many warm-time camps.

It was raining again, and the fire had gone out while Erwyn and Felyn napped. With a hefty sigh, Thalgor took some of their store of dry wood to build a new fire. But he could not get it to light in the damp air. He grumbled and cursed, and finally told Erwyn they would have to settle for a cold dinner.

Without thinking, she moved closer to the fire he'd laid. She pointed one finger at a twig and a small spark appeared. She set flames on two or three of the other pieces of kindling. When Thalgor let out a low whistle, she realized what she had done.

"Magic!" Felyn clapped her hands.

Erwyn had never realized she feared her magic might be taken from her because she had been willing to kill. But now it had been returned to her, she knew that fear had cast a darkness over every day since the renegade's death and turned all her other sorrows into black despair.

Jubilantly she threw her arms around Thalgor's neck. He

embraced her and kissed her face. Then they both froze and stared at each other for a moment. Their lips met in a kiss of a very different kind.

Since Thalgor had come, he had touched her to comfort her or when their bodies huddled together for warmth. But this kiss held both passion and promise. Erwyn settled into it with a sigh, as Thalgor groaned with a need they both knew would have to wait. They ended the kiss with shared reluctance.

"So, are you strong enough to go back tomorrow?" Thalgor asked her after they ate.

"With the help of my staff, if we go slowly."

He took the staff she pulled from beside the fallen tree. He ran his hands over the finely carved surface first, then held the head near the fire to see it more clearly.

"The Witch King," he said solemnly.

"He guards me. Guards us."

"Yes," Thalgor agreed, "but why?"

THALGOR ALWAYS FOUND it a challenge to lead men in wandering and in battle. He soon found it even more of a challenge to lead them on a path that might mean an end to both.

At first his lieutenants argued in ways opposite to the ones he had expected. Gurdek's first reaction to the plan to live always behind a wall was to insist that the risk of staying in one place could not be offset by the protection the wall might offer. Batte, for his part, liked the idea of having a wall to retreat behind after they made raids.

When Thalgor explained there would be no need for raids, Batte rejected the whole plan outright, with the full support of Tynor and their men. Gurdek, for his part, saw that if they did not raid, others might never find their walled camp and would have no need for raids of revenge if they did. After Thalgor took them to the place where the stones were, and Gurdek saw how high the wall would be, he embraced the idea whole-heartedly, as did Sett and their men.

Which left Thalgor, he noted with a weary sigh when they returned to the camp, right where he began. With his lieutenants at loggerheads and a potentially divided camp.

ERWYN RECOVERED SLOWLY, but was well enough to sit at council and listen to the men argue day after day. She understood Thalgor's reluctance to move ahead with his plan while Batte opposed it, but she had sacrificed so much to save the band it was like a new wound to see them in a constant turmoil that put their collective future at risk.

She explained to Gee and Tya how the end of wandering would make the women's lives easier and keep their men alive. Gee spoke in turn to the old women, Tya to the young ones and her mother, her mother to the other women with families.

She did not mean it so, but Erwyn soon noticed that the women talked to their men, their sons, their brothers about the plan. Slowly even Batte's men began to ask him why raiding was more important than peace.

"This is the witch's work," Batte grumbled at council. He cast Erwyn a dark look. "She bewitches my men as she has bewitched Thalgor."

"She speaks only to the women," Rygar pointed out.

"And gives them the power to charm the men in their beds, as she does our leader."

"And as Dara does you," Gurdek added.

Batte's face turned red and his hand flew to the knife at his belt.

For a moment everyone held their breath. But Tynor put his hand on his leader's shoulder. Batte, who had half risen from his seat, sat back down again.

"And as the marauder's midwife charms you," Tynor said amiably to Gurdek. "It is the common lot of men."

"Only *she* is a witch," Batte hissed.

"A witch who has saved us all more than once," Sett noted.

"Yes," Batte agreed, "saved us to imprison us behind this wall of stone so we will be unable to flee when the witches set upon us."

"When have witches attacked men?" Rygar asked.

"There are legends…" Tynor began thoughtfully.

"The legends also say witches are all women to keep them from mounting a battle against men," Rygar reminded them all.

"Their magic depends on their refusal to kill," Thalgor said. "Your fears are foolish, Batte. I suspect you know that."

"To be shut up within stone walls seems like weakness to me."

"Will you go against the wishes of your own men for peace?" Thalgor asked him.

"They wish for peace from their women," Tynor replied with a wry laugh.

"We do not all live for fighting, as Batte does," Sett said with his quiet authority. "Some of us would rather grow food, or raise livestock, or teach our young, or study the skies."

"He's right," Rygar nodded.

The others followed suit, even Tynor.

Erwyn saw on his face the moment when Batte recognized he had lost, but she also knew him well enough to expect at least another day of argument before he agreed. With a sigh, she went to tell Tya the men were ready to eat.

PONDEROUSLY, LIKE A woman about to give birth, the camp

stirred itself to prepare for what most truly hoped would be its last move.

Thalgor felt like the expectant father, responsible for the crisis but dependent on others to do the necessary labor.

As a result, he felt the need to be everywhere at once, to make decisions, to draft plans, and always to talk to people.

He listened to their questions and complaints, and told them over and over why he thought the move would be good for them all. It was like an endless but bloodless battle, with victory very far off and equally uncertain.

So many days in the same camp, even during the dark time, meant things and routines had gotten set in place that now must be dismantled and resettled in a spot closer to the stones. The women put down roots faster, and their children clung to a familiar routine, so most of the price of the move fell on them. That freed the men to go in groups to prepare the stones to protect their new home.

Some of the men remembered old talk handed down from before their fathers' fathers' fathers about how to build with stone. Others seemed to have a natural feel for what it would take to move the great blocks, and what it would take to fix them in place. Gurdek quickly chose several of the best from both groups to lead the others in planning and building the wall.

Rygar was assigned the task of working with those who knew most about livestock to locate food sources for their herds and find ways to preserve and store fodder. Some remembered talk about how that once was done, too, and even how to build wooden pens to shelter livestock in the deepest days of the dark time.

Batte, who had reluctantly agreed to what he still clearly regarded as a foolish plan, was put in charge of developing a smaller, more highly trained cadre of guards that could also serve as a raiding party. He appointed two new captains from among the best warriors, and talked at night to Rygar and the very old men who remembered stories about how battles were fought when the ancient cities still stood.

The dark time was when babies were usually made, not born, so with Tya to help Gee, who had developed a cough no magic could cure, Erwyn could take the time to heal fully from her loss.

At Thalgor's urging, she also spent more time with Felyn, to help ease the mental wounds they both had suffered from the renegade's attack. The girl found the idea of the move exciting enough that she began to talk almost like a normal child, although a single frown or harsh word from any of them could still silence her for the rest of the day.

Thalgor returned from the ruins one night when the first breath of the warm time was in the air to find the tent dark and silent. Alarmed, he burst in through the door. His household sat around the council table. Everyone but Gee, who lay on it, a ghostly rattle as she breathed the only sign she lived.

"We waited for your voice, Thalgor," Rygar said.

"Her body is worn out," Erwyn explained. "I can free her breath and she will live, but I can't see how long. Or I can ease her death now."

Thalgor wanted to roar, to cry, to run, but four faces filled with tears looked up at him. One drop fell from Rygar's eye, as if he had waited for his brother's return to let his grief show.

How was Thalgor supposed to decide such a thing? He decided whether men lived or died each day, one way or another, but the only question then was what was best for the band he led. How could he decide what was best for those he cared about most? Or for Gee, the woman who had cared for him even after he murdered her brute of a son?

"What say you all?" His voice was already thick.

Felyn's response was a sob as she threw herself across Gee's inert form. The child had lost already both mother and aunt.

Erwyn lifted the girl into her arms and rocked her even as she said for herself, "She will not live long."

Tya held Rygar's hand and whispered, "Life is always best."

Rygar sighed and clasped her hand more tightly. "I know what it is to be made to live against your body's wishes." His voice was rusty with unshed tears. "I was young, strong, and in love, and I suffered. She is ..." His voice broke. Tya put her free hand on his shoulder.

Gee was Rygar's grandmother, Thalgor remembered with

a start. A blood tie he had chosen to forget. His own grand-mothers had both disappeared the same night he and his mother had been captured. He didn't know to this day whether they still lived or not. But he knew what a grand-mother was.

A cold wind blew around the tent. Thalgor took the single torch and lit the brazier nearest where the others sat.

Erwyn started to protest, but even before the first puffs of smoke appeared, Gee gave one great gasp. Her back arched up, then fell back down. The rattle of her breathing ceased.

"She chose for herself," Erwyn said.

They all nodded. Tya kissed Rygar's cheek, now wet with tears. Erwyn handed the weeping Felyn to Thalgor, who held her awkwardly. Then Erwyn and Tya began to prepare Gee's body.

Tya's mother came soon with a meal none of them felt like eating. As word spread slowly through the camp, women gathered in the tent to help, each with a story of Gee's kindness and quiet wisdom.

Felyn finally slept. Thalgor laid her in her bed, then went to Rygar.

"I must walk once more around the camp tonight, Brother."

He spoke quietly, so no one else could hear.

"I'll go with you, Brother," Rygar said in a watery voice.

They walked in a silence broken only when one or the

other of them spoke to the guards or responded to condo-
lences from those who knew of Gee's death.

As they returned to the tent, Rygar commented quietly,
"Orphans both now."

"Orphans." Thalgor grasped his arm in a warrior's salute.
"But never alone. Sleep here tonight."

"I will."

The tent was dark once more when they entered, the
main chamber empty. Someone, probably Tya, had made up
a pallet for Rygar near the door. By it sat a cup of tea.
Thalgor lifted the cup and sniffed the wisp of steam that
floated above it.

"From Erwyn. For sleep."

Rygar took the cup and drank it all.

They sat together, quietly talking about the move, until
Rygar yawned deeply.

"Bed," he murmured and lay down on the pallet.

Once assured he truly slept, Thalgor crept into the
chamber he shared with Erwyn. She stirred as he slid beside
her.

"Rygar asleep?" she asked drowsily.

"Yes." His voice felt, and sounded, empty. "Thank you."

"Would it help to talk?" She turned to lay with one arm
across his bare chest.

"No." He raised his hand to the breast pressed against
him. "It would help to touch."

He had not had the solace of her body since she lost their

child. He felt her hesitation and pulled his hand away.

But Erwyn sighed and put it back again. The nipple hardened beneath the fabric of her gown.

"Kiss me, Thalgor." Her breath in his ear flooded his body with a hot, heavy need and, under the need, a yearning he could not name. He ran his hands down her body, then up under her gown and slid it off over her head. Only when they lay skin to skin did he kiss her, claiming her mouth with the same delight he would her body.

His hands stroked her eagerly. Although she was still too slender from her illness, her hips had grown wider with the child she carried, her breasts rounder. The contrast between bone and muscle and soft flesh added more excitement to his exploration of the new, yet familiar paths to passion between them.

When the passion reached its peak and he plunged into her the final time, he felt a wholeness he'd never known existed.

HEALED IN A new way by her re-awakened passion with Thalgor, Erwyn spent her days as he did, overseeing the work of the move and reminding the women of how much better the change would make their lives and those of their families.

Tya took over what little of Gee's work she did not already do, and consoled the grieving Rygar as best she could while maintaining the propriety necessary to her youth.

Felyn began to form friendships with some of the other girls her age. With Gee's loss, first Tya's mother, then the other women began to invite her to play with their children. Erwyn would see her at a distance, running and laughing like any other child.

She was more than glad for the girl's innocent happiness, but troubled by the curse that still hung over her.

The loss of her own child made the girl she once blamed for her parents' deaths unexpectedly dear to her. Once they were settled in their new home, she would ask Thalgor to let her take the girl, an ox, and Rygar, or one of the other men, north to the Wise Witches. If they were unmoved by her own pleas, perhaps the beautiful child with her cursed eyes would convince them to weaken or remove the curse. Or at least to reveal its nature.

Thalgor would argue, of course, but to leave without his blessing was no longer a choice. He was not only her fate but her other half.

Although they would probably continue to argue all their lives, an irrevocable breach between them was unthinkable now. Their passion fed her strength, and her need for him filled her heart. She had never imagined such a oneness between two bodies, two minds.

As she lay beside Thalgor one night, her body still humming with pleasure, the thought crept in unbidden that for such joy she would brave anything.

Break your pledge to another man? A voice inside her asked.

. Yes. She sat bolt upright in the bed, gripped by an icy cold that had nothing to do with the driving rain outside.

Thalgor grumbled in his sleep and turned his back to her, wrapping the cover more tightly around his shoulders.

Had her mother felt for her uncle what she felt for Thalgor?

She remembered how deeply her mother had loved her father, yearned for him long after his capture, mourned him when she could no longer touch his mind with her own and assumed him dead.

Erwyn also remembered her uncle, a great warrior, if a flawed person, the man of her father's sister.

Could he have been moved, without Erwyn knowing it, by her mother's wisdom and beauty, she by his skill as a leader?

Perhaps. The only answer she ever got to such questions.

But would her mother have broken not only her own pledge to Erwyn's father, but also her uncle's to her aunt for less than total passion? To think so was to deny everything Erwyn knew about her mother.

Which left two possibilities. Either her mother had told the truth, however unlikely, about who Felyn's father was, or she had succumbed, as Erwyn had, to a passion that made her betrayal understandable. To Erwyn, if not to her crazed father.

She understood, but could she forgive?

Her head began to ache. Thalgor rolled over and pulled her back down beside him. Wrapped close to his body, she let sleep answer the question for now.

CHAPTER THIRTEEN

THE INTENSITY OF his renewed passion with Erwyn made Thalgor feel truly bewitched by her. One night he decided to combat this new addiction to her body by standing guard with his men so that Rygar, who had a cold, could sleep.

At the depth of the black, icy night he stood silently with two other warriors, sheltered from the raw wind by a few trees on a rise that overlooked the dozing oxen when he saw a movement on the far side of the herd. Then another, and another.

He motioned to the two men half asleep beside him. One ran to alert the rest of the patrol, the other ran back to the camp.

Thalgor divided his men and watched from the rise as half moved around to take the would-be thieves by surprise from behind. When they were close enough to the intruders, he led the rest of his men to where the thieves were trying to cut a dozen or so oxen from the herd and spirit them away.

A raiding party, he judged from the number of oxen they intended to take. That meant they all must die.

His heart heavier than it should have been, he raised his sword high so the fine metal glinted in what little light shone from the stars and a cloud-shrouded moon. Silently, his men fell on the enemy from two sides.

Thalgor fought his way toward their leader. He found him directing battle with one hand and using the sword in the other hand to fend off one of Thalgor's warriors. When that man saw Thalgor, he fell back so quickly the enemy leader had no time to shift his position before Thalgor's sword swept his away.

Thalgor laid his blade against the man's neck just as the clouds moved away and a full moon shone like day on them both.

The face that stared back in his, more in surprise than in fear, was younger than Rygar's.

"Kill me, but spare my men."

The motion of the young leader's throat across Thalgor's sword left scarlet drops of blood on his slender neck. Thalgor drew his sword away a fraction so it did not cut him more.

"Do you know so little of battle?" he asked.

"Enough. But my men are too young to die."

Thalgor gave a gruff laugh. "Younger than you?"

The enemy leader nodded. Thalgor looked around to where his men held the rest of the raiding party captive. Indeed, they were more boys than men.

Anger bristled through him at the need to kill children.

"Why?" he roared at their leader, who still faced him

with calm dignity.

"Our band lost many women to a birthing sickness. Those who should have been our women have become the women of our elders. If we raid and are successful, we have more oxen to trade for slave women in the South. If we fail…"

He shrugged, unable to say they had been sent to die.

Thalgor swore and plunged his sword into the half-frozen earth at his feet.

His men turned toward him. He heard Gurdek's solid steps as he arrived at the battlefield with Sett at his side. Rygar came more slowly, wheezing slightly, followed by the surgeon, the bone-setter, the herbalist, and Erwyn, tying her hair back as she came. The sight of her sleep-softened face sent a sweet flame through Thalgor's system even here.

Without a word she went to the worst of the few wounded men from their band, the other healers following in her wake.

Rygar and the rest looked with astonishment at the young faces of the captive men, and then with even more astonishment at where Thalgor's sword stood half-buried in the ground.

"Would you or your men go back to the camp of a leader who cares so little whether you live or die?" Thalgor asked the young man he had wounded.

"We have our parents, our brothers and sisters."

"But you have no women, nor much hope of any."

"If we capture…"

Thalgor didn't let him finish. "Your leader sent you to capture oxen, not women. And the dark time ends, so your band will move north, not south to buy slave women."

The other man flinched, which made him look younger still.

"And would you want to buy a woman?"

The distaste on the young man's face was clear. Something else to respect him for, Thalgor thought as he pulled his sword from the earth.

The young leader's eyes slid toward the now-dirtied sword, but he showed no sign of fear.

"Why this conversation?"

"You want me to spare your men. But you know I cannot if they will only return to your camp to steal from us again."

The young man sighed. For the first time, he lowered his head.

"But if they wish to become members of my band…" Thalgor went on, then paused.

The enemy leader and his own men all looked at him in open surprise.

"You might find women among us, and we could use strong, young men and brave leaders."

The young man flushed. "My wounded…"

Thalgor turned to Rygar. "Tell the witch to heal them all."

His second nodded and went quickly to where Erwyn was spreading salve on the wrist where a man's severed hand had been.

Satisfied at the approval in Rygar's eyes, Thalgor looked to Gurdek and Sett and saw the same in theirs.

"You have until the witch is through healing your wounded to talk with your men and decide."

Sett led the young man to where the rest of the captives huddled, surrounded by Thalgor's men.

"What a choice." Gurdek laughed grimly. "Join us or die."

"With a leader like the one who sent them, they will die sooner or later anyway," Thalgor replied. "What a fool to sacrifice brave young men so old ones can have women. Better to send them off as marauders, at least."

"But then their families would blame him instead of the enemy who killed them."

"I don't wish to be that enemy. Where is Batte?"

Gurdek hesitated. "His men are third rank tonight."

"He is with Dara?" Gurdek nodded. "You think I care?"

"I'd prefer not to find out from your fist."

Thalgor laughed and clapped him on the shoulder.

Their prisoners, who had been murmuring among themselves, suddenly set up a cry.

Thalgor saw Erwyn approach one of their comrades who lay crumbled on one side, a sword lodged between his ribs.

"They think the witch means to kill him," Sett reported.

"She might need to, if his wound is as bad as it looks. She calls it the gift of an easy death."

Sett shook his head. "I doubt his comrades will agree. It may turn them against your plan. Better to have gotten their allegiance first."

"Not without the witch to tell me if any are unworthy," Thalgor explained.

"A narrow pathway you've drawn for yourself, Thalgor." Gurdek sighed. "And it grows narrower."

He gestured with his head. Batte strode toward them.

"Why do these raiders live?" he asked.

"Because they are but youths," Thalgor answered wearily. "And we could use some young, strong arms."

"You don't mean to take them into our camp?" Batte cast a cold glance at Erwyn, who was cleaning the sword wound on the fallen man she tended. "Are you so bewitched by this she-devil you no longer care for the fate of our band?"

Thalgor found silence the easiest way to control his temper.

"Dara is right." Batte's face reddened with rage. "You are a fool. An utter fool."

Gurdek stepped between them, hand on his sword.

"Do you defy a leader who has saved us all a hundred times?"

Rygar and Sett materialized at Thalgor's side, arms crossed on their chests.

Batte looked at the four men before him and shook his

head.

"I defy no one. I merely speak the truth."

"As you see it." Gurdek took a step closer. "Now."

"As I saw it just a moment ago," Batte echoed with a resigned air.

Gurdek stepped back and took his hand from his sword.

"But I do not trust the witch," Batte added as he strode away again.

"He worries me," Gurdek said.

"He will see things differently in a year or two when those young men have made our camp strong and rich enough to divide so he can lead his own band," Thalgor told him.

"If their women will leave that walled camp of yours," Sett commented with a chuckle.

"Oh, yes, the wall," Thalgor sighed.

Was peace worth losing his bravest, most skilled lieutenant? Was the wall worth losing his oldest friend?

Not questions to be answered at dawn on a battlefield, he decided, and went to find a fire to warm him until Erwyn finished healing the enemy wounded.

THE YOUNG RAIDERS agreed to join the band. None showed a black heart when Erwyn looked into them, so all were welcomed.

Still the air was thick with the acrid smell of danger. It burned Erwyn's lungs as she followed Thalgor back to the tent.

At dawn she rose to wash it from her body, but it lingered on her clothes. She washed them in the stream she bathed in and walked back to the tent through the early morning frost wrapped in nothing more than her cloak, which reeked of danger, too.

Only the tuft of herbs she lit in their chamber on her return drove the smell away so she could dress and face the day.

"What?" Thalgor asked when he came back from his sunrise walk through the camp to eat, and smelled the cleansing herbs.

Erwyn paused in braiding her hair. "Danger."

"Where?"

She spread her arms, one hand still holding the long braid of her hair. "Everywhere."

"Is it this place?"

"In this camp."

He shook his head. "That's impossible. I know every soul in this camp. There is no danger among them. You are a witch. Surely you can see where the danger is."

"I could find a large danger, but this is a small danger everywhere, like the rumble of faraway thunder. Only when it grows loud enough can I see where the lightening is."

"Has it to do with the stones?"

She searched with her mind, but saw only the acid-green cloud all around.

"No."

"I am not the fool Batte thinks me, but I sometimes think I must be mad to share my tent with a witch, much less my bed."

An icy chill ran through her, deeper than the pain at his words. The acrid smell of danger turned darker, more bitter.

She no longer heard minds wondering about her in the camp, but the danger might lie with a few who had moved beyond wondering to anger and fear, their hatred half-buried in the many who no longer wondered because her magic had saved so many lives. But she wasn't certain enough to say anything to Thalgor.

"Tell me if you see more." His tone had gentled. "Do not fear. There is always danger and we are always stronger."

She held on to that "we" as they left the chamber to eat their breakfast and the day began.

THEY MADE CAMP near the stones a few days later. The first job for the stone workers was to build the wall and cisterns for the two springs that fed the creek on one side of the camp.

The first job for Thalgor was to face a rash of disputes over whose tents should be closest to the water.

The usual plan for the camp put barracks on all sides, but the council decided it made no sense to give warriors who ate in a common mess the easiest access to water. So they put the tents belonging to Gurdek, Sett, Batte, and Tynor on the edge near the stream, trading the prize places for the need to feed and house guards. In spite of the fact that Thalgor kept his own tent in the center of the camp, many saw the decision as favoring his lieutenants.

As the dispute grew, Batte and Tynor complicated things by surrendering their tent sites to a very large family and an elderly couple cared for by a daughter with a withered leg. Gurdek, with the midwife's children as well as his own in his tent, and Sett, who also had several children and an aged mother, stood firm.

That only spread the dispute to the next row of tents.

"So, witch," Thalgor sighed after a long day of hearing complaints, "where is your wisdom on this?"

"Am I to blame for human nature?" Erwyn replied, a bit sharply. "It will calm down soon enough. Once everyone is fully settled, no one will want to move."

He rubbed his temples. "What do you have for this headache?"

Before the complaints about the tents faded a new conflict arose.

The stone workers, who did heavy labor every day, felt the herdsmen, who spent their time watching docile livestock, weren't doing their share of the work. The herdsmen, well aware of the lambing, calving, and shearing that came with the warm time, claimed the guards, who waited all day for an enemy who never appeared, were the ones with little to do. The guards, for their part, complained about the few men who, like Rygar, spent their days teaching tales to the children and battle skills to the older boys.

The throbbing in Thalgor's head grew worse each day.

"Every fourth day have the herdsmen move rocks, even if they cannot build with them," Erwyn suggested as she handed him a cup of the nasty tea that eased his pain. "Have the guards watch the herds, and the stone workers stand guard. Have all the teachers do as Rygar does, teach in the morning and work at one of the other jobs in the afternoon."

The council agreed, Batte reluctantly because he had no liking for livestock.

"Teach sword skills, then," Rygar suggested with a smile.

Batte, who was no fonder of children, grunted in response.

"Or tell yourself you guard the livestock rather than herd them, with panthers as enemies rather than men," Sett suggested to the same unsatisfying response.

The disputes grew fewer, the weather warm enough for the women to set up their looms. Building the wall temporarily took second place to the more familiar occupations of planting and birthing animals. The calm of warm time crept over the camp.

But Thalgor was more aware each day that leading a

wandering band was a very different thing than being responsible for a band that lived in a fixed place. Sometimes at night he heard the echoes of those he decided against in disputes muttering as they walked away.

"Batte is right. Our leader is bewitched."

As THE OTHER bands moved north, it was inevitable the camp would be attacked before the wall around it was fully built.

When the day came that scouts reported warriors on their way, Erwyn searched her mind and saw an attack Thalgor's men could easily repulse. She continued to care for the warm time's first new mother as she labored hard to deliver twin babies who would also need Erwyn's care as soon as they arrived.

The tiny pair, their harsh breathing eased by Erwyn's magic and herbs, were enjoying their first meal when Rygar came to say the battle was over and her healing was needed.

Seeing no barracks on the stream side of the camp, the enemy had attacked there. Since they expected a quick and easy victory, they sent almost all of their men into the battle. But the stream was well-guarded and Gurdek's men, although outnumbered, defeated them easily.

Batte's men came on the scene in time to follow the fleeing enemy to their own poorly-defended camp and quickly captured it. The attackers, caught between the two, could only run helter-skelter into the woods or be slaughtered where they stood. In the chaos that followed many were killed or wounded, and the stream beside the camp ran red with blood.

Erwyn healed as she always did, then made her weary way back across the battlefield toward the tent to rest. A hand grabbed her ankle and a rough voice cried, "Heal me, witch."

She looked down and saw a young man she had grown up with among her own people. He must have joined the attacker's band after their camp was destroyed. He was a good man, and a talented flute player. Felyn had loved to listen to him play.

Erwyn greeted the man and dropped to one knee beside him.

"Have you a family now in your new camp?" she asked as she inspected the deep gouge an arrow had carved under his ribs.

"Yes." He drew a sharp breath at the pain. "But this band will take my woman, who carries our child."

"This band does not sell captives as slaves," Erwyn assured him as she reached for her bag. "Would you join us if you live?"

"I will do anything to see our child born."

Erwyn nodded, busy now with his wound. It wasn't until she had finished bandaging it and helped the man to sit that she fully realized what she had done.

And the wounded enemy around her realized it, too.

"Here, witch," called a man with an arrow in his shoulder.

"Please," gasped another with a sword buried in his belly.

The air around Erwyn buzzed, not only with the voices that begged for her help, but also with the yellow-brown danger that was an ever-present part of her life. The calm blue light of her magic opposed it now. Through it all a single sound rang clear.

"Heal," her mother's voice said. Another peal. The voices of the Wise Witches. "Heal."

And another. "Heal," said the voice of the Witch King.

So she eased the death of the man whose entrails were destroyed by the sword in his belly, and mended the wounds of the others most in need of it.

Seeing her work, and perhaps moved by the same spirits that urged her on, the surgeon, the bone-setter, and the herbalist returned to her side to heal the defeated enemy.

By the time they were done the cloud of danger, now a deep yellow-red, was so thick Erwyn was sure it must be visible to everyone around her.

But somehow the cloud, like the healing they had done, went undetected until Thalgor found her standing exhausted among the enemy she had saved.

The rage on his face froze her heart. "Do you care so little for your life with me that you wish to die, witch?"

A different danger, a different fear claimed her. She took a deep breath and fought the anger, the hurt his words brought.

"Are we so well supplied with good men that we can let these die rather than strengthen our numbers?"

"They are a defeated enemy. Why would we let them live? And why would they join with those they would have killed?"

"To have their women and children back."

"What of those who refuse, of those who have none? Will they not fight us again?"

"As marauders or renegades. We have no need to fear them."

He opened his mouth to speak, then closed it again.

Before he found the words he wanted, Gurdek and Batte arrived and repeated the same accusations, with considerably more vehemence.

"I say again you are a fool, Thalgor," Batte declared when the inquisition was finished.

"I say this is a matter for the council."

Batte cast Erwyn a hard look. "The witch did not ask permission from the council before she healed the enemy."

Erwyn started to respond, but Gurdek quickly intervened.

"No, she did not, but she makes a good argument."

Batte swirled toward him, hand on his sword. "You and Rygar, the two who should most want revenge on Thalgor for the cousin and father he killed, always follow his lead, even when he follows the witch. What kind of men are you?"

Erwyn's breath caught in her throat at the insult, but Gurdek moved to stand between her and Batte.

"Men who remember that the man Thalgor killed when still a child was an evil man, even if a great warrior. Men who know how our band has flourished and grown strong with Thalgor as leader. Men who agree with him because he argues well and truly."

"Men as bewitched as he," Batte replied. "The marauder's wife you have taken and that girl Rygar wants feed you poison the witch gives them so you won't question her word or Thalgor's. Dara has seen them practice vile rituals with the cursed child in the woods."

Erwyn's face flushed with outrage, but Thalgor silenced her with a gesture.

"You are the fool, Batte, if you believe Dara's wild tales." Gurdek turned his back and walked away.

"He does not deny it, even if the witch tries to." Although Batte spoke to Thalgor, he clearly had half an eye on the small crowd of warriors that had gathered as they argued.

"No need to." Thalgor spoke to the men around them. "Who has given you more reason to trust, the witch who saves your lives and the midwife who saves your women, or Dara?"

The men shuffled their feet and looked away.

"But she is a witch," called a man at the edge of the

crowd.

Thalgor ignored him. "Go to your Dara, Batte. She no doubt waits for you. We will discuss this in council later."

He directed his men to guard the wounded enemies and gestured for Erwyn to come with him to their tent. Batte was left alone on the battlefield, his face purple with anger.

Erwyn had no choice but to follow Thalgor, too exhausted from healing to sort her anger out from the pain in her heart.

How could anyone, even Batte, believe Dara's lies? One might have great passion for a liar, perhaps even love them, but she always thought Batte, no matter how besotted, knew what Dara was.

"Nothing to say, witch?" Thalgor asked once they were back in the tent.

She slipped the cloak from aching shoulders. "Gurdek spoke well enough. I've never heard him speak at such length before."

Thalgor chuckled. "A man of few words, but a solid friend."

"And cousin to the one who fathered Rygar."

"The man who sired him, more accurately. That one was no more Rygar's father than he was my mother's lover." Hatred rang in Thalgor's voice. "Batte is too young to know that."

"The same age as you."

"But I lived with the brute."

A current in the air made them both turn toward the door of the tent. Rygar stood there.

"I've asked you not to speak so of my father."

Thalgor held his hands up, palms out.

"I seldom do. I was angry at Batte. Angry that he opposes me. I am sorry."

"I heard Gurdek had to defend me from his accusations because you did not."

"He did such an eloquent job I saw no need," Thalgor replied.

"Now I know you lie."

Erwyn stepped between them, her heart tight in her chest.

Rygar's face softened and he smiled. "Gurdek was never eloquent in his life."

Erwyn felt Thalgor relax behind her. She let out the breath she had been holding with a long sigh.

"Did I frighten you, sister?" Rygar asked.

"There is much danger here. I could not bear it if it came from you."

"Nor I," he agreed.

"It is bad enough that it comes from Batte." Thalgor lowered himself to a bench. "He has been my right hand from the beginning. My first lieutenant, when Gurdek was not yet sure of my ability to lead. My fiercest warrior." He paused and dropped his head. "My friend since I was a boy. I would trust him with my life, my people. Yet he believes

Dara."

"The woman is evil." Rygar spoke Erwyn's thought, but without rancor. "A spurned lover is always dangerous."

"I was an idiot ever to let her near me, ever to touch her," Thalgor agreed. "And a bigger one to allow her to think I turned away from her for another."

"Didn't you?" Rygar asked with a sideways glance at Erwyn.

"I walked away because she disgusted me. Erwyn only let me see what I already felt."

"It was the same with me and Tya." Rygar sat beside him on the bench. "Perhaps it is part of her magic, to unite those who belong together and separate those who do not."

Erwyn yawned. "Perhaps it is that men are great fools and it only takes someone who sees clearly to help them realize what is already in their hearts."

"Go to sleep, witch," Thalgor grumbled amiably. "I will wake you when Batte and Gurdek return for council."

BATTE NEVER RETURNED to council. After three days, Thalgor sent for Tynor.

"Batte refuses to come to council anymore," he reported. "He says you are all bewitched, so his words have no power."

"Do you agree?" Thalgor asked.

Batte's second, a broad man like Gurdek but even shorter, craned his eyes up to meet Thalgor's.

Erwyn held her breath. One defection from council could be ignored–two could not.

"I think you hear his words and mine," Tynor finally said.

"Then you will sit in council with us still?" Relief rang in Thalgor's voice.

"Yes. But I will not lead in battle. I am not the warrior Batte is."

Thalgor clapped Tynor on the shoulder. "Summon the rest of the council."

Chapter Fourteen

When the rest of the council arrived, they sat at their usual places at the table. None of them looked at the place where Batte would normally have sat.

Gurdek spoke first. "Those we captured are restless. They fear we still mean to kill their warriors."

"It is too late to kill them," Sett pointed out. "The question is whether we ask them to join our band or send them off with their families to be marauders."

Rygar frowned. "When you say it that way, the question hardly makes sense."

"So do we invite a whole band to become of us, as we have marauders and raiding parties?" Thalgor asked.

"What about the danger of treachery?" Tynor objected. "These men could kill us all in our sleep, or deceive us into a hopeless battle with another band."

Sett held his hands up, palms out. "Perhaps it is best if I do not speak."

"No one here, I think, still blames you for the battle we almost lost," Rygar responded.

"No one here," Tynor repeated in a low voice.

"Is our band weaker or stronger because of those we have added?" Rygar asked.

Only part of Erwyn's mind listened to the discussion as she watched how the yellow-brown cloud of danger grew now thicker, now thinner as the men talked. What Tynor said caused the most change, but other things made a difference, too–whether Thalgor frowned; how much of a common mind Gurdek and Sett seemed to be. Even whether Rygar sighed.

"Stronger," Gurdek answered and the cloud thinned.

Tynor frowned and the cloud grew thicker again. "There is danger if we do not have enough women for all of the warriors."

"We have captured these men's women and children, too," Rygar reminded him, "and except for the raiding party of boys, none have come to us without women of their own."

"If we keep their livestock and send them out to be ma-rauders," Thalgor pointed out, "how long do you think it will be before they come to take back what was theirs by stealth?"

"Even if they join our band, they may do the same from within our camp," Tynor replied.

Erwyn spread her hands in an effort to grasp the words for a future she could see but not quite name.

"We could let them stay with us, but keep them under guard. Let them fight with our men the next time we are attacked. We could tell them that only when they have proved themselves in battle, as the marauders have, will we accept them as full members of our band."

"We will learn much from whether and how they accept the plan," Thalgor added.

A general murmur of approval went around the table. Only Tynor remained quiet. Finally he shrugged.

"Batte will disagree, but I see no problem with that plan. Perhaps I can make him understand it is the best thing we can do if I don't tell him the idea came from the witch."

"Her name is Erwyn," Rygar said quietly.

Tynor looked Erwyn full in the face for the first time. The respect she saw in his eyes made her smile.

"It is a good plan, Erwyn."

She nodded. "Thank you."

For the moment, the cloud of danger disappeared.

The air remained clear later when, one by one, the captured men stood before Thalgor. Erwyn saw that all those who wished to join their band had good hearts. All those she would have refused chose to take their weapons and turn renegade, unable even to get along well enough with each other to form a band of marauders. When many of their women chose to stay with Thalgor's band rather than follow them, those men who chose to leave stalked off with a single weapon each, cursing everyone.

Through it all Batte stood to one side with Tynor and their men, grim but silent.

By the next day, however, rumors flew around the camp that Batte and Dara had argued viciously.

"Sett heard she wanted him to challenge me for leadership of the band, but he refused," Thalgor told Erwyn that night as they lay together in bed.

"Tya heard she told him she had killed another unborn child." Erwyn sighed, reminded of the two babies she had so wanted to keep. "Both could be true. She might throw something like that in his face if he defied her on the other."

Thalgor gave a harrumph of agreement.

She waited for his stillness to turn to passion or to sleep.

After a long silence he said, "Did you give her the herbs?"

Could he still think that of her? "No. It is an herb known to most midwives. There are three in the camp. She could have gone to any of them."

"Not Gurdek's woman."

"No, probably not."

"Do other women come to you for that herb?"

"Women do not come to me. The midwives send for me when a birthing troubles them."

"So even our women do not trust you, unless they have to."

"No." She could see the cloud of danger rise around them. "No one trusts a witch."

WHEN THE COUNCIL met the next day, Batte was still absent.

"He says we should meet without him, for the same reason as before," Tynor told them. "Why did you call us here?"

"The attack across the creek showed two flaws in our plans," Thalgor answered. "Even with many guards, family tents on that side make it vulnerable, and when the battle comes, our water supply is dirtied."

"The women in my tent and others along the creek have spent every day since the battle making sure the water is pure," Gurdek explained, "but still bits of bone and flesh appear."

"The springs are clean," Sett reported. "Still, we need the stream clear as well so all can have easy access to water without emptying the cisterns too quickly."

"We must build the wall first along the creek," Thalgor concluded.

Tynor shook his head. "I don't disagree, but you know some will see it as more favors for your closest lieutenants." He hesitated, then went on. "And you know Batte and that woman will fan those flames."

"Tya and I could talk to the women," Erwyn suggested. "They will understand about the need for clean water."

"The women aren't the problem," Rygar replied. "They know very well how their lives will be better if the wandering and the raiding end. It is their men who tire of the work and listen to Batte when he calls for a return to battle."

"Perhaps we can convince the stone-workers, at least."
Thalgor rubbed his temples. "We know it is the best plan.
Even Batte must see that."

"It is only the best plan if we stay here and build a wall,"
Tynor pointed out. "That is what Batte believes is foolish."

"Perhaps I should speak with him face-to-face," Thalgor
suggested. "We are friends, comrades. He will listen to me."

"He stopped listening to you when he began to listen to
Dara," Sett warned him. "He is no longer your friend and
only remains your comrade because he is afraid to challenge
you."

Thalgor had known that. But to hear the words still hurt.

"Has it gone so far?" he asked Tynor. "He accepted it
when we allowed the captured warriors into the band."

"Because we had little choice, once your witch healed
their wounded."

Thalgor felt Erwyn go tense beside him.

"Back to 'witch' now, Tynor?" Rygar asked with a smile.
"Even Thalgor's witch?"

Tynor flushed red. "When Batte speaks, his words make
sense. When Thalgor speaks, his words make sense. It is hard
for me, for many of us, to know who speaks most true."

Because there was no truth to it, Thalgor knew. Only
two visions of how to live; as they always had, in wandering
and war, or as legend told them their ancestors had, in peace
and prosperity. He could not give Batte a guarantee his
vision was best. He could only offer his dream of something

better.

"Is it time to split the band?" Sett asked hesitantly. "Let those go with Batte who want to wander, the rest stay here?"

"We do not have enough warriors for two bands," Gurd-ek responded immediately.

"I fear most of those we have would go with Batte," Rygar added sadly.

"But their women would not follow," Erwyn said.

Thalgor waved away the idea. "We are not enough yet, and I would not divide the band or families in that way."

"You could challenge Batte, if he will not challenge you," Tynor suggested.

When they all turned to stare at him, he shrugged.

"It would be easier to hear only one…voice."

One leader, Thalgor knew Tynor meant to say. The throbbing in his head grew more intense. He could surely defeat Batte, but at what cost to the band? And to himself? He had not only lost his comrade, he might also lose his position as leader. Still, to kill his friend…

"The wall?" Erwyn prompted quietly.

"We will build the wall first along the creek," Thalgor declared. "It is necessary to protect our people."

"Agreed," the others all said, Tynor last.

After dinner Thalgor drank the tea Erwyn gave him for his headache and fell into a deep, troubled sleep.

He awoke much later from dreams of blood and water that flowed in rivulets down stone walls. But what had wakened him?

Erwyn screamed again and scrambled across him. Her body left a hot, wet trail across his chest.

Groggily he turned toward the tent wall where she slept. In the light of the single torch he saw two slits in the cloth, both stained dark red.

He sat up. Erwyn searched among her potions and herbs with one hand while the other held a clump of her gown against her side, but still blood trickled down her bare thigh.

"You've been stabbed." His tongue was thick from the herbs.

She cast him a look, then sat by his feet, her free hand gingerly testing the wound in her side.

"Sword or knife?"

"If it was a sword, I would be dead." She gave a gasp of pain. "If you cannot help me, please get Tya."

That "please" told him more than anything else how badly hurt she was. He didn't trust his own head, still muddled by the tea, so he rushed to the room where Tya and Felyn slept.

Tya refused to let him watch while she tended his woman's half-naked body.

"Should I fetch the herbalist?" He couldn't bear to simply stand there while Erwyn bled.

"Just go away," she told him, her voice tight with pain as Tya's inexperienced fingers spread salve on the wounds.

He went into the main chamber to wait. Anguish and

rage battled with the grogginess for control of his mind.

When the wounds were cleansed and bound, Tya went to make Erwyn a cup of the same tea Thalgor drank earlier so she could sleep. He declined a second cup for himself and went into their sleeping chamber.

"It was a sword." Erwyn's voice was still taut. "But not thrust deeply enough to kill."

"A warning?"

"Or someone unused to wielding a sword."

"A warrior must be able to respond to every alarm, so his woman sleeps next to the tent wall. A warrior never expects an attack from within his own camp."

"Whoever it was attacked me, not you."

"But in such a way that I could not protect you."

"How else to do it? You are an imposing foe, Thalgor."

He paced the small chamber. "None of my men are cowards, to sneak around and attack a woman as she sleeps."

"Are you sure it was a man?"

"It could be one of the men we captured."

"I healed them, Thalgor. I saw into their hearts."

He stopped and rubbed his forehead. "One of my people?"

"Someone afraid of my power."

He looked down at her in the flickering lantern light, unsure of what it was he felt. Tya had dressed her in a clean gown. The old one lay crumpled and blood-soaked in a corner. He made a silent vow to burn it at first light.

Tya came with the tea, and he knelt to help Erwyn sit up.

"Take a torch and mend the tent now," he told Tya.

Erwyn made a noise to protest, but he waved her silent.

"No one must know of this but we three, and the one responsible. Then none can say it was the men we captured. And to keep it secret will help me find who did it."

Tya nodded and slipped away.

Erwyn drank the tea, then he laid her back on the bed and took the cup to the scullery. By the time he returned she was half asleep. He crawled into bed beside her. When he pulled her to him, she nestled closer and drifted off.

He lay awake even after Tya finished mending the tent. Who in his camp would want to kill his woman? Dark thoughts, but better than the memory of the black moment when he thought he'd lost her forever.

ERWYN DREAMT OF battle inside the camp. No enemy attacked. Brother fought brother, father, son. Rygar and Gurdek were at each other's throats. Panic ruled. The ground was soaked with blood.

She woke as she had in the night, not sure of the source of the sharp pain in her side. She screamed. A second pain, sharper.

She screamed again and sat up, fully awake.

Tya and Felyn appeared at her side, eyes wide. Reality rushed back.

"Sorry," she mumbled. "I had a bad dream."

The other two relaxed. Tya handed her a cup of warm broth.

"Thalgor said you would not want a full meal."

Erwyn managed a smile, despite the burn of her wounds.

"He was right." She drank the broth gratefully and handed the cup to Tya. "Is it midday yet?"

"Not quite."

Erwyn shot Felyn a quick glance. "Could I have a cup of the tea you made before?"

One of the wounds burned deeper than she'd thought at first. Her magic could heal them more quickly, but pain made it impossible to use it just now. So she drank the tea when Tya brought it. She hoped that, even if she could not sleep, it would ease the pain enough for her to get up and find a stronger healing salve to put on the wounds.

After Tya and Felyn left, Erwyn lay in the still room and listened to the sounds of life around her. Half-awake, the dream crept back over her, the death and destruction as clear as a vision. Again, the image of Rygar and Gurdek locked in battle with each other forced her to clear her mind.

I must leave, she thought when the last wisp of terror faded. I must take Felyn to the Wise Witches as soon as the weather warms enough. Not for the child's sake, but to keep Thalgor's dream alive.

And not with any hope she would ever return to this camp that had become her home, to the man she loved so deeply.

Once she was gone from the camp, the suspicions Batte and Dara spread within the band would dissipate like fog in sunlight. No one could or would question Thalgor's leadership on his own account. Only the fear of her magic, of her power over him, gave the distrust Batte sowed any room to grow among their men. If she left, her awful dream of the future would be erased.

And all the joy would go out of her life.

On that thought she slept again, and dreamed the Witch King stood beside her bed.

"Do you not know a vision from a dream?" he asked her.

Her mind was instantly clear despite the pain and the tea.

"You are a dream."

"I am a vision."

"And the other, the battle inside the camp?"

"Was a dream, a bad dream such as Felyn might have."

She wanted so much to trust his words she forced herself to doubt. "Why should I believe you? The battle was as real to me as you are."

"Trust your heart."

She closed her eyes and felt the truth resonate from the Witch King to her core. When she opened them, he smiled down at her and his smile eased the pain in her side.

"Why have you come here?" she asked him.

"You must stay with Thalgor. Only then will the warfare and wandering end. Only then will you find the answers you seek about Felyn, and about your mother."

"But the dream…"

"Was a dream. I am the future."

She slept again. By evening her pain had eased enough she could use her magic on the wounds. The next morning only two ugly red welts remained, but she was still so weak that Thalgor insisted she remain in bed.

In mid-afternoon she heard a woman call Tya from the door of the tent. Bored and restless, Erwyn went to see who it was.

Dara stood in the main room of the tent. A pot sat on the table, so hot that steam still circled above it.

"Hello," Erwyn ventured.

Dara jumped in surprise, and looked even more shocked when she saw it was Erwyn who stood there.

"You are well?"

"Yes. What did you want of Tya?"

"I thought she might be too busy taking care of you to cook, so I brought a pot of stew for your dinner."

A cold prickle crept up Erwyn's spine.

"Why would she need to take care of me?"

"Because you are ill."

"Clearly I am not. Why would you think otherwise?"

Erwyn shifted her weight carefully so Dara would not

know the wounds ached again.

"Everyone knows you are ill."

"How can that be when I am not?"

"You've not been out of the tent in two days."

If only she dared sit down. But something told her to stay away from that pot on the table.

"Why would anyone watch closely enough to know whether I leave the tent or not? Perhaps I have been at an especially difficult birth. Or out in the woods practicing my magic. Don't you know witches can make themselves invisible?"

She stirred the air around her and smiled at the shock, then horror on Dara's face when she seemed to find herself alone.

Hidden, Erwyn went to the pot Dara had brought. She didn't have to smell the stew because as soon as she drew near it the cloud of steam over it turned black with warning.

She stirred the air again. Dara screamed and jumped back when Erwyn reappeared across the room from where she vanished.

"The stew is poisoned." Erwyn kept her voice calm. "The mushrooms, I suspect. How careless of you to pick bad ones."

Dara took another step back. Afraid she might flee, Erwyn cast a quick spell that locked the other woman's feet in place unless she moved forward.

"It was an honest mistake." Dara tried to step back again

but could not. Her face went white with fear.

"Was it? You must hope so, in any case. Do you not know of the curse that falls on any who cause the death of a witch?"

"More witch lies," Dara spat. "Batte warned me of them."

"He knows you meant to kill me?"

Dara looked away. "Why do you insist I did? You can't prove the stew is poisoned."

"It is true I cannot prove it was you who stabbed me."

Dara's face flushed from white to red with anger.

"And since I cannot prove it," Erwyn went on, "and since no one is around to hear, I'd like to know why."

The other woman stepped forward and gave a hollow laugh.

"Are you so dense, witch, that you do not know? Your brain must be as weak as the spell you cast a moment ago. Or tried to. You didn't do it very well, since I can move now."

She took another step forward.

"Hmmm." Erwyn mimed a puzzled look. "Apparently I didn't."

"Think, witch. If you lived, as you do, no one would suspect a woman. If you died, Thalgor would blame Batte, who would challenge him as he now refuses to do. One would die and the other would be leader. And that one would be mine."

Erwyn shuddered. She had faced evil before, but always based on passion, lust, or anger. This calculated, purely selfish evil chilled her to the bone. She felt no fear, but to breathe the same air as Dara seemed unclean. She undid the spell rather than have her magic touch the other woman.

"Do you think Thalgor would have you again? Or that Batte would not know who caused him to kill his friend?"

Dara smiled a serpent's smile. "I am no witch, but there are ways of clouding men's minds that do not rely on magic. The plan was foolproof because it relied on them both being fools."

"But I lived, and now know for a certainty who stabbed me."

"Which of us will be believed, if not by Thalgor and his henchmen, by everyone else? You, a witch, who says I, a woman, took a sword to you, or me when I say Thalgor stabbed you when he escaped for a moment from the spell you cast over him?"

Erwyn sighed and shifted her weight again. The pain grew worse every moment.

"Most likely few will believe either story."

"Which serves my purpose just as well."

"What about the poisoned stew?"

"An honest mistake, as I told you. Those who don't believe I tried to stab you will see no reason I should poison you."

"What if it killed Thalgor?"

Dara shrugged. "If he dies, Batte will be leader. Besides, I hoped to find a way to keep him away from the tent until after you were ill or dead. It would not be hard to convince Batte he had some grievance Thalgor needed to address immediately."

"But what about the others—Rygar, Tya, Felyn?"

"You can't win a battle without a few dead."

Erwyn's body shook with such disgust and rage she feared Dara could see it. She refused to give the woman the satisfaction of knowing her words hit home.

"I know now the stew is poisoned."

"You suspect it is poisoned."

"I can see the death that hovers over it."

Dara tapped her cheek lightly with her hand. "Oh, yes, a witch. Luckily for me, no one else can see what you do."

"No, but if I can prove the stew is poisoned, everyone will be much more likely to believe you stabbed me as well."

"How could you prove it if no one eats it?"

"Easily enough. Dump it at the edge of the camp. Depending on what kind of mushroom you used, the crows will either smell the poison and refuse to eat, or eat it and die."

"What if they eat it and fly happily away?"

"They won't, will they? Guards!" Erwyn called quickly when the other woman looked as if she might escape.

"Please." Panic replaced arrogance when two warriors appeared. "No one was hurt."

Erwyn raised her hand to the ache in her side. "No one?"

She sent one of the men for Thalgor while the other remained to guard Dara.

When Thalgor arrived and gestured for the guards to leave, Dara ran to him.

"Thank goodness you are here. Your witch says I brought you poisoned stew when I only thought to make life easier for Tya."

Thalgor's eyes met Erwyn's over the other woman's bowed head. Erwyn saw surprise, then understanding.

"Why would Erwyn accuse you of something like that?"

"Because it would weaken Batte's position among your men. You're too noble to use treachery against a friend who in good faith questions your decisions, but your witch is not."

Thalgor grimaced. "It is true at least that I am noble."

"So put it to a test." Dara lifted her hands to his chest, but he stepped away. "Dump the stew at the edge of the camp. The crows will eat it unharmed, and prove it is not poisoned. Then no one ever need know of the witch's evil accusations."

"Why not test it by eating some of it yourself?" he asked.

Dara went pale. "I ate a bowl of it as it cooked. I can't eat any more right now."

Thalgor cast Erwyn a questioning look. She gave a nod in answer.

"All right, we will try your plan," he said.

The two women followed Thalgor through the scullery

and out of the tent in an awkward procession. Dara carried the pot at arm's length, as if afraid to breathe the cloud of poisonous steam Erwyn could still see hovering over it.

He led them along seldom used paths to a large, flat rock just beyond the edge of the camp nearest the barracks, empty during the day except for the sleeping warriors who had night guard duty.

Dara poured the stew out of the pot onto the rock. A flock of crows began to circle almost at once, cawing loudly.

"There's no need for us to stay." Dara looked sideways at the two of them, then quickly away. "If we come back at sunset, it will be gone. That will be proof enough the witch lied."

Erwyn thought to point out she had not spoken at all, but chose silence instead.

"Agreed," Thalgor said.

Dara quickly walked away, the empty pot still at arm's length. She stopped at the edge of the camp and looked over her shoulder to make sure Erwyn and Thalgor followed her.

When Dara went into her mother's tent, Erwyn pulled Thalgor down a path back to the edge of camp.

"Where are we going, witch?"

"The long way back to the rock."

"Oh. And maybe on the way you can tell me what's going on."

There were no bushes near the rock they could hide in, so Thalgor climbed a tree some distance away and helped

Erwyn scramble up beside him.

Soon Dara appeared and walked back to the rock. She kept looking over her shoulder and jumped at every scurry in the grass. She scraped what remained of the stew into the pot, then picked up two crows that had already died from its poison.

Thalgor jumped down from the tree and walked toward her. "Your test worked well."

Dara screamed and dropped the dead crow she held between thumb and forefinger. But she quickly pulled herself together.

"Well enough to fool Batte and the others." She gestured to a small group of men that came toward them from the camp.

Erwyn went to try to slow their approach while Thalgor dealt with Dara.

"I don't think this will fool anyone." Thalgor picked the dead crow up by one foot.

Dara looked from Thalgor to Erwyn to Batte, who approached with a stormy look on his face. With a cry of panic, she turned and bolted into the woods.

Erwyn expected the cloud of danger to thin. Instead it grew thicker and so dark she could barely see through the burning yellow-brown haze.

CHAPTER FIFTEEN

BATTE STARTED AFTER Dara, but Tynor stopped him with a nod toward Thalgor.

As Thalgor watched the men come toward him, he felt a chill creep from Erwyn's body to his. He understood the reason when he looked into Batte's eyes.

"What have you done to Dara?"

"Confronted her with her own treachery."

Batte spat at his feet.

Thalgor saw the moment when he became the leader of the band on a battlefield not far away. The man who led after his mother's murderer lay dead. Gurdek had fallen with a wound that might have been fatal. Batte, Gurdek's second then, had caught an arrow clean through his sword arm. He'd turned to Thalgor, a bit younger but a head taller and untouched by the enemy. Thalgor had met his gaze and raised his sword. As he'd cried out to rally their warriors, Batte had echoed the cry and stood by him, despite his wounded arm, throughout the long battle that had saved their camp and made Thalgor their undisputed leader.

Undisputed until now.

"She tried to poison my family." Thalgor's tone was placating, despite the men who stood around them and listened.

The eyes that had made him leader now condemned him in a stare of fear and rage. Next to that, what the others might think meant nothing.

Batte shook his head. "She told me she wasn't sure about the mushrooms. That's why she came back here to clean up the stew."

Why is the man so blind? But Thalgor knew the answer. A woman was always the answer. Women brought nothing but sorrow and loss.

"Out of compassion for the endangered crows?" he asked.

"It was an honest mistake."

"Do I have to show you the wounds on my woman's side?"

"She is a witch, Thalgor, not a woman."

Thalgor was reluctant at the moment to disagree. "She is mine. As Dara is yours. Or as you think she is yours."

Batte's hand went to his sword. "Explain yourself."

Thalgor glanced at those around them and wished for a quiet place where the two of them could talk alone, friend to friend.

"Dara loves battle. Perhaps she should have been a man. As it is, she belongs to any man who can bring the thrill of battle to her."

"Liar!" Batte looked around at his men, but none of

them met his eye. "Liar," he repeated more frantically.

He knows what she is, Thalgor realized sadly, and loves her still. A mad blindness to match Dara's mad passion for battle. All love risked such madness. Even a son's for his mother.

"Go after her, if you will," he told his friend with resignation. "But she cannot live free in my camp any longer. She must be guarded at all times."

Scorn curled Batte's lip. "Why cost the camp you call yours a warrior to guard a woman?"

"So she does no more harm to what is mine."

"Be careful, or you might find that nothing is yours."

"Do you wish to take Dara and turn renegade?" Thalgor looked at the hand that still rested on Batte's sword. "Or do you wish to challenge me?"

Batte dropped his hand. "We will finish this when I have found my woman and all can judge the truth of her story against the witch's."

Thalgor nodded. Batte gave a few orders to Tynor, who headed back to the camp. Then Batte disappeared with the rest of his men in the direction Dara had fled.

Thalgor turned to Erwyn. He gestured for her to go with him back to their tent.

"Sometimes I still think you are more trouble than you are worth, witch," he said with more force than he meant to.

"You have no right to judge my worth. And you have not yet begun to see trouble."

In his heart, Thalgor feared she was right.

RYGAR WAITED AT the door of their tent, his face dark.

"How bad?" Thalgor asked him.

"Bad enough. Rumors fly as never before. The men are split. Some believe Erwyn; some believe it when Batte says Dara made an honest mistake. The women believe Erwyn, but if trouble comes too soon, they will not have time to convince their men."

"Gurdek?" Erwyn knew only she heard the pain behind the question.

"Openly calls Batte a fool, as does Sett."

"Call a council." Thalgor's voice was less burdened now. "We must decide who will judge Dara, and how." He held out the dead crow he still carried. "And find a safe place for this."

Rygar looked at the filthy bird and started to say something, but Erwyn caught his eye and gave a small shake of her head. Thalgor's anger flowed too hot and too close to the surface for even his second to question him.

Rygar grimaced and carried away the dead crow, muttering under his breath.

To Erwyn's relief and surprise, Thalgor chuckled as he went into the tent.

She didn't follow him. She knew he would not want her

at this council. She went instead to the tent of a woman she'd helped through a hard birth the day before she was wounded. She hadn't seen the child since and wanted to make sure it did well. She wanted, too, the assurance of her worth to Thalgor's people, if not to Thalgor himself.

By nightfall the whole camp was tense as it waited for Batte and Dara. Erwyn returned to the tent late, exhausted from another birth, her wounds sore, her spirit heavy with the danger that clouded everything around her.

Thalgor sat alone at the table, a bowl of food beside him. He gestured for Erwyn to sit and pushed the bowl toward her. Wearily she shook her head.

"Eat, witch. You are no use to me dead."

"And little use to you alive, to hear you tell it."

Her pride demanded the words, but all her traitorous heart wanted was to crawl into his arms and weep.

"Eat." He said it more gently this time, then added, "I will leave if you do not wish to eat with me."

She sighed, picked up the bowl, and sank to the nearest bench. "Don't be a fool, Thalgor. I do not ever expect you to be other than you are."

She took a few bites and found the meaty stew eased her tiredness, if not the ache in her side.

"And how am I?" he asked, one eyebrow raised.

"Loyal to those you love. Loyal to me and distrustful of me. Unsure I deserve the respect you so grudgingly give me."

"You forgot unreliable."

She frowned and took another bite of stew.

"No. You will reliably defend me because, as you say, I am yours. But each time you give me, and everyone else around us, reason to wonder if this is the one time you will turn on me."

"Strange. I always wonder if this will be the one time you turn on me. And I suppose the others do as well."

She wanted to say "I will never turn on you." If she were simply a woman, it would be true. But a witch was not simply a woman, and her magic had laws even more binding than the oath she shared with Thalgor. Even more sacred than her love for him.

"I believe some do not, but you may be right," she told him with a shrug, as if it did not matter.

"I must check the guards." He stood and put on his sword.

Erwyn nodded a farewell, then finished her meal alone.

He woke her when he came to bed by kissing her wounds.

"They still pain you?" he asked when she pulled away.

"Yes," she replied drowsily.

"Shall I put salve on them?"

Surprise brought her fully awake.

"Please. I was too tired to do so before I slept."

He found the right jar in her bag and smoothed the fragrant ointment on her tender flesh.

By the time he finished his hand trembled. She took it in

her own and kissed the herb-scented fingers. He tipped her face up to his and kissed her lightly.

"Your wounds…" he murmured against her lips.

Beyond him, outside the tiny space of safety and calm they created between them, she saw the dark cloud of danger loom. And she felt his remorse.

"You will be gentle enough."

Despite the need for oblivion she knew raged in him, he was.

They were awakened at dawn, still in each other's arms, by an uproar in the camp.

Thalgor waited while Erwyn dressed so they could leave the tent together. She ached for the comfort of his hand in hers as they walked toward a danger she felt in her bones and could not yet see, but she knew better than to reach for him.

They emerged from the tent to find what seemed to be the entire camp arrayed between them and Batte, who came toward them. In his arms was a bloodied body barely recognizable as Dara's.

The crushing grief on Batte's face tore at Erwyn's heart. She wished she had a potion that would show him how completely unworthy of his love the woman whose remains he carried was. But there was no magic, no words to convince him, any more than there were words or magic to ease the pain of Dara's death for him, to ease the pain of wondering if he might have saved her.

A murmur ran through the crowd. "A panther."

Felyn, who stood with Tya to one side of the tent door, gave a small cry when the word reached her and threw herself at Erwyn.

Stunned, Erwyn knelt beside her. What she saw in the child's eyes froze her to the core. And revealed a secret she knew she would carry to her death.

She hugged the small, trembling body to her. Felyn seemed to find some comfort in the gesture because the tremors eased. With a sigh the child looked up at Thalgor, who towered over them. She gave a little nod and stepped back to grasp Tya's hand fiercely in hers as Erwyn stood once more beside her man.

She saw now the bloody, gaping throat on the corpse Batte carried, the missing arm. She closed her eyes against the terror the body screamed at her. They echoed in her own wounds, which throbbed and burned as if fresh. Dara's revenge before the fact.

The wave of agony passed. When she opened her eyes, Batte stood before them. He dropped the body he had carried so gently at their feet.

"This," Batte said loudly enough for all to hear. "This is what your witch brings us, Thalgor."

Thalgor stepped between Erwyn and his lieutenant. "Do you challenge me, Batte?"

"If that is what I must do to rid us of the witch."

The crowd around them froze for a moment with dread, then began to stir. The women slipped away and took their children with them. Tya and Felyn lingered but, at a nod from Thalgor, Rygar led them back into the tent. The old men stepped back from the confrontation. The warriors eyed each other, trying to gauge who was still friend, who was now foe.

"Who stands with Batte?" Thalgor asked.

Rygar, Gurdek and Sett came to stand at his side, blocking Erwyn's view, but not before she saw the majority of the warriors step away from Batte.

"I do not wish to divide the camp," Batte said. "I only wish to free it of the witch."

"It seems you have failed to divide it, in any case," Thalgor replied. "I offered you the chance to go renegade yesterday. I offer you and those who choose to follow you the freedom to become marauders today."

"Not while the witch lives to poison your mind and put the band I was born into at risk."

"Do not make me choose."

Erwyn heard the plea behind Thalgor's threat. But she knew Batte did not.

"A personal challenge, Thalgor."

Rygar, Gurdek and Sett stepped away. When Erwyn remained frozen to the spot with fear, Rygar pulled her to one side.

Batte directed two of his men to pick up Dara's body and carry it away, then pointed to the bloodstained dirt at Thalgor's feet.

"Your blood where hers fell."

Erwyn felt a pain inside Thalgor as if he had been split in two. Not between her and Batte, she realized with surprise. It was the band he saw threatened by his lieutenant's defiance. And the band he defended when finally, with great reluctance, he said, "My blood, or yours."

Everything went still. Erwyn wanted to curse the already cursed Dara for the stupidity and blind deceit that led to this awful moment. How could Dara's twisted desire so distort her view of the world she actually wanted this battle between two men who once trusted and loved each other like brothers? And for what? Her own pleasure? She was beyond any pleasure now.

Erwyn shuddered at the how shallow the other woman's evil had been.

With characteristic bravado, Batte stepped back and drew his sword. The crowd of men drew farther away to make space for him.

"Batte," Thalgor said grimly, one last time.

His lieutenant raised his sword and brought it down with a swift slash. But Thalgor's shield blocked the blow. He pulled his sword and struck low, toward Batte's legs.

"Not to wound." Batte's voice mocked. "To kill."

He thrust fiercely at Thalgor's midsection. The larger man stepped aside, but Batte's sword sliced the flesh below his ribs.

"First blood," Batte said with relish, his eyes already

dimmed by the battle lust.

Thalgor brought his weapon down hard on the shoulder of the other man's sword arm. It struck bone with such force that it bounced away again, but the wound wasn't deep enough to stop Batte's enraged attack.

Erwyn watched with horror as the two men, matched in strength and trained in the same ways of battle, continued to hack away at each other's bodies, glancing blow for glancing blow. Some struck home, so those who watched gasped, but none wounded enough to bring the fight to its inevitable bloody end.

When Batte paused, panting, to re-grasp his sword, the hilt slick with his sweat and Thalgor's blood, Thalgor asked, "Truce?"

The other man's only answer was to lunge expertly at his belly, a move Thalgor parried with his own sword. He turned on his attacker smoothly enough that his sword slipped under Batte's, past his shield, and struck home upwards into his chest. The blood lust faded from Batte's face, which took on an unearthly calm.

"Well fought, Thalgor."

He smiled, then fell dead where Dara's blood stained the ground.

Thalgor stared down at his lieutenant's inert form for a long time. No one else moved. Even the air seemed frozen in time.

"A quick death, at least, old friend."

Erwyn wondered if only she saw the tears that fell to sink into the ground with the dead man's blood.

"Bury them together," Thalgor told the grim-faced men who came to carry Batte's body away.

Slowly, solemnly the crowd dispersed. Finally Thalgor turned and went into the tent. Rygar and Gurdek followed him. Erwyn was the last to enter.

Her mind was dark, not with the danger. That had died with Batte. The darkness came from what she sensed would follow.

Thalgor sat at the far side of the table, as if at council.

"This is your fault, witch."

She shook with the force of his words, but stood straight and met his eyes.

"No, it is yours. You tolerated Batte's challenges too long. You should have driven him out of the camp while Dara still lived."

"Your gift of sight is of little use after the fact."

"It took no gift to see what you needed to do. Only an unclouded eye."

"She speaks the truth," Rygar ventured from the bench where he sat with Tya and Felyn.

"Silence, archer. If she were not a witch, Batte could not have been turned against me so easily by Dara's cunning words. If she were not a witch, none of my men would have been swayed by Batte. If she were not a witch, Dara would not have been exposed and fled into the woods."

Erwyn stepped between him and Rygar. This was a battle she must win for herself.

"If I were not a witch, Dara would have poisoned us all. If I were not a witch, you would have been defeated in battle how many times, Thalgor? If I were not a witch, Rygar would be long dead. If I were not a witch, you would not have wanted me for your woman."

"That would have been best. Leave my sight, witch."

Pride froze the tears in her throat. "I will do more. I will leave your tent."

"Good," Thalgor roared. "And take that accursed child with you. The two of you have brought me only grief."

"And you have brought us only pain."

Erwyn swept out of the tent. Her heart drummed and her knees trembled as she walked. To her surprise, Felyn, face wet with tears, ran to her side and left with her.

Where would they go now?

The answer came from Rygar. While Tya packed their few things and gathered Erwyn's herbs and potions, Thalgor's second ordered the tent that had been Gee's set up near Tya's family.

He led Erwyn and Felyn there, grim-faced, and helped them settle before he hurried off to post his men on guard duty.

Felyn didn't ask why she was uprooted once again. She said nothing, as completely silent as when they were first captured.

Other than that, she and Erwyn acted as if nothing were out of the ordinary. Erwyn chattered cheerfully as they arranged their things in their new home. As evening fell, she built a fire, and they went to get water in the one large jar and one small one Tya had given them.

Silence greeted them as they walked through the camp, but after they passed whispers hissed and crackled behind them like green wood burning.

When they returned to their new home, Rygar appeared to light the fire and leave food. He said little, clearly torn between his loyalty to Thalgor and his friendship with Erwyn.

And his fondness for Felyn, who clambered into his lap the moment he sat down on the single bench that stood next to the narrow table on one side of the small tent.

He stayed and held the child while Erwyn cooked their meal, then left to eat in the warriors' mess, perhaps still simmering with too much anger on their behalf to eat in Thalgor's tent.

Erwyn had gone through the motions of the day as if in a dream. Her body still worked, but her heart was numb with shock.

Once Felyn slept, Erwyn sat alone in the unfamiliar tent, lit by a single torch, warmed by a single brazier. She let the tears stream silently down her face and wrapped her arms around her knees to stifle sobs that might wake the child.

She'd been torn in two, as Thalgor had been earlier, right

through the center of her being. It amazed her that she yet lived, that blood didn't gush from the wound, that she still breathed, although at times even that seemed almost more than she could manage.

And tomorrow would be another day exactly like this. Tomorrow another night without Thalgor by her side. An endless life of empty days and lonely nights stretched out before her.

She gave one low sob, in spite of herself. And why?

She sniffed and wiped her face on the sleeve of her gown. Because, she reminded herself, she could no longer live with Thalgor's uncertain temper. His distrust of what she was. His failure to respect her magic. She refused to be blamed for everything that went wrong in his life. Better to suffer one clean, deep wound than to die slowly from a lifetime of small ones.

Have you no magic…? A voice inside her asked, but she silenced the thought unfinished.

There were legends of witches who used magic to win a man. But, even if based on truth, such stories only proved they were not true witches, not the kind of witch she was raised to be. Not the kind of witch who could ever win Thalgor's respect.

Not that there was any hope of that now.

She forced herself to lie down beside Felyn and pulled a blanket around her, then summoned up a half-forgotten spell to put herself to sleep.

The second day was easier because she expected it to be harder. Rygar brought food again and stayed with Felyn when Erwyn was called to help with a difficult birth.

The third day was worse. Anguish came with every breath. Felyn was silent and sulky. There wasn't even a glimpse of Rygar. Erwyn suspected that Thalgor had found some pretext to keep his second away, perhaps to protect him from her, perhaps to hurt her. She didn't know which was the more painful possibility.

Tya appeared the fourth morning, eyes red from crying.

To her shame, Erwyn welcomed the chance to focus on someone else's sorrow.

"What's wrong?" she asked as she offered a cup of tea.

"Thalgor sent me away the day you left. Neither he nor my father want me in his tent without you there. Thalgor only has me come to his tent a short time each day to keep things clean. He eats at the warriors' mess."

The girl stopped and gave a forlorn sniffle. Despite the searing pain at the sound of Thalgor's name, Erwyn patted her arm.

"It is hard to return to my mother's tent," Tya went on. "When Rygar came to see me, there are children everywhere. When we tried to walk alone together, they follow us. And now Thalgor has sent him off with a scouting party for who knows how long?"

Again sorrow burned through Erwyn, but she put her arms around Tya, who wept helplessly beside her.

"Would your father let you live here with us?" she suggested when the torrents stopped.

Tya looked up and brushed damp hair out of her face. "With you?"

Erwyn nodded. "You could still do what…" She stopped and took a deep breath. "What Thalgor needs from you. I am often called away to help with births or illness. It is awkward to take Felyn, and I do not want to leave her alone at night."

"You truly need my help?"

"Yes. Felyn could use a more cheerful playmate than I can easily be, too. She's stopped talking again."

"Poor child." Tya looked over to when Felyn idly shifted through the stones from the game Thalgor have given her. "I'll ask my mother. But I'm sure she'll agree. She was complaining again this morning about how many of us she had underfoot and cursing her weakness for my father's smile."

Tya giggled. Erwyn made an appropriate sound, but her heart bled at the memory of Thalgor's rare but seductive smiles.

Tya gave a contented sigh. "And when Rygar returns we can talk alone together again."

Erwyn quickly discovered she needed Tya's help for more reasons than she'd thought.

The girl's cheerful presence not only eased Felyn's sorrow but gave Erwyn herself minutes at a time when she was able to forget her pain.

She was busy with births, too. She hurried to and fro in the camp, mostly at night, but managed not to cross paths with Thalgor as she went.

But it was impossible to avoid him completely. At least they met in broad daylight, and Gurdek was with him. She almost ran headlong into the two of them as she rushed from one birth to another, her face damp with tears for a baby she had not been able to save.

Thalgor stepped in front of her. With no way around him, she stood and waited, breathing an almost unbearable effort.

He looked as if he had not slept. And the glare of his eyes told her he blamed her. His face was gaunt. He looked awful.

"You look awful," he greeted her. "Are you ill?"

"Do you care?"

"I care if Tya becomes ill, since she still does the work of my tent."

Erwyn tried to slow the pounding of her heart, but without any luck. She was forced to push her words around it.

"I am well. There is a birth…"

"There is always a birth, as I remember. How is the child?"

"She mourns."

"Me?"

Erwyn shook her head in disbelief. Arrogant man!

"Her home. Rygar, since you sent him away."

"Oh. Good company for Tya, since they both miss him."

He stepped aside.

She hurried on her way on legs so weak they scarcely held her.

Rygar returned the next day. He brought Gee's loom with him and set it up outside the tent. Then he played the stone game with Felyn before he took Tya off on a long walk alone.

Erwyn set the child to carding wool and settled at the loom, pleased at her friend's return. Still, she wondered at the reason for it, as she had wondered at the reason he was sent away.

As she wove her seemingly endless sorrow into the warp and woof of her work, Gurdek came and sat on the stool by the tent door.

"How are you?" he asked solemnly.

"Why is everyone suddenly so concerned with my health?" she snapped.

He held up his hands in a gesture of innocence. "It was a greeting."

She nodded an apology and waited, still focused on her work.

"Thalgor mourns," her taciturn visitor finally said.

She gasped at the tear in her heart at her lover's name. "For Batte?"

"For all he has lost." Gurdek shifted his thick body uncomfortably on the stool made for Gee. "He calls no council."

"Hmmm." She stared more fiercely at the loom.

"He means to name Sett his lieutenant in Batte's place."

"A wise choice. Did he send you for my approval?"

"Sett did."

She allowed this new pain to flow through her.

"Because he sensed Thalgor would be uncertain without it," Gurdek quickly added.

The new pain shattered into another, less familiar hurt.

"Well, you can tell them both that, if a council were called and if I were told of it, I would support Thalgor's choice."

"Those are welcomed words." Gurdek pulled himself to his feet. "For all of us."

He laid a hand on her shoulder. She looked past the grizzled beard and saw the fondness in his eyes.

"My woman, the midwife, worries."

"She need not." Erwyn managed a smile.

With a sigh, Gurdek dropped his hand and walked away.

The days melted into one another. Erwyn wept only at night, when she dreamed of Thalgor. Finally she decided to go into the woods to perform the ritual of loss.

She would need to make herself invisible because the panther that killed Dara still lurked about to prey on their sheep. And because, if she were seen going into the woods at night, word would get back to Thalgor, and he might think she left to meet a lover.

When the moon was full, and both Tya and Felyn slept, Erwyn stirred the air around her and slipped from the tent. She crept through the silent camp unseen by the guards and out one of the four openings in the rapidly rising wall of cold, gray stone. As she neared the woods, a lone figure appeared in the moonlight, walking along the path that circled outside the wall.

Thalgor.

CHAPTER SIXTEEN

ERWYN KNEW IT was Thalgor by his size, by his walk, by the way her heart leapt with need at the sight of him.

As he came closer she took advantage of the moonlight and her invisibility to fill her eyes with him.

He had lost so much weight his tunic hung loose over muscle and bone. His face was thinner, his eyes sunken. Deep lines bracketed his mouth, their grimness echoed on his brow.

He looked so alone she almost called to him, yearning to take him into her arms and make him whole again.

She stopped herself in time, grateful he could not see her.

Great tears rolled down her face as he walked away. When he disappeared around the bend in the wall, she went on into the woods, no longer certain why she was there.

She ended the invisibility spell, impatient with the drain of energy from the thoughts that buzzed through her mind like swarming hornets. No two led in the same direction, so all tumbled about in one agonized confusion.

As she walked toward the sacred circle she began to wonder if she was right to leave Thalgor's tent. Clearly the disruption in their lives had upset Felyn, who only now began again to whisper a few words to Tya or Rygar. But Erwyn never meant for the child to leave with her. That was Thalgor's choice.

Her own pain Erwyn considered the price, if a high one, of living as she needed to live. But Thalgor's pain...

Perhaps he mourned Batte, grieved that his friend died at his hand. Even so, his solitude would make the pain worse.

And he probably missed Felyn, as the child missed him.

Enough grief to keep him from calling council, to slow his naming Sett to replace Batte, to make him walk the perimeter alone at night.

But not to eat, not to sleep was something else. Even after she lost their child, even after Gee's death, he ate and slept, if badly at first. Could Batte have meant so much more to him?

She reached the calm of the witch's circle and sat to one side of it, her back against the rough bark of a tree. The moonlight turned the air silver. The rustling sounds of the woods at night faded away. She sensed others here, all the witches who had come to this place over the ages. Yet she felt as alone here as she did in the bustle of the camp at midday.

What if Thalgor mourned her?

Then he can come and ask me to return to his tent, a voice inside her huffed indignantly.

Could he? Even without Batte and Dara to spread lies about her, many in the camp still feared her and her power.

They would have to make it appear he bent her will to his, and the need for that pretense would make a man as honest and proud as Thalgor twice as reluctant to ask her to return.

Could she return to him unasked? At what price?

Would he allow her to?

The thoughts began to buzz again until her head ached.

She'd never before questioned her choices. She'd always relied on her witch's sense of what was right. Not that she'd never made mistakes, but as soon as she'd seen them for what they were, she'd undone them the best she could without hesitation.

Now she was all hesitation. Had she made a mistake? If so, how could she undo it? If she could not see her way clear, could not heal her own pain, how could she heal Thalgor's?

Her magic was no help. These were a woman's problems, not a witch's.

As the gold of dawn sliced under the darkness in the east, she started back to the camp, more distraught than when she left.

Distraught and exhausted, so she did not sense the panther's presence until it stood right in front of her.

She didn't scream and run, as Dara would have. Instead she froze. Even her heart stilled. She knew enough to keep her eyes fixed on the great cat's hindquarters so she could see the telltale flick of its tail and tension in its muscles if it decided to pounce.

The panther sniffed the air.

Did it smell that she was a witch? Or did it smell the fear that coursed through her?

Perhaps this was not the panther that had killed Dara. Or perhaps it had already eaten for this night. In any case, it seemed to ponder for a while, then swung its tail wide and melted into the grayness of the pre-dawn woods.

Erwyn let out a long breath and rushed back to the camp. In the relief of her escape, she forgot to make herself invisible. With no choice but to brazen it out, she nodded a greeting to the guards as she passed the gate. She managed to slip into the tent without waking the others and was soon asleep. She dreamed of a talking panther who seemed to be her friend.

When she emerged from the tent at mid-morning, Sett sat on the stool outside the door. He stood when he saw her, his scarred face grim.

"You are well?"

She bit back the hard answer she'd given Gurdek.

"Yes. Why do you ask?"

"My men were on guard duty last night. They said you returned from the woods at dawn, alone. I worried that someone took you there. Someone who might have hurt you."

She shook her head, puzzled at the force of his reaction.

"I went to the witch's circle."

"You shouldn't go alone. The panther that killed Dara

still stalks the camp. And once one learns humans are easy prey..."

For a moment she wanted to tell him what happened, wanted to cry out her fear on that broad, strong chest.

But the only chest where she could find true comfort was Thalgor's, and he offered none.

"You forget, I am a witch."

"But flesh and bone. If something happened to you..."

Would Thalgor blame Sett if she were killed because his men failed to stop her from leaving camp?

She looked up into Sett's eyes. What she saw there made her dizzy, as if she'd stumbled and hadn't quite righted herself yet.

"Why were you worried?" She already knew the answer.

Sett raised both hands and held them near her shoulders, but well away, as if afraid to touch her.

"My woman..." He swallowed. "My woman was crushed by a tree in a great storm a few years ago. I thought never to take another. But if there comes a time when you..."

He must have seen the truth on her face because he stopped.

"I am Thalgor's woman. I shall never be with any other man."

His hands fell and he stepped away. "Of course. But the thought of you injured..."

"I'm sorry."

He nodded and walked away.

His words left Erwyn stunned. She had never thought of any man but Thalgor and assumed no other man thought of her. Who, as her uncle had so often said, would want a witch?

Thalgor's lust for her body had led him to want one, but it was not lust she saw in Sett's eyes. His desire was mixed with an admiration she'd never expected, admiration not only for her as a woman but also for all she was, witch as well as woman.

Seductive, though she had no inclination to be seduced by it. She had seen such admiration in Thalgor's eyes only once, when she'd saved Rygar. The one he loved most.

The buzz in her head continued all day. By evening she longed for the Witch King to appear in her dreams. He would know what she should do. But he stayed stubbornly away.

THALGOR LOOKED AT the man and woman before him, unable to decide between their competing claims for judgment. Both widowed, they had come together, each with children and possessions. Now, as they separated several years later, accusations flew, and Thalgor knew no way to sort out true from false.

"He cannot take what was mine to start a new life with that …that child he shares a tent with now," the woman declared.

"I have a right to what was always mine," the man countered.

Thalgor's head hurt. He glanced over to where the man's new woman sat. Pretty enough, but young. Dara's sister, he realized with a start.

Would she want a man that age, and his children, without the goods he claimed? Thalgor thought not, but he couldn't separate what his witch blood told him from the taint of her sister's memory the young woman might not deserve.

Rygar noticed how Thalgor rubbed his forehead and gave him a look that clearly said "Erwyn" but Thalgor shook it off.

He let the separated couple wrangle a while longer, then asked a few questions.

"Can your children verify this was yours before?" He pointed to a well-made table.

The man grimaced. "I made it after we were together."

"Why?" Thalgor rubbed his forehead again.

"Because neither of us had a table large enough for all the children."

"So, because you were one family?"

The man nodded. His former woman was on the verge of tears.

"Which of you has the most children?"

"She does. But only one more, so with my new woman,

the number will be the same. If she and I have more children…"

The older woman wiped tears from her face with the sleeve of her gown. A weeping woman always made Thalgor's heart ache with memories of his mother. Sadness mixed with an anger he'd never understood filled him, but he could base no decision on that.

"What if she takes another man and they have children?" asked Erwyn as she entered the circle where he sat in judgment.

Sett moved into the edge of the crowd, avoiding his eyes.

The man stiffened at the witch's words. "She is too old."

"Too old to have children, perhaps, but not too old to take another man," Thalgor said thoughtfully.

The woman looked up. She was still handsome.

"Do you want her?" the man growled at Thalgor.

"If I were older I might."

Erwyn spared him a lightening glance.

The look was a sword to his heart. Could the witch think he wanted, could ever want, another woman in his tent? At least the pain stopped the searing need in his body that had sprung to life when he saw her. Against his will he sniffed the air, lonely for the scent of her, even if it brought back that need redoubled.

"And if she takes a new man, and he has children," Erwyn said, "they will need a large table."

"Not a table I made with my own hands," the man protested.

"Did she not weave and sew the clothes you wear with her own hands? Would you go to your new woman naked?"

The man flushed. "Does the witch speak for you, Thalgor?"

"The witch asks useful questions. What is it all worth, the clothes she made for you, the meals she cooked for you, all the work she did to keep you and your children?"

"But I worked, too. I fought. I hunted. I herded sheep."

"You worked for the band, but she and her children would be cared for in any case," Erwyn said. "She worked only for you."

"The witch speaks true," Gurdek's woman, the midwife, added from the other side of the circle.

The rest of the women in the crowd nodded their agreement.

Thalgor did not like where this was headed. If women and men began to count up who did what when they shared a tent, squabbles as painful as this could break out all over the camp.

"The woman keeps what she can use, all except your clothes and your children's." Everyone turned to stare at him. "You and your new woman can replace what you need. She cannot do that alone."

"But the witch says she will take a new man," the younger woman protested in a whiny voice.

Erwyn hid a smile. "I only said she might."

The man turned to Dara's sister with a new look on his face.

"This matters to you, whether we need to make new things for the tent we share?"

"Of course. I do not wish to work all the time. I suppose your children can do most of it."

"My children do my woman's work?" the man asked in a tone Thalgor knew should have warned her.

"What else are they good for?"

Rather than have this very private conversation continue in his makeshift council, Thalgor declared, "I have made my judgment," and walked away.

The man and the younger woman continued to argue as Thalgor made his way back to his own tent, each speech louder than the last so he heard it all the way across the camp.

"Sett," he called as he entered the tent.

To his surprise, his lieutenant followed right behind him.

"You brought the witch to council."

"You refused to call it a council," Sett reminded him. "Could you have settled the dispute without her?"

"I can do anything I need to do without the witch. Remember that in the future." He looked around at Rygar and Gurdek, who followed them both. "All of you."

"Yes, leader," Rygar replied with a mocking bow.

Given only the two choices, and afraid he might do the younger man permanent damage if he struck him, Thalgor roared, "Get out!" and they left him alone. Always so alone.

He was more than surprised when, a short while later, Erwyn called his name from outside his door.

His body flamed alive again at the sound. Did she come to beg him to take her back? His heart pounded in his ears. His face a careful mask, he stepped out of the tent.

"Have you changed your mind, witch?"

She frowned. "About what?"

His world crumbled, but he managed to keep the same frozen indifference on his face.

"Rygar tells me you have headaches," she said.

He'd started to rub his forehead and quickly pulled his hand away. "How would he know? Why would he send you?"

"I am a witch. I heal people." She spoke as if to a small, not very bright child.

"If I need healing, the herbalist has teas."

"But without a witch's help, he cannot be sure which herbs will ease your pain."

Her tone suggested his pain meant little to her.

"So heal me, witch. For Rygar's sake, since my headaches, if I have them, bother him more than they do me."

Liar, her look said, but she silently placed one forefinger on each side of his head and closed her eyes. Her scent shot through him like lightening. Her skin against his brought a mixture of pleasure and pain that soon became unbearable.

He was about to step away when she suddenly released

him, as if the contact pained her, too.

"No wonder your head aches," she said. "You never sleep."

"My bed is cold."

"I am sure many women in the camp would be more than happy to warm it for you."

He made the gruff sound that now served him for a laugh. "The women have all taken your part. They turn their backs on me as I walk by. The men are scarcely better. Those who followed Batte blame me for his death. The others let their women persuade them I treated you badly. Rygar barely speaks to me, and Gurdek only grudgingly. Even Sett told me I was a fool."

Something crossed her face that caused his eyes to narrow.

"What is Sett to you?" A murderous rage began to burn in his belly.

"Nothing." The rage froze at her tone and the truth his witch blood heard in her words. "I merely reacted to the wisdom of what he said."

He wanted the rage back, wanted to rant at her, wanted...

"Dara's sister walked away from the man who came to you for judgment," she went on, as if they were having an ordinary conversation. "I suspect he will be back with his other woman by the day's end."

"Because of the things he wanted to keep?"

Erwyn smiled and shook her head.

"Because you suggested she might take another man?"

"And because you helped him see her in a new light when you said you could be that man, if you were older."

He wanted to say something–but what?

"I will send your tea with Tya."

Say anything! But she was already gone.

WHEN RYGAR CAME to see Tya that evening, Erwyn asked if Thalgor's headache was better.

"Better!" Rygar said with uncharacteristic heat. "I send you to help him and you make wild accusations about other women!"

Erwyn's body flooded with anger, need, and sadness. She took a deep breath before she dared speak.

"I merely suggested he might look for another woman. It would be the natural thing for him to do."

"Natural when he pines away for you?"

"Pines? That giant of a man? Hard to imagine, Rygar."

"You've seen how he looks, felt the agony in his head."

She started to object, but what he said was true. Could Thalgor suffer that much over her? A man who never yet told her he loved her?

"What do you want me to do?"

"Return to his tent, to his bed." Rygar's voice was a plea

that cut through her like a frozen blade.

"Does he want me to return?"

Her friend threw up his hands. "Haven't you heard what I said?"

"He might pine, as you put it, and yet not want me back."

Rygar sighed. "Yes, he wants you back."

"Then let him ask me, instead of sending you."

"He didn't send me. He need not ever know I spoke to you of it. Just go back, as if it were your own idea."

She stood up from the bench where she had been mixing herbs and faced him, hands on hips, temper barely in check.

"Go back as if how he treats me is of no importance?"

"Are a few angry words worth so much both of you have to be alone the rest of your lives when you belong together?"

She turned away so he could not see the pain on her face. If she could not make Thalgor understand, perhaps at least Rygar could be made to see it from her point of view.

"He will be alone only so long as he chooses to be."

"That's not my point, Erwyn."

"It was more than a few angry words. You know that. I cannot go back to his tent until he respects me for what I am."

"He respects you, values your magic."

"When it serves him. When it doesn't..." She turned back to him. "Words can do as much damage as blows, over time."

Rygar's face went cold. "You forget my father killed my mother with his blows."

She froze. Was she to lose her dearest friend over this as well as her man?

"I'm sorry." She put her hand on his arm and sighed with relief when he covered it with his own and gave her a thin smile.

"I am, too. It is hard to watch the man who is my brother and the woman I love as a sister hurt each other so."

"Then you should help Thalgor understand why Erwyn won't return to his tent," Tya suggested from where she sat with Felyn asleep on her lap.

"You take Erwyn's side, of course."

"I know how I would feel if you loved me less because I was not a witch and only a woman and sometimes berated me for it. I assume it is much the same for Erwyn when Thalgor acts as if he would prefer she were only a woman and not a witch."

Rygar turned away from her, as if her words hurt him.

"What do you know? You are only a child."

Tya's face crumpled. "Are you so devoted to Thalgor you cannot see the truth of what we say?"

Rygar rubbed his forehead as Thalgor had earlier in the day.

"I need to check on the guards," he muttered and left.

"Oh, dear." Erwyn sat down next to Tya. "I didn't mean for the two of you to argue."

The girl shrugged. "Sharp words where he is so distressed aren't an argument. It merely took me by surprise. He will be back with flowers or a honeycomb for me in the morning."

Erwyn knew it was true, so she returned to mixing her herbs. But what Tya said lingered in her mind. Thalgor's sharp words when he was distressed were what had started this. Sharp words wounded, as she had told Rygar, but why could she not let them go, as Tya did? Because she was older? Or because Tya was sure of Rygar's love?

Erwyn never expected Thalgor's love. She knew what loving his mother had cost him—his childhood, his innocence. She knew how he suffered over Rygar's illness, the loss of their child. He told her in every way but words he would never put himself at the same risk of pain by loving her. He was not capable of it.

Respect. Trust. Those were what Thalgor could give her in return for her devotion to him. Without them she was nothing more than his willing slave. But how to make him, and Rygar, see that? Two tears dropped on the herbs and spoiled her work. She sniffed and patiently began again.

Rygar did not return until the next evening, but he brought flowers for Tya and a honey-comb for Felyn, who gobbled it up and went to sleep. Happily reconciled, Rygar and Tya went out for their usual evening walk. Erwyn sighed and began to settle the tent for the night.

Soon after they left, Thalgor appeared in the doorway.

For a moment Erwyn thought she might be ill with the shock.

She swallowed the bile in her throat, hoping he could not see the flush on her face or the way her hands shook.

"May I come in?"

She nodded, not ready to trust her voice.

He sat on the bench. She dumped the pillows she'd been readying for sleep on the floor and sat on them.

He leaned his elbows on his knees and kept his eyes fixed on the ground as he spoke, his voice raw as if he were in pain.

"Rygar says I need to ask what I must do to have you back in my tent."

His suffering hurt her, so she made her words harsh. "In your bed, you mean."

"In my life."

She knew at once she could resist no more. She could not force the admiration she saw in Sett's eyes, but she could make it difficult for Thalgor to hurt her so badly again.

"You must accept that I am a witch, that you cannot have me in your life without my magic."

He frowned. "I never wish you to be other than you are."

"Yes, you do. Every time something goes wrong, you blame my magic, as my uncle did. I cannot live like that any longer."

"You punish me for your uncle's faults."

"I punish you for your faults, which are much like his.

Like him, you think your skill as a warrior means you know more than I can see. My uncle trusted my mother's magic because my father did, but after her death he would ask what I saw, do as he thought best, and berate me for what happened. It is a hard way to live when you share a tent. An impossible way to live when you share a bed."

He opened his arms wide.

"What do you want from me?"

She sensed he feared she would demand words of love he could not give. But she loved him too much for that.

"If you want me back in your tent, you must promise to trust what I am, even if you cannot respect it, as I trust that you are a warrior."

"Do you not respect that?"

She thought a while before she spoke. Every word must be true, this moment more than ever.

"Now, I do. But when you lived by killing and capture—that is hard to respect, even if you are better at it than any other. I always trusted your skill as a leader and a warrior, but only now can I respect it."

He nodded solemnly. "And this is what you ask of me?"

"Yes. Woman to man, man to woman."

Her breath stilled as she waited for him to respond.

His scowl didn't fade, as she so hoped, but grew darker, deeper.

"I will consider it." With that he was gone.

ERWYN WOKE AT dawn with a headache so bad she could scarcely move. She lay still until Tya stirred, then asked her to brew some tea. But the headache weakened her magic, so the tea merely allowed her to sleep, which she did.

Tya woke her for more tea and some bread at midday, then Erwyn slept again until she heard Rygar's voice when he came to take Tya away for their walk. She ate more bread, drank more tea and sent them on their way, but asked them to take Felyn, wide awake this evening, with them.

She had dozed off again when Thalgor burst into the tent and rushed to kneel at her side.

"You are ill!"

She sat up and pushed away from him, then grasped her head at the pain shooting behind her eyes.

"My head aches."

"Rygar says you slept all day."

"My head aches," she repeated, her mind still fuzzy.

"You aren't ill?"

His hand reached out to stroke her cheek. It trembled against her flesh.

She was suddenly fully awake, headache gone. "Would it matter to you if I were?"

"You might die." His other hand joined the first to frame her face with fingers that still shook.

"Then you would have no witch."

"I would have no life."

She took his wrists in her hands to still them, but she trembled as much as he did.

"What you wish of me," he said in an unsteady voice, "I will try to do. I swear. If I fail, you need only remind me of this promise. But promise me you will come back to my tent and never leave again."

She raised her hands to his face and kissed his cheek. And promised all she could.

"I will come back to your tent."

She brushed the tears first from his face, then from hers.

"One other thing," she said, unable yet to surrender to joy.

He frowned and pulled away. "Is my promise not enough?"

"For me, yes. But before I can return to your tent, you must go to Felyn and tell her that you were wrong to make her leave, that you miss her and want her to return. You hurt her, and I cannot take her back to your tent otherwise."

"You said she did not mourn me."

"I may have implied that, but I never said it."

"You lied to me, witch," he said gently.

"Because you deserved it."

He lowered his head. "I did. And I have missed the child's laughter in my tent."

His words undammed the relief and joy she'd had to hold in check. Delight flowed like liquid sunshine through all the channels the pain of their separation had cut into her heart and healed her as it strengthened her. She was Thalgor's again, as he was hers.

CHAPTER SEVENTEEN

ERWYN LEANED FORWARD and kissed Thalgor lightly on the cheek.

"We will return tomorrow."

"Not now?"

She smiled at the look on his face. "Your men will expect their leader to have more self-control than to scurry me back to his tent in the middle of the night."

"Then I will sleep here."

"With Tya and the child in the same room?"

"They aren't here now."

Her joy spilled into laughter. He reached again to pull her into his arms, but she shook her head.

"They might return at any time, with Rygar."

"Then I best leave now, before I even kiss you. It has been so long, one more night alone will not make any difference."

He didn't look as if he believed his own words, but she gently pushed him away.

He grinned at her and hurried out of the tent with only one backward glance of longing.

He came the next morning and spoke to Felyn as Erwyn had asked, then went on guard duty with his men. Tya quickly packed her things and the child's while Erwyn gathered her clothes and her herbs and potions for the move.

Rygar appeared at mid-morning with two of Tya's brothers to carry their things back to Thalgor's tent, then the men dismantled their temporary home.

They all shared the meat Tya cooked at midday except for Thalgor, who had taken Rygar's guard duty.

Erwyn understood why he kept away from her, but still felt strangely alone while Felyn, Rygar, and the others celebrated in Thalgor's tent.

He came to her late that night. With hesitant hands he cradled her face and kissed her. He seemed so reluctant to move beyond the sweetness of that first, chaste kiss that she slid her tongue between his lips to lure him deeper into passion.

Her daring succeeded beyond her wildest dreams. His caresses exploded into a savage need that spurred an equal savagery in her. They met in a primal act of joy, like the joining of sea and earth that created life itself.

Afterward, in the dark after he extinguished the single flickering torch that had illuminated their reunion, he said with a raw craving, "Do not leave me again, witch."

Sadness flooded her. She could not give him the reassurance he wanted, just as he could not say the words of love she craved. If her magic demanded that she go, she could not stay.

Despite the rapture they'd so recently shared, her silence enveloped them both like a shroud.

THE WALL AROUND the camp was nearly complete. When a small raiding party attacked, the men herded the livestock in through the four gates, then filled the space with warriors to drive the attackers off. The outcome of a stronger attack was uncertain.

With Erwyn back at his side in council, Thalgor felt more sure of what needed to be done next.

"Closed gates will shut us in as solidly as they shut enemies out," Gurdek objected.

"Wooden gates can burn and set the whole camp on fire," Sett added, and Rygar nodded his reluctant agreement.

"If we coat the wood with the same clay we used as mortar to build the wall," Erwyn explained, "they cannot burn."

"Perhaps you can enchant them, too, witch," Gurdek huffed.

Thalgor was surprised to find his old friend had taken up Batte's role of challenging Erwyn on every point, perhaps because he sensed a need to balance Sett and Rygar's reliance on her. Sett, who was older than Tynor and so had taken Batte's place as Thalgor's lieutenant, was as quick for battle as the man he replaced had ever been, so council continued much as before.

"Raiding parties come most often from the south," Thalgor mused aloud. "What if we put gates at all but the north opening, and see whether they make us stronger or weaker?"

The others argued around his suggestion for a while, but eventually agreed, as he knew they would.

He allowed his own ox cart to be dismantled first to provide the wood for the south gate, both because his cart was the largest and because it marked his decision to wander no more.

Once the wall was finished, crews of his men built the gates while Gurdek and then Sett took their men out on raids to compensate them for their loss at council.

Sett returned with more than livestock, tents, and goods. He brought back a woman.

Thalgor heard word of it before the main body of the raiding party reached the camp. He met Sett as he led his men through the open north gate.

Thalgor blocked his lieutenant's path and gestured toward the woman. "We take no captives on raids."

The woman was no longer young, but beauty lingered on her face and slender body. Great emerald eyes stared at him like those of a snared rabbit.

"She came willingly," Sett said.

Thalgor glanced at Erwyn, who stood to one side of the small crowd that had gathered. She looked intently at the woman for a moment, then gave a small nod.

But he still hesitated to accept his lieutenant's story. If his men began to see raids as a way to take women, everything about the battles would change. As would everything in the camp, he suspected.

Sett had no woman, but Tynor, Gurdek and his new second did. What if one of them returned from a raid with a captive woman, even a willing one? And despite Erwyn's agreement that the woman came freely, the captive shook with fear.

While he thought things through, the woman broke free of Sett's hand on her arm, which seemed to hold her erect, and half fell, half threw herself at Thalgor's feet.

"Please do not send me away. He...they will find me. Kill me or sell me for a slave. Do anything you wish with me but let me be taken back to that camp."

Thalgor quickly agreed as Sett and Tynor helped the sobbing woman to her feet. Tynor's woman appeared and led the woman to their tent, speaking to her in low, soothing tones.

Sett gave Thalgor a questioning look.

"You rescued her. You did not capture or steal her. You and your men did well. Tonight we feast in honor of your success."

Sett nodded and raised his sword to lead his men through the camp in the usual victory march. But he did not smile.

"A great evil lives in the camp the woman came from,"

Erwyn said as she and Thalgor watched the warriors celebrate.

"Is it a danger to us?"

"Not in the time I can see. They head north to make a warm-time camp. But they take their own cold and darkness with them."

"Is there evil magic, witch?"

He knew the answer, but wanted the assurance of her words.

"No. All witches are taught the rules of our magic and the cost of breaking them. But some men with strong witch blood, like yours, use the power it gives them to serve an evil the magic did not create. Her mind has been damaged by such a man. I will do what I can to help her, but I'm not certain that even then Sett's love will be enough to heal her."

"Love for a woman he just met?"

She gave a small laugh. "Have you never captured a woman because you knew at first sight you wanted her in your tent?"

He smiled. "Not a woman. A witch."

THE WARM TIME was full upon them. The men tended crops and livestock. The women spent the long days at their looms. The children splashed in the pool that formed just below the point where the stream left the camp.

Gurdek and Sett lost their eagerness for battle, Gurdek because he was in charge of the food stores, Sett because of Lana, the woman he had rescued.

She seemed well and whole by day, and even into the night, he confided in Erwyn, but in the hours before dawn she dreamed dreams that woke her, trembling with terror. But she refused to come to Erwyn for a remedy.

"She says she will never let anyone into her mind again," Sett explained to Erwyn sadly late one warm, lazy afternoon. "She will not even speak of it to me."

Erwyn gave him an herb tea to help Lana sleep. It calmed her terror most nights, he reported later, but when the air of the warm-time night was calm and the sky clear, she still woke up screaming and lay awake the rest of the night in terror.

Otherwise the camp was peaceful, the adjustment to a settled life, if not complete, well under way.

Then one day their scouts reported a large group of warriors moving toward them from the north.

"A raiding party?" Thalgor asked Tynor, who brought the report to council.

"Too many men who move too slowly. They bring oxen with them and some carts."

"But no women?" Gurdek asked.

"My men saw a few, but no children."

That meant they were probably slave women, to be used by all the warriors. The council fell silent for a moment.

"Marauders?" Rygar suggested with his usual optimism.

"Too many men, too few women and oxen, no sheep."

"What do you see?" Sett asked Erwyn.

She pushed the plight of the slave women out of her mind and closed her eyes, then opened them and shook her head.

"Only what Tynor says, the men and what they bring with them. Between my mind and theirs lies a dirty gray cloud, like dust on a windy day."

"Another witch's work?" Gurdek's second asked.

She shook her head again. "I think not. Sometimes it is hard to see. I am weary from a birth this morning. Perhaps tomorrow the vision will be clearer."

"If they don't attack before then," Gurdek grumbled.

"Have scouts watch them constantly," Thalgor said. "Gurdek's men will guard the open north gate in three shifts from dawn to dawn. Rygar, take our men to guard the rest of the wall and the three closed gates. Sett's men will scout and carry on with normal guard duty. They will not take us by surprise."

The others agreed and went to carry out his orders.

The cloud in her mind troubled Erwyn. She lay down after the council and hoped for sleep, but the cloud only darkened.

There was tension in the camp that night, but no fear.

Erwyn drank a tea made from an herb that might help her see more clearly before she slept, but it made no difference.

Her vision still unclear, she was searching among her things for another herb to try the next afternoon when the guards at the north gate raised an alarm.

She tried to see the battle about to take place, but the dirty cloud only closed more tightly around her. With a call to Tya and Felyn to take shelter with the other women and children, she followed the warriors who hurried to defend the camp.

But no sounds of battle rent the air. No clash of swords, no swoosh of arrows, no cries of the wounded and dying.

When Erwyn reach the warriors gathered inside the north gate, they created a path for her to where Thalgor stood with his lieutenants shoulder to shoulder across the open space.

She touched Sett's shoulder and he stepped aside so she could stand beside Thalgor and see what had set off the alarm.

The warriors the scouts had reported stood well away from the wall, perhaps forty of them, their hands not touching the weapons that hung at their sides and on their backs. Only two men in the first rank stood with arrows notched on their bows. In front of them, two other men walked, unarmed, toward Thalgor.

The dirty cloud grew so thick in Erwyn's mind she was forced to push her magic aside to see the men more clearly. They were both pale, with watery blue eyes reddened by dissipation. Clearly brothers, if not twins, neither seemed tall or strong enough to lead the mass of burly warriors behind them.

As they neared, one of the strangers scanned the ranks of men arrayed behind Thalgor and his lieutenants. The other focused on Erwyn with an oily smile that clenched her stomach.

"We come in peace." The first man's voice sent a crawling sensation across her skin.

"You have something that belongs to us." The other man's tone was one of arrogant dismissal as his eyes devoured Erwyn.

"Can you prove ownership?" Thalgor asked in a guarded tone.

The second man put his hand on his chest above his heart. "She has a scar here."

Sett gasped and dropped his hand to his sword. One of the enemy archers swung his notched arrow toward him. Sett froze, but Erwyn felt his body tremble in silent rage.

"She?" Thalgor's voice was a mix of anger and disbelief.

"One of our leader's women," the first man explained.

"Why are you so sure she is here?"

"We weren't, until this man saw him." The second man pointed first at a man from his own ranks, his body twisted, one arm gone, then at Sett. "He swears on his life this man is the one who stole her."

Erwyn put her hand on Sett's arm to keep him from

drawing his sword despite the arrows aimed at him. The men behind them stirred uneasily.

"You must give them both to us, so they may be punished," the first man said.

Thalgor grimaced. "Do you think me a fool, to surrender one of my men because of a woman who may not even be here?"

"We have no wish to do battle. We only want what is ours," the second man replied in a wheedling tone.

"What you say is yours."

The first man looked from Thalgor's men to his own, then back to Thalgor's again.

"Perhaps if you come back with us to where we are camped, we could provide further proof the woman belongs to our leader."

Thalgor laughed out loud. "If further proof is to be offered, it will be in my camp, in my tent."

"So you can kill us at your leisure?" the second man whined.

Thalgor held out both hands, waist high, palms outward. "I pledge you shall both walk out of my camp alive."

"May we bring our personal guards with us?"

Thalgor's indignation that leaders would have such guards washed through him with such force Erwyn felt it as clearly as he did.

"No. Your only chance to reclaim what you have come for is to talk to me alone in my camp."

The men turned to each other and conversed in a hurried whisper. They looked now at Thalgor, now not so much at their own men as past them, toward something beyond them to the north.

Clearly Thalgor never expected the strangers to comply with his unheard of demand. Erwyn and the men around her were shocked when the two turned back to him and said in one voice, "We agree."

Thalgor's warriors grumbled at the offer to allow two strangers into their camp, but the ranks opposite them stood unmoving, as if indifferent to their leaders' fate.

"I will have a dinner prepared for us." Thalgor turned to Erwyn and spoke quietly, as if to give her orders. "Serve us yourself. Keep Tya and Felyn both well away from these two."

She needed no warning. She had seen how they looked at her, and remembered the terror in the face of the woman Sett had rescued from their camp.

As Erwyn walked to the tent, she spread the word for the women to remain hidden and keep their children with them. She sent Tya and Felyn to Tya's mother, and began to make dinner.

She was brewing a special tea when Sett's woman came in through the outer door of the scullery. In her hand was the sword Sett had used before Thalgor had given him the better one that had been Batte's.

Lana held the hilt of the sword toward Erwyn.

"Kill me. Give them my dead body. Then they will go away without harming anyone."

Erwyn's heart tripped. She took a deep breath to steady herself and find words that would not wound. "I cannot."

"You must. I would do it myself, but it must be done by another as if to punish me. They will only exact a bloodier revenge if they think Thalgor allowed me to kill myself."

"Are they such monsters?"

"They serve such a monster. You are a witch. Do you not see what they are? Kill me quickly so they will leave."

Erwyn bowed her head. "I cannot."

"You are as brave as a man, I have heard. And you've eased death for many. Why refuse a simple sword stroke to save me and your camp both?"

"Thalgor's warriors can defend us against these men, and you as well. You cannot think he would surrender you to them."

"But you do not know their treachery. Kill me."

Lana thrust the sword at Erwyn with such force she cut her own hand. Blood dripped into the tea. Erwyn pushed the sword aside and started to throw the tea out, but Lana stopped her.

"The taste of blood will please them and hide the bitterness of the herb." Lana wrapped her cut with a cloth. "But herbs and magic will not save your camp. You must kill me."

Erwyn looked at her with the unsettling sense she spoke the truth, at least so far as she understood it.

As if in confirmation, Lana lowered the shoulder of her gown to reveal the scar the strangers had referred to. It was not the jagged line of a wound. Someone had intentionally carved the rough outline of a bird's head on her flesh.

Erwyn stepped back. Her head reeled with visions of the pain and terror Lana had endured at the hands of the man whose emissaries now sought to reclaim her.

Erwyn's stomach turned so hard she needed to step out of the tent to empty it into the dust by the scullery door. Dizzy and drained, she sat on the bench by the fire and forced her mind free of what she had seen.

When she went back inside, Lana had pulled her gown back in place and neatly bound her wound.

"You see now death is better," she said.

Erwyn spoke the first words that came to her.

"How can you let Sett touch you, after what that man did?"

The other woman sighed. "Sometimes I cannot, but when I can I would allow it out of gratitude, even if I had not come to love him. He is so different, so gentle, it hardly allows me to consider that other one a man. Sett weeps so at my scars I dare not tell him the rest, for fear it might destroy him entirely."

"You are fortunate to have found each other."

Lana nodded as she picked up the sword with her uncut hand and again held the hilt out toward Erwyn.

"I have known more joy these last days than I ever expected to know in my life. You need not fear I will die unfulfilled."

"I cannot kill you." Erwyn held up her hand to stop the woman's immediate protest. "I am not sure whether I would if I could, but I cannot. If I murder, with or without my magic, I will lose my power. I would sacrifice much to protect you from what you have endured, but I will not surrender what I am."

"It must be so?"

"It is a law of my magic. It must be so."

Lana lowered the sword, her face so pale Erwyn thought she might faint, but she just took a deep breath and said, "So be it."

Erwyn felt a faint stir in the air that warned her Thalgor and the strangers would soon reach the tent.

"If you fear to be in Sett's tent, take the others there and go to Gurdek's woman. She will welcome you without question and comfort Sett's children, if you cannot." Erwyn paused, uncertain whether to say more. But the horror she saw in her vision pushed her on. "If the worst should happen, Gurdek's woman has an herb we use with newborns who have no chance to survive. She will know how much to use in a tea for you. But you must promise not to ask of her the act you asked of me."

Tears filled the other woman's eyes. "Thank you. I will not ask her that."

She slipped out with a final "Thank you," leaving Erwyn

alone to face what was to come.

THE MAN WHO guarded the tent pulled up the cloth that served as a door and Thalgor led the two strangers inside to the square table where he held council. The benches on the sides had been pushed against the walls, so when Thalgor sat in the great chair, the other two were forced to share the bench that faced him.

Thalgor settled uneasily onto the gilded and jeweled chair he seldom used. Made for the man who had killed his mother, it always gave him the panicky feeling he might yet become that man. But the strangers would expect him to sit in it, a message reinforced by Erwyn when she ordered the benches moved.

The less whiny of the two men's eyes widened when he saw the gilded chair, then narrowed as he scanned the space for further signs of wealth. Finally his eyes lit on the chest Thalgor had taken from Erwyn's captor where he kept the colored jewels and bits of wrought gold his band had taken over the years.

"Where are your slaves?" the other man complained. "I am thirsty and hungry. You promised us food."

Thalgor suppressed a shudder. "We keep no slaves."

"Who does your work?"

"My people do their own work."

"Yes, but the work of your tent? Surely a leader does no work himself." The first man still ogled the gilded chair.

"Leading is work. My woman cares for my tent, as with any man, with the help of a girl."

"You have only the two women?" the second man asked.

"I have only one. The girl is promised to my second."

The man shook his head in clear disbelief.

"And the witch?" The first man pulled his eyes to Thalgor's face.

"What witch?"

Both men laughed.

"We have enough witch blood to know one when we see her," the second man said, "even if she were not such a tasty piece."

Rage boiled through Thalgor. He satisfied himself with imagining their dead bodies in the dust and remained seated.

"The witch is my woman."

"You do not strike me as fool enough to let a viper like that live free in your camp, much less sleep in your bed," the first man objected.

"A captured witch can be bent to your will, of course," the other man said, "if you hold those she cares for hostage."

Thalgor winced at the reminder of how he had captured Erwyn.

"But once you no longer need her magic, or want her body, it is safest to kill her. Only fools truly believe that to kill a witch will bring on a curse," the man went on. "And it is best done slowly, to serve as a warning to other women who might think too much of themselves."

Before Thalgor could forget his promise and kill both of the strangers with his bare hands, Erwyn slipped in from the scullery with a tray that held three bowls of savory stew and two loaves of bread.

She had put on a light warm-time cloak with the hood pulled low to hide her face, but he saw her grimace when she came near the strangers, as if the nearness of their bodies, or their minds, caused her pain. His own head throbbed already.

It promised to be a very long meal.

THE FILTH OF the two strangers' minds choked Erwyn so that it became hard to breathe. The one imagined Thalgor's dead body and the wealth they could then so easily take. The other raped her in his mind.

She erased the images with a powerful blue cloud. Her magic met no resistance in the minds of the two men, only a sort of wordless surprise. She served their food and drinks with an air of calm subservience, then escaped to the scullery where she could cleanse her mind of their evil and watch them without being seen.

The three men ate their meal in silence. The visitors greedily pushed the meat and fresh bread into their mouths while Thalgor pretended to eat but only moved food around his plate.

When they were done, she cleared the plates and brought tea.

Forced close to the strangers, she felt their rotting fear of Thalgor, smelled and tasted their vile greed, the one for gold, the other for her body. Worse, she saw the blackness of their souls.

"You eat meat every night?" the stranger who cared only for wealth asked as he sipped the blood-tainted tea Erwyn had given them.

"You are guests." Thalgor cast her a quizzical look when he noticed his cup held only water.

"Your witch cooks well." The would-be rapist reached out for Erwyn, who danced around his grasping hand. "I wonder what else she does well," he added with a leer.

Thalgor's rage sizzled in the air, shackled by his pledge.

"Why do you cover up the woman, when you allow all to see the jewels and gold on your chair?" the first one asked.

The second one laughed. "You display what can be stolen and hide what can be used by many with no loss to yourself."

Erwyn used his distraction to read deeper into his mind and met a dark shape that frightened her, but she couldn't see it clearly enough to know why.

She found the same shape in his brother's mind. Her fear multiplied by ten.

She fled back to the scullery, so weak with the effort of keeping her mind free of their visitors' evil she needed to pull a stool near the door into the main chamber to sit on while she peeked through the curtain and listened to what they said.

When they finished their tea, the first stranger said solemnly, "We ask you to surrender to us what is ours and the one who stole her. If you do, we will leave your camp in peace."

She knew even Thalgor could see the vile black smoke the lie left in the air. The man waved his arm, as if to brush it away.

"Why not just attack us and take them?" Thalgor spoke as if it were of no consequence.

"We might fail," the second man answered with a tremor of fear. "Or she might be killed, or kill herself."

"Walls," the first man added. "We've never fought a walled camp. Victory is…was not certain."

"I cannot do as you ask," said Thalgor.

"Why would you risk battle over a woman who is not even yours?" the second man objected.

"My lieutenant has taken her for his."

"He stole her. He has no right to her," the first man responded fiercely.

"She came willingly."

"The slut will go with any man," the second man replied. "One night when our leader chose another, she went with me."

The man fingered a scar across his throat, but spoke with such relish Erwyn knew he had raped Lana. Thalgor's scowl told her he knew it, too.

CHAPTER EIGHTEEN

"THAT WAS WHY our leader marked her, so all men would know she was his and his alone," the first man explained.

"I promised her shelter here," Thalgor told them.

"A promise to a woman means nothing," the second man spat.

The two men exchanged a look, as if they read each other's mind. Witch blood to witch blood, Erwyn thought with a shudder.

"If you give us the woman, we will let the man live," the first one declared with the air of someone doing a great favor.

"No."

"Why did you bring us here, if not for such a compromise?" the second one asked.

"You offered more proof the woman was yours. I hear none."

"Summon her. Her fear can be proof," the first man said.

"Any woman in this camp would be afraid of you. Even my woman hides in the scullery rather than eat with us."

Both men grimaced. "Eat with a woman?" the second

said.

"So, do you have any other proof?"

"The mark on her breast," the first man answered.

"Which proves only that, if she is yours, she was not cared for as a woman, as any person should be."

"She belongs to our leader," the second man reminded him. "How he cares for his women is no concern of ours."

"But bringing this one back is your concern?"

"It is what we have been sent to do," the first answered.

"Then you will have to tell your leader you have failed, because I will not give her to you."

"Failure," the second man hissed, "has too high a price."

"Then an attack is your only choice." Thalgor stood up to his full height. "I have no more to say to you."

"You will find our men ruthless on the field of battle," the first man said as they, too, rose unsteadily to their feet.

"And our revenge swift and sure," the second added.

"Revenge assumes a victory you have already admitted is uncertain. Perhaps it would be wiser to let the woman go."

Both men blanched and swayed on their feet.

"You know nothing of what is wise," the first told him.

"You will regret your choice a hundred times over," the second one said. "Why risk so much over a trifle?"

"My word is not a trifle, nor is any woman."

The two men traded another look and left.

Thalgor gestured for his guards to follow them as they made their way through the camp to where their men waited.

Erwyn picked up a bowl of herbs she had already prepared, lit them, and took it into the main chamber to clear it of evil.

"They will attack at dawn." Thalgor's voice, heavy with contempt, cut through the fog in her mind.

"Not after they drank that tea," she corrected. "They will sleep until noon, then pretend to leave peacefully. The second day they will split their men and attack with half from the south. When our men are engaged there, the other half will attack through what they think will be a poorly defended, open north gate. They intend to kill us all except the woman and Sett."

"But they will rape as many of our women as they can first."

"In front of our wounded and dying men," she agreed solemnly.

"I scarcely needed a witch to see through them." He sat on one of the benches against the wall. "What do you suggest?"

Still exhausted from wandering in those evil minds, she settled on the bench next to him.

"That we use the day the tea has bought us to build a north gate. That will be one surprise. And we should have the old men and older boys take the livestock as far as they can before dark, so we will not have them in the camp during the battle."

Thalgor nodded. "What if we also divided our men? We could send Gurdek's into the woods for the night, so while their men at the north gate are confused because it is closed, Gurdek can come around their men at the south gate and catch them by surprise."

"With Gurdek's men on patrol today, they may underestimate the size of our forces," she agreed. "They surely underestimate the power of men who fight to protect what they love."

"They would not know what it meant."

They sat in grim silence until Rygar and the others came to learn the outcome of the unsettling meal with the strangers.

That night Thalgor stayed in the tent, quiet and restless.

Erwyn was too tired to be bothered by his strange mood. Perhaps he saw the dark shape deep inside the strangers, too. When he sat beside her, she leaned her head on his shoulder, but he turned to face her in the dim light.

"Tell me, witch," he murmured as he put both hands on her neck in a gesture that was half caress, half threat. "Did you bewitch me as you did those men?"

She was used to his lingering distrust, and understood it as part of the balance of their life together, but still she rallied her strength to meet his eyes and combat it.

"I have no power but the power to see and the power of fire." She paused and put her hand over the broad, misshapen scar on his belly. "And the power to heal."

They both saw the moment when she had saved his life.

"And the power to kill," he added solemnly.

"When it is a kind of healing."

"Come to bed."

"Their minds were ugly and evil."

"I know. But I want you near me in the night."

The day of the battle broke calm and damp. Inside the walls it was strangely silent with the older boys, always restless and noisy before a battle, gone. The clay on the new north gate was not yet dry, but the gate was solid, built with the last of the ox carts. The band would wander no more.

A sentry on the south wall reported Gurdek's men could not be seen where they hid in the woods. Then he leapt quickly to the ground as an arrow whizzed past his head. The attack was on.

The women and children were gathered in a few tents in the center of the camp, a cordon of warriors around them. Erwyn sat just outside the cordon with the surgeon, the bone-setter, and the herbalist. They listened to the battle until arrows felled the first warriors, then set about their grisly work.

As she eased the death of a dying man, Erwyn heard the warriors whisper that the enemy shot arrows of fire at the south gate. She soon saw the clouds of smoke created as they burned out against the clay that protected the wooden gate.

One of the flaming arrows flew over the wall, followed by another. A third hit one of the tents and set it ablaze.

Quickly the warriors nearby went for water from the cistern and doused the flame, but it drew them from the battle.

Erwyn exchanged a few quick words with Tynor, who led those stationed around the women and children. Between them they organized the women into a line to pass buckets of water from hand to hand as other tents burst into flames around the camp.

Erwyn was surprised to see Sett's woman among those who fought the fire.

"Sett's children are with Tynor's woman," she explained, breathless from the effort of passing the heavy buckets. "Your people lose their tents for me. And perhaps if some of the women must die, I will be able to be one of them."

As if to confirm her fear, an arrow flew past them and landed with a thud to quiver in the ground at their feet.

A cry went up from the north gate. Erwyn could not tell if it was their warriors' alarm at the second wave of attack or the sound of the enemy's dismay when they found the way blocked.

Soon arrows flew from both directions, but those from the north were not lit, so the fires were no worse. Still, the number of wounded doubled with the number of arrows.

Erwyn worked steadily, pausing only now and then to drink some water. When she did, she looked around for Thalgor's head above the others.

He stood now with his own men at the north gate, now with Sett's at the south, now with those guarding the gates to the east and west. He praised his men and urged them on, and shot his own arrows with what she knew was unfailing accuracy, aided by his advantage in height.

The smoke of the fires took the place of dust, so the camp was no different from any other battlefield, despite its wall. Perhaps worse.

The smoke meant the attackers didn't fight for the goods of the camp, except perhaps Thalgor's jewels and bits of gold. They wanted revenge.

Erwyn's eyes burned as she went from wound to wound, and the stench of burning tents twisted her stomach even more when mixed with the smells of battle.

But eeriest of all was the strange quiet everywhere.

The cries of their wounded were dampened by the smoke, those of the enemy by the wall. No swords clanged on breastplates or helmets. The whirr of arrows, the crackle of fire, the cries of the wounded, and the hushed voices of those who fought to save their camp were all she heard. It was so quiet she could hear a baby or young child cry now and then from inside the cordon of warriors.

Gurdek's orders were to wait with his men until the battle at the north gate was well under way and the enemy at the south gate began to flag. The cisterns were perilously low when Erwyn heard the roar that told her his men had finally made their attack. The burning arrows stopped as the strangely welcome sound of sword on sword came over the south wall.

She continued to heal, but knew at once when first the battle to the south, then the one to the north fell silent. Gurdek's second came to take her out the now open south gate to the wounded among their men there.

As she moved about the battlefield, she came across the body of the would-be rapist she had once fed. No arrow or sword had killed him. He had been stabbed in the back by a knife. She looked at the enemy who stood passively around their fallen leader's body, but saw no remorse or guilt in any of them.

Once their wounded were all tended to, she turned to the enemy wounded. A surprising number fell to sword wounds, given the relatively short time between Gurdek's attack and the end of the battle. Had they turned on each other?

Then she saw a wound that was clearly self-inflicted. And another. They did not turn on each other, she realized with a wave of revulsion. They turned on themselves.

But why? Even if Thalgor chose to kill the defeated men, it would be a quick, clean death. It was the way of all bands.

A sudden darkness filled her mind.

But perhaps that was not the way of their band, their leader.

She moved to the north gate and immediately picked out the body of the other brother who had led the attackers there. He lay face down in the dirt, his head pointing away from the camp, an arrow in his back. A coward in addition to all his other evil.

As she healed, Thalgor's men gathered the captured enemy, and Sett's men found and returned with the oxen, carts, and women they had brought. Of over a dozen women, all young and lovely, only a few clung to a captured warrior or searched among the bodies and threw themselves weeping on one of them. The rest stood in a forlorn clump, faces frozen with fear.

By the time all were healed who could be, Erwyn was almost too weary to stand. Not only from healing, but from the reluctance of so many of the enemy to be healed. She leaned on Rygar as they went to where Thalgor faced the piteous captives.

Before he could speak, one of the older men stepped away from the woman who clung to him and fell at Thalgor's feet.

"Kill us quickly," he pleaded. "Before you take our women."

Tynor pulled the man to his feet. "We do not kill captives."

"But if you sell us as slaves, he may find us," the man objected with horror.

"We do not deal in slaves," Thalgor said with distaste.

The prisoners looked at him in astonishment as Thalgor made his usual speech about accepting the captives into the camp.

"You mean this?" the enemy spokesman asked.

Thalgor nodded, but still the prisoners stood rooted to the spot, as if they waited for the killing blow to fall.

Finally, when it did not, a woman pulled one of the men forward. "You will let us share a tent of our own?"

Thalgor nodded again. The woman looked at the man by her side. He looked down at her and even in her weary state Erwyn felt the love and the good heart in both of them.

"We will join you." The man's voice was thick with emotion.

Thalgor looked at Erwyn, who still leaned on Rygar's arm. When she nodded, he said, "Done."

The others quickly followed, first the men with women, then the others. Only one or two of the men chose to become renegades, and they were the only ones Erwyn would have refused.

She wondered that none of them chose to return to their own camp to reunite with their women and children. But the same blackness that filled her every time she thought of that camp told her men there had no women they could truly call their own.

She remembered the badly maimed man who identified Sett as the one who had taken Lana. And she finally understood that to return to that camp after a defeat meant a slow, painful death.

As the men stood one by one in front of Thalgor, Gurdek's woman had gone to the knot of women without men and those grieving the dead to speak with them in her soft, calming voice.

When all made their choice, Thalgor spoke to the older man who served as their leader.

"We have lost many tents to the fire your arrows brought, and our camp is in disarray. Until it is set to rights, your men will camp outside our wall. We have lean-to's for the men with women, and the other women can share a tent in the camp. But for now you will all eat with us."

"We celebrate the death of those who led us, as you celebrate your victory," the man said, and the others murmured their agreement.

"Why would they follow men whose deaths they celebrate?" Thalgor asked Erwyn as he led her, leaning heavily on him, back to their tent.

"Because the one they once served has such power," she explained, the dark cloud so thick around her she stumbled.

Thalgor nodded and, without a word, picked her up to carry her to their bed. She was asleep before he reached the tent.

THE DAMAGE TO the camp, and the dazed reaction of those who had been captured to their freedom from the tyranny of their former leader, made the next days hard for all. The women of the camp began to make new tents out of the remnants of those too burned to repair, and weave cloth for more, while Thalgor and his men salvaged what they could of the household goods and taught the new warriors their ways. Unused tents, like Gee's, were hauled out and set up by the older boys.

Only the captive women who had no men or had lost theirs in the battle remained fearful. They huddled in their tent when not helping with the work of the camp.

Lana took it upon herself to convince them of the good faith of their new band. She all but moved into their tent to work with them. Thalgor joked with Sett that their women both cared more for others than for the two of them.

But Thalgor wasn't so sure it was a joke for him.

The pain of the new additions to the camp, and the horror that filled their dreams, tore at Erwyn even when she stayed away from them and had Tya or Gurdek's woman take them sleeping teas in her place. The evil that was done to all of them seemed to soak into her and left her weary and distracted. So much so that some days he wondered if she carried a child, but she quickly assured him she did not. He didn't know if it was sadness or relief he felt at her words.

Finally the day came when one of his older warriors, a widower with half-grown children, asked one of the older captive women if she would like to go for a walk after dinner. His simple act was like the first drop of rain. A torrent followed.

The captive men chose to court women from Thalgor's band, if they courted at all, perhaps to avoid painful shared memories. The men without women from Thalgor's camp flooded the paths around the captive women's tent. The women blossomed under the wish of his warriors for women to keep in their tents, not merely use. Soon the dilapidated old tent was empty and turned a home for one of the new couples.

The camp restored, and the captives becoming a part of them, they all began the preparations for their first dark time within the wall. The men harvested the food they grew, the women preserved it, and all prepared themselves for the dark and cold.

The dark time was when the bands wandered south and battled. And if a wandering band sought revenge on a walled camp, it would not be hard to find it. Thalgor pushed those thoughts aside and went about the task of leading his people.

Except at night. Then his dreams were filled with a great darkness he could not understand.

As the first frost came, the darkness began to invade his days as well. Just now and then, when he met one of the recent captives in the camp, stronger yet when he saw Sett's woman. And strongest of all when he returned to the tent late at night to find Erwyn awake, so afraid of her own dreams she sought refuge in his arms.

Lana's nightmares had returned as well, Sett confessed one day when he almost fell asleep at council. The others nodded without comment and went on with their business. But the groggy explanation left a cloud above the meeting that lingered in Thalgor's tent for days.

One night after the stream that ran through the camp froze solid, he found Erwyn crying when he came in from his last circuit of the wall. He gathered her in his arms and soon changed her tears to need. She gave herself to him with the same rage and despair, the same need for comfort that drove him to take her. It was a time he knew he would remember, a passion so pure and shared another man might have called it love.

Afterward, as he kissed her absently along the angle of her jaw, a scream tore through the icy night air.

He barely had time to look up before a small body threw itself through the curtain that hid their bed. Ignorant of what their intertwined bodies meant, Felyn burrowed between them until her head rested on Erwyn's naked breast.

"Erwyn," the child sobbed. "Erwyn."

Tya appeared at the curtain with Felyn's cloak wrapped around her sleeping gown as if she pulled on the wrong one as she chased after the child.

"It's all right," Thalgor told Tya gruffly, embarrassed she should see he was naked except where a blanket luckily hid what most needed hiding. "Go back to bed. Erwyn will care for her."

Tya looked at Erwyn, who nodded and stroked the child's head. After Tya left, he was able to find his tunic and pull it over his head without any indecent display. Not that Felyn would have noticed, her head hidden in the soft flesh of Erwyn's body.

He sat up and gently pulled the child into his lap so Erwyn could slip on her gown, but Felyn strained against his hands, reaching and crying for Erwyn, who finally took the sobbing child into her arms. She soothed her with sweet, musical words so like his mother's that Thalgor's eyes filled with a painful mist.

When the child was calm enough to speak, Erwyn asked her gently, "What is it? A nightmare?"

Felyn only shook her head, her lips tightly closed, her jaw clenched against the words that threatened to escape.

"I cannot help you, if you do not tell me what it was."

The child cast Thalgor one quick glance, then leaned closer to Erwyn, as if to hide her words from him.

"You must take me to the Wise Witches. Now. Tonight. We must be gone from this place. You must take me. Please."

Felyn still spoke rarely, never more than a few words here and there, but this speech was clearly said, without any hint of the childish lisp he sometimes heard from her.

Erwyn looked down at the child, puzzled. He realized she could no more read that small mind than she could his own. More proof that, despite Erwyn's protestations of uncertainty, the child was as much a witch as she. And so her sister.

"Why must I take you there? What have you dreamed?"

"Not dreamed, seen," the child wailed. "You must take

me." She began to sob again.

As Erwyn rocked her in her arms, she looked over the child's head at Thalgor. He couldn't quite read the look. Surely she didn't intend to do as the child asked.

"It is the dark time," he reminded both of them in a low voice. "You cannot travel so far alone, and I cannot ask any of my men to go with you and be so long from their families."

Felyn looked at him, her strange eyes full of sadness.

"You must take me," she said to Erwyn. "We must go now. We can make it there safely, if we are careful. Your magic will help us. Please, please. We must get away from this place."

"Thalgor is right. We cannot go there in the dark time. You do not know how far it is, how dangerous the way. Even in the warm time I almost died before I reached their citadel." She looked at him again, a question in her eyes. "Perhaps when the warm time comes Thalgor will give us an ox…"

"No, no! That is too late. We must go now. We must."

Thalgor stood and ran his hand through his hair, then rubbed his forehead, where an ache had begun to build. He was about to go to the scullery to make a tea to help them sleep when Tya appeared again with four steaming cups on a tray.

Felyn didn't protest as Erwyn and Tya urged her to drink.

He sipped his tea in the far corner of the small sleeping chamber, reluctant to leave for fear Erwyn might agree to the child's mad demand.

Even to have her leave him for so long in the warm time filled him with an emptiness that sickened him. To risk losing her in the cold and dark was beyond thought.

The child's head soon drooped on Erwyn's breast. Tya led her back to their chamber.

Luckily he sensed she would return and kept his tunic on so she didn't find him naked again.

"She sleeps," Tya told them from the doorway. "I'm sorry she disturbed...um, disturbed you."

"You could not have stopped her," Erwyn assured her, and Thalgor nodded in agreement.

"What should I do if it happens again?"

"Try to calm her, listen to her if she will talk to you, give her tea, and tell me what she says," Erwyn answered.

Tya nodded. "That will at least give you some warning." Her face, already rosy, turned scarlet.

"Good practice," Thalgor told her in a too hearty voice, "for when you and Rygar have your own."

Tya smiled and took a drink of her tea.

"Go to sleep," Erwyn said softly. And when she was gone, to Thalgor, "Come to bed."

It was a long time before either of them slept.

For days the child's screams interrupted their sleep. Thalgor hoped no one outside the tent could hear, so piteously did she cry and demand to be taken to the Wise Witches.

Tya was never able to calm her, so each night the child ran to Erwyn with the same plea. And as the sun rose each day the child's fear evaporated with the cold dark time fog.

One day Thalgor woke at dawn, his heart frozen. The child had not come. Had she died in her sleep? Fled the camp alone?

He pulled on his tunic and rushed to the chamber when Felyn slept. He pulled back the curtain to find her sitting on her bed, clearly just now awake, a sad smile on her face.

She slid from her bed and took his hand, then solemnly led him away from where Tya still slept, snoring daintily.

Absently Thalgor wondered if Rygar knew of that snore, but he had no doubt a love such as his brother's for Tya was most likely deaf as well as blind.

Felyn sat on a bench in the main chamber, and he lowered himself down beside her.

"No nightmare?" he asked.

She thought a moment before she answered. "I saw the same vision as always. But the Witch King…"

"The Witch King," he interrupted, then quickly lowered his voice back to a whisper. "You know of the Witch King?"

"He calls me 'sister'." The child frowned. "I think. It is hard to know, since I am always asleep when he comes."

Thalgor shivered. "What did he tell you last night?"

Even as he spoke, his heart turned over, less with fear

than with a certainty he did not want to hear what the Witch King had said.

"Not to be afraid. That what I saw had to happen, and I could not run away from it." She lowered her head. "He could not promise…"

"Promise what?" Thalgor asked when she stopped.

She reached up her small hand and touched his cheek, his lips. "Keep silent," she said in that eerie voice beyond her years. "The Witch King tells those who need to know."

Before he could probe further Tya burst from their chamber, cheered by her full night's sleep.

"Good morning," she said brightly. "Are you both ready to eat something?"

Felyn became a child again. He knew he would learn no more.

He wanted to tell Erwyn about his strange conversation with Felyn, but while he made his morning circuit of the camp she was called away to a birth. By the time she returned, he and Rygar had gone on patrol with their men. When he returned late to the tent she was already asleep.

Tomorrow would be soon enough.

CHAPTER NINETEEN

LATE THAT NIGHT Erwyn woke him.

He thought at first the child's nightmares had returned, but the tent, the whole camp lay silent under the frosty dark-time sky.

"What?" he grumbled, half-asleep.

"I must go to the forest."

"Why?"

"I must fly."

He sat up, fully awake.

"Fly where? Why?"

She sighed as she pulled on her heaviest gown.

"You have enough witch blood to see the dark cloud that lingers over the camp. Even Felyn sees it in her dreams."

He started to tell her about the child's last dream, but she put her hands to his lips to silence him, as the child had.

"It grows larger, darker every day, but I cannot see where it comes from or what causes it. I must fly to see. And it must be soon. Tonight."

She quickly gathered a bag of herbs and pulled her cloak around her, waiting silently by the curtain that separated their chamber from the rest of the tent. She knew he would not allow her to go into the forest alone. He clambered to his feet and pulled his tunic on in the same movement, as if for an attack.

And an attack it was, he thought as he put on his sword. An attack on the contentment he had felt these last few days, despite interrupted sleep and the dark cloud he, too, saw in the air over them. Erwyn's words had set off a jumble of feelings and fears he neither wanted nor understood. As he wrapped his cloak around him against the icy night air he cursed witches and witch blood, just quietly enough for her to know his anger.

But her thoughts were clearly busy elsewhere. Before they even left the tent she made herself invisible, as though her mind leapt ahead of them to the sleeping camp.

If the guards at the gate wondered why he asked them to let him out, they hid it well, or perhaps it seemed more rational a request to their sleep-hazed minds than it did to his.

Once out of sight of the camp, Erwyn appeared again and took his hand.

The night was clear, the forest strangely still as they walked in silence to the clearing. No owls hooted in the dark. No small animals rustled through the fallen leaves that covered the frozen ground. No panther called over its prey.

He built the tiny fire on the flat stone in the clearing while Erwyn drew what she needed from the bag she carried.

Soon sharp flames cut the darkness. She arranged large leaves on top of the fire. He stood at the edge of the clearing, his cloak across his face as the aromatic smoke filled the air.

When she let her robe fall to the ground and took her gown off to stand naked he could scarcely bear to look at her.

Her body was white in the moonlight that suddenly escaped the leaden clouds that covered it until then. Her beauty always amazed him but in this witch's circle, she stunned him.

Humbled at the knowledge that she was his, he watched as she repeated the same ritual as before. When her body fell limp to the ground, he caught her and laid her gently on her gown, covering her with her cloak against the chill.

Then he lowered himself to the ground with his back against one of the trees that ringed the circle, helpless to do anything but wait.

The fire was out, the eastern sky bright when Erwyn finally stirred. Despite the heavy cloak that covered her she shivered. Great tears streamed down her face.

He knew better than to ask why, but helped her pull her clothes on and allowed her to lean on him, like an old woman, as they walked, until they came in sight of the camp. Her hand shook with effort of making herself invisible, and she leaned on him still as they passed the drowsy guards at the gate.

ERWYN SLEPT ALL day, her dreams restless, painful.

Thalgor brought her food at sundown, then stared at her as she sat on their bed to eat. She let him wait. She knew what would happen once she spoke.

Finally she set the remains of the meal aside and stood to look him full in the face.

"The two we defeated," she gestured toward the past, "were crows. The one who comes now is a raven. Twice as powerful, ten times as wise in the ways of battle, with strong witch blood and a mind capable of unimaginable evil."

"Why would one such as that take those two as his lieutenants? The one died like a dog at the hands of his own men, the other died a coward's death. If he has no better, he cannot be as you say."

"They were his brothers, the only ones he could trust."

"If his evil is so great, it is no wonder." He sighed. "You say he comes here?"

She closed her eyes against the vision. "He marches this way for revenge, for blood and rotting flesh. He has half again as many men as you do and brings no women or livestock."

"A raiding party. How long?"

He took one of her hands. She opened her eyes and touched his hair with the other.

"Three, maybe four days."

"Can we defeat them?"

She lowered her head as her eyes misted with tears. "No."

"Defend ourselves?"

His voice was thick with anger, but she knew him too well to feel a fear he meant for others.

"I do not know." The words felt forced from her lips.

She knew he wished to ask more, but her eyes drooped with exhaustion. She closed them to hide her tears. He laid her back on the bed, dipped his head in salute, and left. She felt the plans for battle that already filled his mind.

Late in the night he returned.

"Can you kill the raven?" he asked in a hushed voice when he saw she was awake.

Somewhere between sleep and waking she had wondered the same, and found the answer in a magic her mother had taught her, a magic from long ago, before witches and men found a way to live together. Before killing a witch brought a curse, and a witch's power was lost if she killed. A magic now only whispered from mother to daughter, in case that war should ever erupt again.

"I can." She refused to lie to him, despite what it could cost her. "But I won't."

His face darkened. At which confession, she could not tell. Perhaps at both. That magic was a secret long kept from men.

"Why not?" was all he asked.

"My gift is not for killing."

He brushed the explanation away. "You kill after every battle."

"I ease death."

"Sett, Gurdek, and the others are afraid. They don't see how we can defend ourselves against a force that large."

She was afraid, too, but she could not tell him that.

"They wish to flee, to wander once again," he went on. "The time we should spend in preparations for the battle they want to use to build new carts and train the oxen to pull again."

The loss of his dream. Another cause for grief.

"What did you tell them?"

"That what they ask is impossible. They knew that, but it offered some hope. I told them you would find a way to save us."

His words, his trust, would once have buoyed her, perhaps even only the day before. Now they were an added burden.

She wanted to cry out in pain, grief, and fear. Instead she told him the plan that had come to her while she waited for him.

"You could send some of your men to the forest, as you have done before. Once the attack begins, they can come around behind the enemy's weakest flank."

He thought for a moment, strategies flying through his mind.

"Are you certain that will drive them off?"

She could only shake her head. She was certain of nothing.

"Then you must kill the raven."

"No." Despair reduced her voice to a reedy whisper.

He grabbed her shoulders as if to shake her, but she lifted her eyes to his in silent warning and he immediately let her go.

"Why would you let us all die?" he bit out.

"I cannot murder."

"You say you know magic that can kill the raven."

"Yes, but if I murder, my gift will be gone."

He waved his arm toward the main room of the tent.

"We can do as well without your gift. I am grateful for it, but it is only one of many things you can do."

"My gift," she repeated with as much force as she could master. "Not only my gift to see, but also my gift to heal."

"So my men will die harder. And someday, so shall I."

"And what would I be without my gift?"

"My woman still." He looked at her intensely. "Always."

Something that had grown slowly inside her over these last months formed a tender bud, as if it might someday bloom.

But the battle she saw threatened much more than their lives together. It threatened the peace they brought to their people, the dream of a life without warfare and wandering.

"A warrior's 'always' can be very brief."

She hoped he did not hear her heart break as she said it.

The intensity in his face hardened into pain. "How can you refuse to save us?"

"How can you ask me not to be what I am?"

His face softened as he drew one hand across her cheek. "You are…" He dropped his hand and looked away.

She took a deep breath. "Would you not be a warrior?"

His only answer was to wrap his arms around her and pull her down to the bed in wordless surrender to what would come.

A SOMBER COUNCIL met the next day. Scouts brought word of the mass of armed men moving south toward the camp.

Rygar marked the enemy's progress on the map spread across the council table. Thalgor began to see lines of force shimmer on the map. He smiled slowly. There might be a way.

"They must come down this valley." He drew a line from the enemy's position to the camp with the back of his sword point, then glanced at Erwyn, who nodded. "If we attack them there, before they reach the camp, we will have surprise on our side."

"How can you surprise a leader with as much witch blood as you say this one has?" Gurdek asked.

Thalgor frowned as the thoughts formed in his mind aided, he sensed, by Erwyn, who sat silent beside him.

"The man has witch blood, but is no witch. The same cloud that hides his movements from Erwyn conceals ours from him."

"Are you certain?" Sett prodded.

Thalgor sighed. He was certain of so little.

"And even so," Rygar mused aloud, "his scouts will see our men as we move toward the battlefield."

Thalgor was on firmer ground again. "We know this land. His men do not. We can move out in small patrols and follow different paths. At most the scouts will think they are raiding parties. By the time the enemy is fully aware of how many of our men they have seen pass, it will be too late."

"But that leaves the camp undefended," Gurdek said. "The guard we usually leave behind will not be enough if even a part of them escape our ambush, they are so many."

"We will attack only with my men and Sett's. Mine from head-on, Sett's from their weak flank. Your men will remain to guard the camp. If they defeat us, we will send messengers to alert you in time to have most of your men take the women, children and livestock away from here, into the woods, and leave your best warriors and the old men here to stage what defense they can. By the time the enemy discovers the camp is empty, those you lead will be a day or two's march away. With any luck," he added under his breath.

A dark silence fell. The plan might thwart the enemy, but what would be left of their band? More women and children than the few warriors who survived could protect from other bands when they made dark-time raids. His people would become marauders. At best.

But what other choice was there? He saw the dark cloud clearly now, could almost make out the form of the one Erwyn called the raven in the black mist. His men could not see, could not know the terrible vengeance that awaited their people if the enemy won. He had tried to tell them the day before, but they could not believe such savagery was possible. Nor would he if his visions had not shown it to him.

Sett, who had been silent, finally spoke. "There are worse fates than a marauder's life."

His tone invited no dispute.

"I will organize our warriors to teach the older boys all they can about how to defend a camp," Rygar said.

"And I will get the old men to teach them how to build one," Gurdek agreed with a sigh.

"Teach the women, too." Erwyn's voice, when she spoke, was rough. "Both of you."

From her seat to one side, Tya let out a low sob.

Only the day before Thalgor had been glad to see Felyn play with the other children in the light snow that had fallen during the night. Now all he could think of was the terror her nightmares about the coming battle had brought her.

They all sat in bleak silence for a long while, until Gurdek's woman appeared at the door of the tent to summon him to eat. Slowly they all stirred themselves and went about their appointed tasks with heavy hearts.

THE CAMP WAS strangely quiet by day as they prepared for the battle to come. The nights were strangely noisy as women and boys listened to the old men tell them how to build and defend a camp while the men worked to make arrows, bows, and knives, not only for themselves now, but for their women and sons as well. A hurried desperation shrouded everything they did.

On the second day Sett's warriors began to leave in groups of six or eight to circle quietly through the woods to the valley where Thalgor's men would attack the enemy. Their farewells were grave and earnest. Their women wept only after the men left, as their children clung to them in sad confusion.

That night the remaining council met to plan the departure of Thalgor's men the next day.

"I will go with the first party," Rygar said, "and Thalgor can come with the last."

Thalgor had dreaded this moment all day. "You stay here."

"Here?" Rygar asked in disbelief.

"You are needed to guard the camp."

"Gurdek's men will guard the camp. That was your plan."

"You are needed to guard my tent."

"Is your tent more valuable than any other, Thalgor?" Rygar rose to his feet. "Because, perhaps, of the jewels and gold on the chair you took from my father?"

Gurdek and the others gasped, but Thalgor remained calm.

"Because of the girl you love who lives here, Brother."

"Look at her, Thalgor. She is a girl no longer. Even her father agrees. After this battle she is to become my woman. But that does not make her more dear to me than my duty. And my duty is as your second, until you say otherwise. The blood of the leaders of this band from back before memory flows in my veins, and I will fight with our warriors to defend it."

Thalgor stood slowly. "You must protect the witch."

"I love Erwyn like a sister, Thalgor. She saved my life. She has saved us all. But I am a warrior, and the battlefield is where I must be. With your leave or without it."

He chose to ignore the threat in Rygar's words. "And who will lead with us both dead?"

"Gurdek will lead. That is the path you chose yourself. It is a wise path. He is best suited of us all to lead marauders."

Thalgor sank back on the bench. "Would you take all hope from me, Brother? All possibility those I love will survive?"

"What must survive," Erwyn said in a voice hollowed out by pain, "is the band. No one person is more than that."

"Then kill the raven!" he spat at her in a hushed tone.

The others looked at them in confusion.

"Thalgor," Gurdek said in a placating tone, "this is not the time to fight with your woman over birds."

Thalgor's mind searched frantically for a way to protect those he loved, but he waved his hand for Rygar to continue.

"I will go with the first group, you with the last. The witch, the bone-setter, the herbalist, and the surgeon will go in my group and meet in the woods with Sett's men, who will hide them until the attack."

Thalgor sprang back to his feet. "Who gave such an order?" he roared, turning toward Gurdek.

"I did," Erwyn told him calmly. "I have my duty, as Rygar has his and you yours. Mine is to heal."

Thalgor shook his head in disbelief. Would this witch never do as he wanted?

"Your duty is to do as your man tells you. You will stay here with the other women and keep yourself safe."

She looked up at him, eyes defiant. "There is no safety to be had in this battle. You know that. I will not hide docilely to be taken captive. You have never asked that of me before. Do not ask it of me now."

"You hid docilely enough the night I captured you," he reminded her grimly.

"The child was with me. And I had no weapon."

"You had your magic."

"And I will have it on this battlefield as well."

"Kill – the – raven," he bit out.

Gurdek made a sound of disgust. Rygar came to stand behind Erwyn, his hands on her shoulders.

"She is right, Thalgor," he said. "You know she is right."

"Clearly you have no need of a leader." Thalgor stood. "Make what plans you wish, then tell me what I must do. Like any warrior, I have weapons to ready for battle and farewells to make." Then he left.

THALGOR CAME TO their bed late that night. Erwyn thought for a moment of pretending she was asleep, but decided it was unworthy. If he wished to argue, she would listen, but she would not change her mind. Not about killing the raven, nor about going with his warriors to heal them after the battle. If any of them still lived. If she still lived.

But rather than argue, he slid into the bed beside her and pulled her tenderly into his arms. Her body responded even before she got over her surprise.

He took her in a slow, solemn mating, done more as if to forget a pain than to remind himself of pleasure. It became a kind of healing for her as well. They slept wrapped together like new lovers, but both dreamt of the battle to come.

At noon she left with Rygar's men. She and Thalgor had said their farewells before they rose from their bed. When the time came, she hugged Tya, whose eyes were red from a night of crying over Rygar, and knelt beside Felyn. The child stroked her face, then kissed her cheeks. Erwyn echoed the gesture.

"I love you," she whispered, only for the child to hear.

Felyn nodded and stepped away, the feelings behind that face so much like her own hidden even from Erwyn's magic.

"With a woman along, we will look even more like a raiding party, or a band of marauders," Rygar told Thalgor cheerfully.

Thalgor glared. "Do you fancy yourself Erwyn's man?"

"Are we not far beyond that, Brother?"

Thalgor nodded and the two men embraced.

Then the small patrol and the four healers were on their way.

Erwyn's legs soon began to ache. She had gotten soft behind the safety of their wall. She said nothing, but the other healers, older men also unused to walking so far, complained openly. The warriors laughed at their weakness, but walked more slowly.

The sun shone on shallow, crusted snow. A few hardy birds chirped and warbled as they moved through the woods.

Half asleep as she walked in the drowsy afternoon, Erwyn sensed enemy scouts nearby. They watched the patrol's progress, but did not seem alarmed by it. Perhaps Thalgor's plan would work.

She let Rygar know by gestures where the scouts were, but he nodded and kept on walking, confident in the plan. Or perhaps reluctant to warn the enemy of their intent by an attack on the scouts, who equaled their warriors in number. His farewells to Tya had been those of a man who doubts he will return.

They were met just before sunset by four of Sett's men, who led the healers to their patrol's campfire while Rygar and his men turned back to meet up with the rest of Thalgor's warriors and prepare to fight at dawn.

Erwyn never failed to be amazed at the cheerful air a camp took on before a battle. Especially among Sett's men, who were the most thirsty for battle of all in the band, just as Thalgor's were the best fighters and Gurdek's the most stubborn and solid. Like the men who led them.

The men told stories about other battles around the campfire, some they had fought themselves, some from legends or from the stories of their fathers and grandfathers.

She listened impassively so her distaste and worry would not mar the ritual the warriors needed to be ready for the next day. But their tales haunted her dreams and woke her in the night, alone on the hard ground and shivering.

AT FIRST LIGHT Thalgor crept to a rock that overlooked the valley where the enemy camped. The enemy warriors below were preparing for the day's march as a few men, slaves by their tattered clothing, took down the leader's tent and cooked breakfast gruel over a single large campfire.

In the midst of the carefully ordered chaos stood a man Thalgor knew at once must be the raven Erwyn had described. He was taller than the others, perhaps taller than

Thalgor himself, his black hair streaked with white, his face fierce, even at this distance, as he wielded a whip meant for oxen against the slaves who dismantled his tent and cowered near the fire.

Evil radiated from this man. Not the craven obsessions of his brothers, but an evil Thalgor had seen only once before, in the first man he had killed long ago.

But this man's evil was darker yet, fed by witch blood, a link to the ancient magic as strong and vital as Thalgor's own.

Magic made him think of Erwyn. He looked to the hill where he knew she camped with Sett's men. And then down behind him to where Rygar's patrol had spent the night. What he would not give to have them both safe inside the walls of the camp. But they chose their duty over their love for him, love he never doubted.

Erwyn chose it doubly—her duty to heal and her duty not to murder, not even the unspeakably evil man below him who now turned his whip on one of his warriors.

What a thing was duty. What a thing was love.

Had he ever told Erwyn he loved her? He scarcely knew it himself until these last few days when he realized the laws of magic that bound her bound him, too. He could only love her as she was, even if the cost was his own death. Or hers. A world without Erwyn was unthinkable. So he ceased to think and became nothing more than a warrior intent on victory.

A victory every instinct told him, as he looked out over

the mass of men camped in the valley, was all but impossible.

Almost silently Rygar moved into position next to him.

"All the patrols are ready," he reported. "When do we attack?"

"Now."

Thalgor stood, drew his sword and raised it over his head so that it shone like a beacon in the early morning sun as he led his men down the hill toward the unsuspecting camp.

ERWYN LOOKED OUT over the enemy camp from her hiding place on a hill thick with evergreens.

She saw their leader at once and watched how he treated those who served him. Her heart filled, first with horror, then with something like hope.

His brothers' arrogance had helped Thalgor defeat them, but bolstered by his far more powerful witch blood, the man below her was ten times as arrogant as they. That might be the difference Thalgor's men needed to win this battle.

She heard a cry. Thalgor's battle cry. Her blood froze.

But the element of surprise served them well. Thalgor's men were past the sleepy guards at the edge of the camp and half-way to the leader's tent at its center before the enemy gathered his forces to meet them full-on.

Once they did, the battle became slow and grim. She saw an archer who might have been Rygar from his size take an arrow in the left arm. He merely pulled it out, tied a rag around the wound and raised his own bow again as if nothing had happened.

She would never understand how the blood lust protected men from the pain of their wounds. If they went on fighting, their wounds were often harder to heal later, but this time, at least, she was glad for the oblivion brought by fury.

Thalgor was easy to find by his size in the dust and confusion of the fighting. She almost thought she heard his voice above the clamor of metal on metal, the whoosh of arrows, the moans of dying men, as he urged his warriors on. Already he clearly searched for the enemy leader, in hopes he could bring the battle to a quick end. But it was as if his opponent fled him. Not from fear, Erwyn was certain, but to prolong the bloody battle, to delay the moment he thought inevitable when Thalgor would fall beneath his sword.

Rather than search for Thalgor, the enemy leader walked up and down behind the jagged line of his warriors to urge them on.

Occasionally he would strike a man who didn't fight as his leader wished across the back with the broad side of his sword. The dead and wounded he stepped over like so much fallen wood. When one of Thalgor's men broke through the line and plunged at him, the enemy struck him down with a single blow to his heart, then stepped back behind his men and returned to pacing.

Erwyn heard the restless shuffle of Sett's men around her, knew he watched as she did for the time and place when a second attack would be most effective.

She saw it a moment before he did, a break in the enemy line that cut a full quarter of their men off from the main battlefield.

Sett called the charge at once. In a wave of fierce resolve, his men stormed past Erwyn and rushed into the battle. To win, or die. Or both.

CHAPTER TWENTY

THIS SECOND SURPRISE threw the isolated enemy warriors into total confusion and what few still lived after the onslaught took flight. With a roar that echoed over the battlefield, Sett turned his men to where Thalgor's men were beginning to tire as they fought an equally weary enemy.

But instead of breaking their opponent's will, the success of the second attack seemed to revive them as the more compact mass of warriors began to push back at the line of Thalgor's men that moved implacably through their camp.

Erwyn watched with mounting dread as the enemy took the offensive and slowly drove the attackers out of the camp and down the valley. Thalgor's men fought valiantly, but the numbers were against them, even with the loss of the quarter of the enemy Sett's men had scattered. Their opponents fought like men possessed, driven on by a leader they feared more than the enemy, more than death itself.

The battle had moved so far down the valley that Erwyn, the other healers, and the two young men left to guard them, were forced to leave their hiding place and move cautiously along the ridge, careful to stay as much as they could in the thickest part of the woods.

The guards led them past the fighting, so they could take shelter again well behind Thalgor's men, where the valley narrowed before it opened out onto the plain where Thalgor's walled camp stood, Gurdek's men its only protection.

There in the narrow pass Thalgor would have to make his final stand. Erwyn saw the three scouts he sent back to the camp to tell Gurdek the battle went badly, so he could move the women and children into safety in the forest. She sent Felyn and Tya strength with her thoughts, but knew the others would care for them until she returned. If she returned.

That she truly might die only now came to her. To die in battle with Thalgor, at his side in mind if not in body. A well of love and pride filled her at the thought. She hoped it would give her the strength she would need not only to die, but perhaps worse, to live on without him.

As the valley narrowed, numbers counted less. It mattered less if five ranks of the enemy faced only three of Thalgor's men if Thalgor's fought better, were braver, and had more at stake, so they struck down their opponents more freely than they fell.

Erwyn didn't know if her witch's sight or the excitement of the guards told her, but she saw the tide of the battle turn.

Now only three ranks of enemy forces faced Thalgor's still almost three. Now two. Outnumbered, the enemy fought more viciously, but Thalgor's line stood firm.

The lowering sun glinted off those swords not completely bathed in blood and off the metal of shields raised in defense, then lowered in attack.

The enemy leader put on a helmet for the first time. Covered entirely in gold, it hid his raven hair but not his size or the way he used his sword on his own men, if they got in his way, as viciously as on the enemy.

The golden helmet would make it easy for Thalgor to find the enemy leader in the roiling humanity of a last-stage battle. She watched with ice-filled veins as the man she loved made his way unerringly to his target. He brushed aside the last line of men around their leader as if they were so many flies on a warm-time afternoon.

Finally the two leaders faced each other. The fighting continued around them, but it seemed to still, as if everyone kept half an eye on the battle that mattered most.

Leader to leader, to decide victory or defeat. A fight to the death.

THALGOR WAS TIRED. The battle lust had ebbed and flowed through him so many times in the day that even his heart felt weary as it beat in his chest.

The enemy, who had prodded more than fought himself, held his head high despite the great weight of that golden helmet, his body straight, his sword at the ready.

This was not a normal man. Thalgor sensed the witch blood in him, felt him try to probe his mind, to weaken him with visions of what would become of his people if he lost.

More than the witch blood, though, he sensed the man's evil. An evil he had seen the likes of only once, but then he had lived with it every day for more years than he wished to remember. Most evil was stupid and so easily defeated. But not this.

If he had never faced the likes of this intelligence before, Thalgor would have feared much more than he did. He knew this evil. He knew its power was its greatest weakness.

The brute he'd slain before did not think a boy could make a killing blow. This monster would make a similar mistake. Thalgor only had to fight and survive long enough to give him the chance to make it.

He dropped his shoulders to feign greater weariness than he felt.

An arrow whizzed past his left shoulder. A row of enemy archers stood with arrows pointed directly at him.

Bitter rage coursed through him. A tradition since before time said leaders fought each other one on one. Another arrow flew by and he felt his opponent's smile broaden.

The third arrow brought a death-cry from the men who still fought behind Thalgor. Was it Sett's voice? Rygar's?

Thalgor pushed the thought away. His enemy sent it. He sent one in return– the golden helmet on his own head. A loss he knew the enemy feared as Thalgor did the loss of friend or brother.

A volley of arrows from his own ranks answered the opponents' and most of the archers across from him fell.

As the two leaders circled, each looking for a weakness in the other, Thalgor saw that his opponent expected their ranks to collapse and Thalgor's men to flee if he was killed, so the enemy could capture his camp and destroy his people without opposition.

But that would never happen, at least not at once. If he fell, Sett and Rygar would hold the line fast and, if all here died, Gurdek still had a full third of their men with him to defend a camp that by now should be empty of all but warriors.

Was this man so bent on revenge he would follow the remnants into the forest? Even if he did, he would never catch them all. Some of Thalgor's people would survive, and with them the legend of a walled camp, the dream of a time without war or wandering. That knowledge made him smile in his turn.

The enemy tilted his head at the smile and the afternoon sun glinted off the gold of his helmet.

Suddenly Thalgor saw that the helmet offered so much protection his opponent held his shield lower than usual to better protect his chest and belly. And when he moved just so, a line of flesh was exposed between helmet and shield. The vulnerable flesh of a human throat.

Thalgor's smile widened.

Certain of what he must do, he lunged toward his opponent's sword hand. But his blade met only a stout shield as his own felt an answering attack. The duel was on.

The two of them circled and traded stroke for stroke, but none hit home.

Silence seemed to fall around them. Even the air felt still, but Thalgor knew—lunge, parry, strike again—that the battle raged on all sides, if less fiercely, that their swords clanged, that they both breathed hard with the work of it. Such duels always quieted the battle. The narrowness of his focus always drew an invisible circle around him and his enemy.

But this was different. This was more.

Perhaps it was the witch blood that flowed so strong in both of them, perhaps something else, but their duel had an air of eternity about it. Not just death and victory hung in the balance, but the future of the land. Peace or terror.

They moved in the slow dance for as long as he ever remembered it lasting. The short dark-time day would soon fade.

Suddenly the other man made a quick downward stab at Thalgor's leg and caught him just above the knee. It was not a serious wound, but the blood flowed freely and wet the ground between them.

His enemy paused for a moment and lifted his head to breathe the smell of blood as a man might the scent of a woman as they mated. He made a thrust at Thalgor's heart, but only sliced a hole in his breastplate.

They began to circle again. Thalgor favored his wounded leg more than was necessary to draw his opponent's strikes in that direction and pull him slightly off-balance.

Thalgor feinted to the right and brought his sword down sharply, striking his opponent on the wrist of his sword hand.

The enemy looked up at him in obvious surprise, then called something to his men Thalgor could not hear. The movement exposed a ribbon of flesh between helmet and shield.

Now.

Thalgor's sword cut through that flesh. His senses were so alert he felt the hesitation before the skin gave way, heard the crunch as the sword cut through the bony voice box, heard the sound of the man's dying gasp.

The spurt of blood almost blinded him as the enemy fell dead with one last cry of rage.

Thalgor was again the boy who had killed his first man with a similar blow. Killed and freed those he loved from a horrible evil. Man and boy, it was a good day's work.

A cry went up around him. As much from the enemy warriors as from his own men.

He dropped his bloody sword and shield, and pulled the golden helmet from the dead man's head.

He held the helmet high in the sinking sunlight for all to see with a victory cry of his own.

A whirr, a thud.

Everything went black.

ERWYN COULD NOT make herself watch the duel between Thalgor and the enemy leader. Instead, she convinced the guards to lead the healers down the steep hillside at the narrowest part of the valley so that, if Thalgor was victorious, they could immediately set to their work. And if he was not, they could return to the walled camp to await their fate with Gurdek's men.

She was battered and scratched from clambering down rocky slag and through heavy underbrush before they reached the more level soil of the pass.

The guards found them a hiding place behind Thalgor's men where they could hear the clamor of battle but see nothing of how it went, or how Thalgor fared in his duel with the enemy leader.

Then the sounds changed. The last rank of men began to talk excitedly among themselves. The guards crept forward to hear what they said. Erwyn followed while the surgeon, the herbalist, and the bone-setter stayed safe in their hiding place.

One of the guards heard her behind them, but rather than send her back, he only whispered, "Thalgor has wounded his opponent's sword hand."

She was past them before they could stop her. When she reached the battlefield, she heard the cry that went up when Thalgor struck at the enemy's throat. Spurred by a power she did not understand, she struggled through the next rank of warriors, all of them oblivious to her presence in their intense focus on the duel.

Thalgor's victory cry pushed her through the front ranks and into the midst of the now-frozen battle.

She caught sight of Thalgor just as he fell.

With a scream of pure terror, she rushed forward and reached him while the arrow lodged deep between his ribs still quivered where his breastplate had been cut open.

On his right side. She struggled to calm the edge of hysteria in her mind. Not in his heart.

He lived. But something was still very wrong.

Rygar and Sett were arguing over the body of an enemy archer, Sett's sword plunged deep into his belly.

"You did not need to kill him," Rygar said.

"A better death than he deserved for such treachery," Sett replied as he pulled his sword free.

"He only obeyed the orders of his leader."

"After the leader was dead."

"Rygar," Erwyn called, as much to stop their arguing as because she needed him. "Rygar, come here."

He came at once, while Sett began to create order on a battlefield where the captive enemy still slightly outnumbered Thalgor's victorious warriors.

"Thalgor is wounded," she said in a reproachful tone.

"It is not his heart. He will live," Rygar replied.

Thalgor groaned and fine pink bubbles formed on his lips.

Everything inside Erwyn froze.

Rygar blinked twice and reached down to touch the foam. He smelled it to learn what Erwyn already knew. It was blood.

Time stopped as they looked at each other, brother and woman, and absorbed the awful truth.

A moment passed. Perhaps an hour. Perhaps a lifetime. Erwyn could not have said.

Someone, maybe the surgeon, called for torches in the fading light of day. Still she and Rygar stared at each other.

Thalgor groaned again. Again the bloody foam.

"Can you heal him?" Rygar finally breathed.

"I don't know."

But she did know. Knew her powers were not enough to slow Thalgor's breathing at the same time she healed and mended all the layers of wounded flesh in his lung. With two witches, it might be done. With only one there was no hope.

Still, she reached into her bag and pulled out cobwebs. Perhaps the wound was not so bad as she thought.

"Take out the arrow," she told Rygar.

He grimaced, then pulled the arrow free.

With the arrow came not a spurt of blood but, more sinister, a hollow sound from Thalgor's chest. And more bloody foam.

Erwyn clasped the cobwebs over the hole, but felt the suction threaten to pull them inside Thalgor's body when he struggled for another breath.

"No," she cried aloud as the fear swallowed her.

Those nearby fell silent. Torches gleamed in the twilight.

Rygar cursed and threw the arrow toward the dead man who shot it. He sighed and touched her head as she knelt at his feet, holding the cobwebs against the hole in Thalgor's chest.

"No," she wailed again. "He cannot die."

Rygar lowered himself down beside her and put his good arm around her shoulders.

"No," came on a sob this time. "We have a life to live together yet. I want his child."

"Can you save him?"

"Not alone." Panic took over her thoughts. "But if his mother had witch blood, you do. I can show you how to still his breathing..." She spoke quickly, as if that would make it true.

"Only he inherited what witch blood our mother had. You should know that. You do know that. Think, Erwyn. If you cannot save him alone, you must ease his death."

"How can you say that? You are the one he loves most. I must try to save him. Don't you see that?"

Thalgor groaned and struggled again to breathe.

"How long?" Rygar asked gently.

"He is strong, but…" The hollow ring of her own voice shocked her, as if her body knew what her heart could not accept.

"Will it be an easy death?"

She looked up at him, at that face so like Thalgor's. "You need not play the fool with me, Rygar. I am not so far gone with grief as that. At least not yet."

"Then ease his death, sister. As you would for anyone."

Pain wracked her body. Even as she knew the truth of his words, knew her magic demanded it, she whispered, "I cannot."

Before Rygar could respond, Thalgor's eyes flickered open.

"Erwyn." His voice, robbed of air, could barely be heard.

"Do not talk," she told him automatically.

Thalgor smiled thinly. "Erwyn," he said again.

Resigned, she replied, "I am here."

He reached his right hand up to cover hers where they held the cobwebs to his wound.

"Erwyn, I love you." He coughed up a mass of pink foam and closed his eyes again.

"Now can you ease his death?" Rygar asked, with more wisdom than she would have expected.

She shook her head. Tears flowed down her face and damped the hand that was still clasped with Thalgor's.

Let him die easily, she silently begged.

Night fell. The surgeon tended Rygar's wounded arm.

Someone brought food they ignored. Sett came to speak in hushed tones with Rygar, who still knelt beside her, but she could not care what they said.

She lived only for each quavering breath Thalgor drew, lived only on the wish that each would be his last.

He loved her.

The words freed her. Her heart soared above the clouds of the dark-time twilight into the clear purple sky beyond them.

The words bound her, to this one moment in time, to this endless, hopeless vigil.

Most of all, the words deafened her, drowned out the cries of all the other wounded and dying men around her who needed her healing. Drowned out the call of her magic. Drowned out her duty to give Thalgor the easy death he deserved. She heard only those word –and his every strangled breath.

She was as incapable of easing the death of the man she loved as she was of saving him.

It was full dark when a stir among the warriors around them roused her from her stupor. A man stepped into the circle of light cast by a fire someone had built without her noticing.

She would have taken him for Rygar, if Thalgor's brother did not still kneel beside her, as numb with grief as she.

The man cast back his hood.

The Witch King!

She started to cry out to him, to beg for his help, but he gestured for her to remain silent and pulled back his cloak.

From out of the dark folds stepped Felyn.

Before Erwyn got over her shock, the Witch King was gone and the child stood alone before her, cursed eyes wide with fear.

"Why are you here?" Rygar asked her gently.

"The Witch King brought me."

"But why?"

"So I can help Erwyn save Thalgor."

Erwyn lifted her eyes to Felyn's and for the first time saw her sister.

Her mother had told the truth. The warmth of that knowledge, after all this time, eased the icy chill of this new loss.

More, when she looked at Felyn she saw a second witch.

Thalgor groaned and shifted beneath her touch. There was still time!

"Kneel with his head in your lap," she told Felyn with sudden calm. "Put your hands by his eyes and find his mind with yours. It will be deeply asleep. Tell me when you have it."

"Can I help?" Rygar asked.

"Not here," she told him. "Go to Sett and help him organize the march back to the camp. Was Gurdek told of the victory?"

Rygar pulled himself to his feet and smiled down at her.

"Welcome back, witch. I won't go far, in case you need me."

She nodded and carefully lifted her hand to free it from Thalgor's grasp without letting the cobwebs move.

"Erwyn," Felyn whispered.

"Do you have his mind?"

"Yes." The child gave a small sob. "I'm afraid."

"Don't be. You are a witch and the magic in our blood-line is strong." Fear was their enemy just now. "You do not need much magic to do this. Even Thalgor managed it, after a fashion, when I healed Rygar. We will save him. Together."

The child nodded. Erwyn told her how to slow Thalgor's breathing to the barest minimum and how to tell if it was too slow. Then Erwyn began the long, delicate process of using her magic to heal the hole in his lung.

Around them the warriors settled into a battle camp. Someone added wood to the fire and brought more food. The smell of it teased her empty belly, but she dared not pause to eat.

At long last, just as the moon set, Erwyn told Felyn to let Thalgor breath normally again. No air sucked against the cobwebs that covered the wound. She lifted them gently away. No bloody foam rose in the hole that still gaped open in his chest.

She placed her hand on the skin above the damaged lung and let it fill fully with air. Thalgor breathed it out on a sigh.

She sank back on her heels and moved her stiff shoulders.

"Thank you, Sister," she said softly to Felyn.

The child released Thalgor's head and set it gently on the ground. Then she lay on her side and immediately went to sleep.

Someone, Sett perhaps, carried Felyn to a makeshift bed near the fire. Rygar took her place at Thalgor's head.

"I can tell you if he starts to wake," he whispered.

Erwyn nodded. With a yawn she began the relatively ordinary task of treating the broken tissue inside Thalgor's chest wall, then the muscles of his chest, and finally the tattered skin over the wound. She used magic lotions now, as there was no need to heal completely, merely to cleanse and bind so his body could heal itself.

The pungent smells of her potions mixed with the dying fire brought a grimace to Rygar's face. She laughed softly, overwhelmed by joy because Thalgor would live. Rygar laughed back with the same jubilant sound.

She bound the wound and took a moment to cleansed and bind the gash on Thalgor's leg. Then, like the child, she slept where she fell.

THE LIGHT BLINDED. Thalgor's chest was on fire.

Were they burning his body as legend said his ancestors, the great kings, were burned? He tried to call for Rygar, but no words came.

The searing pain in his chest told him he still lived. He tried to call out again, but every breath was agony.

Then he remembered he had said what he needed to say.

He had told Erwyn he loved her.

He tried to draw a deeper breath against the pain, but his chest was tightly bound with cloth and cobwebs. Erwyn's work.

He felt about him for her with his hands, but found only earth still damp from his own blood. And, no doubt, her tears.

He reached higher to touch the legs where his head rested. A man's legs. Rygar. His brother snored and shifted, asleep where he sat.

One leg ached. Thalgor stretched out the other and found a soft bundle that was surely Erwyn asleep beside him. He smiled, turned his face away from the weak dark-time sun as it rose, and sank back into welcome oblivion.

THE ENEMY'S LEADER had never considered the possibility of defeat, Erwyn was sure. Thalgor's men held his warriors captive outside the walled camp. The camp where their women and children were guarded only by a few old men and boys nearly of warrior age was several days' march away.

After much discussion, the council decided there were

too many to bring into the band. Instead Sett was chosen to return the captives to their people with as many of his own men and their families as were willing to go with him. The one Erwyn still thought of as the raven had feared to have anyone else capable of becoming leader of his band, so the captives easily agreed to accept Sett as their leader, in alliance with Thalgor.

That alliance, Erwyn could see now, would plant the seed of peace and an end to wandering for all the bands.

Tynor replaced Sett as Thalgor's lieutenant after Rygar declined to fill that role.

"I'm a poet, not a warrior," he told Thalgor with a smile.

Erwyn knew his choice would please Tya.

In the midst of all the turmoil, Thalgor healed slowly, drained because he insisted on sitting at council when he should have rested. But she said nothing. It was enough just to have him alive. And to know he loved her.

She began to teach Felyn to use her magic. As the child checked Thalgor's wound each day, Erwyn taught her to see with both eye and mind that it healed properly all the way through.

"Two witches," Thalgor sighed one evening when the child had left them alone in the light and warmth of their room and gone to her bed.

"You knew all along she was a witch, didn't you?"

He nodded. "Why didn't you?"

She sat beside where he lay on their bed. "My uncle had

no witch blood. If she was not a witch…" She shrugged. "I was young when it all happened. It was easier to blame her than to blame my father. I loved him very much."

"What of Felyn's curse?" he asked somberly.

"We wait. It will not show itself until she is grown."

"The curse cannot be removed?"

She shrugged. "I doubt even the Wise Witches can do that."

They were both silent for a while. Finally Erwyn said, "Rygar takes Tya as his wife tomorrow. We will need a new girl to help with the work of the tent."

"You have one in mind, of course."

"Gurdek's youngest. He coddles her."

"He would." Thalgor sighed again.

"What bothers you? Did Felyn disturb your wound?"

"I scarcely know it's there, her magic works so well. No, I was thinking how to ask…"

Absently he reached over and took her hand in his.

Puzzled, she waited. What could he need to ask of her now? He knew he was not yet well enough to take her to their bed, as much as they both yearned for it.

He cleared his throat. "With two witches, even if one is a girl, it would not be so inconvenient to have you with child."

She gave him a look. "Not so inconvenient?"

"Let me start again." He took both her hands in his. "I love you and want you to have my child. Perhaps more than one." He paused and added with unaccustomed meekness,

"If you still wish to have my child."

A thrill of more joy than she could have imagined filled her heart. Tears stung her eyes.

"I wish nothing more."

Mindful of his healing wound, she took his face in her hands and kissed him. The kiss of a woman who loves with all her heart and is loved as fully in return.

Somewhere, she knew, the Witch King watched them—and smiled.

THE END

If you enjoyed *Thalgor's Witch*, you'll love these next stories from Tule Publishing…

The Farrier's Daughter by Leigh Ann Edwards
Book 1 in the Irish Witch series

Blood Bound by Traci Douglass
Book 1 in the Blood Ravager's series

Animal Instincts by Patricia Rosemoor

Available now at your favorite online retailer!

ABOUT THE AUTHOR

Nancy Holland recently began to live her dream as a full-time writer. After being a finalist in the Romance Writers of America's Golden Heart© contest and publishing two short contemporary romances, she is thrilled to return to her first love and write fantasy novels for Tule Publishing.

Despite dark pasts, heart-breaking betrayal, and a future that is always at risk, her fantasy heroes and heroines accomplish amazing feats of valor and magic to create a better world for everyone. More importantly, her characters refuse to give up on themselves, struggle to improve their lives, and learn to trust each other.

After years spent studying and writing about words written long ago and far away, she loves to travel with her husband to explore the cities where she can feel the lived experience behind the words.

Visit her website at www.NancyHollandWriter.com.

Thank you for reading

THALGOR'S WITCH

If you enjoyed this book, you can find more from all our great authors at TulePublishing.com, or from your favorite online retailer.

TULE
PUBLISHING